The Benefactor

THE BENEFACTOR

JOHN MORAN

FIVE STAR
A part of Gale, Cengage Learning

GALE
CENGAGE Learning™

Detroit • New York • San Francisco • New Haven, Conn • Waterville, Maine • London

GALE
CENGAGE Learning™

Five Star Publishing, a part of Gale, Cengage Learning.

Set in 11 pt. Plantin.

Printed on permanent paper.

LIBRARY OF CONGRESS CATALOGING-IN-PUBLICATION DATA

Moran, John, 1954–
The benefactor / by John Moran. — 1st ed.
p. cm.
ISBN-13: 978-1-59414-771-5 (hardcover : alk. paper)
ISBN-10: 1-59414-771-X (hardcover : alk. paper)
1. Murder victims' families—Fiction. 2. Murderers—Fiction. I. Title.
PS3613.O6817B46 2009
813'.6—dc22 2009005237

First Edition. First Printing: June 2009.
Published in 2009 in conjunction with Tekno Books and Ed Gorman.

Printed in the United States of America
1 2 3 4 5 6 7 13 12 11 10 09

For Trish,
as promised

Chapter One

"The police? *Again?*"

Kay Daniels only had to hear the words "husband" and "no appointment" to assume her secretary was referring to the detective who had questioned her five times in the past month.

"No," Linda replied on the intercom. "The gentleman says it's business. He's asking for ten minutes."

Oh God, Kay thought. Another poor investor who had been screwed over by Bernard. She sighed.

"All right. Send him in."

Kay glanced at her watch. 4:30 P.M. If she could get rid of the guy in ten minutes, she could then make that begging call to Citibank's V.P. of Commercial Credit and be out of here by five o'clock. Kelley's soccer practice would be over at that point, and she would only have to keep her waiting a few minutes. She sighed again. It was all so much easier when she was a stay-at-home mom. When she had no marketing plans to create, no out-of-state conventions to attend, no employees wondering if their next paychecks would actually be worth something beyond a guffaw from their local bank teller. But that was a different time. A time when Bernard was alive and—

The door opened and a man entered. Linda, standing behind him, winked, her usual seal of approval for any potential mate.

"Good afternoon, Mrs. Daniels," he said. "I'm Nikolas Seifer."

Kay introduced herself and, while shaking hands, had to agree he *was* good looking. But at around forty, he was fifteen years too old for Linda. Or perhaps Linda viewed him as a possible replacement for Bernard. He was at least six feet tall, the fit, muscular physique and erect posture suggesting "military." His eyes, blue and unmoving, stared into Kay's. The charcoal gray suit, perfectly knotted crimson tie, and brown leather attaché case seemed the standard outfit of a businessman. But Kay sensed a toughness that no mere clothing could mask.

She gestured to the chair in front of her desk.

"Please, have a seat, Mr. Seifer."

"Thank you very much indeed."

The overly formal expression sounded unusual, somehow foreign, though she detected no accent.

"So," she said, when Linda closed the door. "You knew Bernard?"

"No," he replied. "Not at all."

"Oh? My secretary said you had some business dealings with him."

"I murdered him."

"I beg your pardon?"

"I'm responsible for your husband's death."

"But—but my husband was killed in an auto accident. I met the woman who was driving the vehicle."

"An associate of mine."

He looked around the office, like an appraiser at an estate sale of less-than-interesting items.

Kay picked up the phone. "I'm calling the police."

"And tell them what?"

The appraising eyes were now on Kay. He held up his right hand, palm facing her.

"Please, Mrs. Daniels. Put down the phone. I have another appointment shortly. And you have to pick up Kelley from soccer practice."

Kay, startled at the knowing reference to her daughter, placed the receiver in its cradle. "Who *are* you?"

Seifer smiled. "Think of me as your benefactor."

"My benefactor?"

"Yes."

He reached down and picked up the attaché case. After touching some numerals on a small keypad, he opened the case and withdrew a folded newspaper.

"Is this familiar?" he asked.

He handed it over but she didn't need to read the story. The headline from the Metro section of *The New York Times* was all too familiar. "Connecticut Businessman Arrested for Assault. Wife Seeks Restraining Order."

"Your arm has healed sufficiently?" Seifer asked.

She responded only by nodding.

Seifer spoke again. "And it wasn't the first time, was it?"

"First time?"

"That he'd beaten you."

How do you answer such a question? she wondered. How do you acknowledge that the man you loved once—no, the man you *thought* you loved—could take such satisfaction in raising his fist to you? She blamed the alcohol, initially. Then, she blamed the pills he was taking for his unending depressions. Finally, she blamed herself for staying and enduring it. That's when she moved out to her sister Janet's house and filed the restraining order. "What are we going to do now, Mom?" Kelley had asked, and Kay had mumbled some incoherent reply. Kay had no money of her own, and no job. She and Bernard were partners in the business, but the articles of incorporation stipulated that neither could buy out the other for a minimum of ten years. Whatever she could get out of him would have to be hacked by attorneys and judges and court orders from the thicket that was Bernard's finances. Janet talked about a "new start," but words were cheap; rents were not.

And then, as if by magic, the problem disappeared. Bernard, as he usually did, went out for his evening jog around the neighborhood—another of his ploys to beat back the clock since he'd turned fifty—and he was hit by an SUV. It was absurd. Life wasn't like that. No one you know ever wins the lottery. And yet, as if God snapped His fingers, Bernard was gone.

And she got the company and his estate—he had never found the time to re-write his will—and she got his life insurance. No wonder that detective had been hounding her. She'd have been suspicious herself. But she had been at a PTA meeting that night with twenty other parents providing a cast-iron alibi. Marilyn Jarvis, the driver of the SUV, was from Nebraska and had never even visited Connecticut before. She had no criminal past. She was a chartered accountant, living the uneventful life that chartered accountants live. There was no alcohol or illegal substance found in her system. She'd called 911 immediately and then ran to the nearest house for help. It was a freak accident. If the streetlight at the corner of Munson and Deepdale hadn't been out, Bernard would have been easily seen. But Jarvis had failed to see the jogger in the darkness as she made the turn.

"I don't believe that's any of your business, Mr. Seifer."

"Actually, it *is* my business. It is precisely my business. Mrs. Daniels, as Kelley would say: 'Get real.' You were in a violently abusive marriage; your husband was ruining your life—as he was ruining your company. You had obtained a restraining order against him and, no doubt, you were about to divorce him. I did you a favor. An enormous favor. Now you have your freedom, your health. And all this." He raised both arms to encompass the office and, evidently, the entire company. "Now you can rebuild your life."

The phrase was almost the exact one Janet had used after the funeral. All the mourners had left the house. Kelley was in the kitchen, starting on the dishes, and she and Janet were in the living room collecting the debris from the reception. Kay had looked at Janet and knew she was correct. The shock of it all—identifying the body, the wake with the oh-so-disapproving in-laws, the police interviews—had worn off. Driving away from the cemetery she had had a curious—almost shameful—reaction: Relief. She was *free,* she realized. She and Kelley. They could start afresh. She had responded to Janet: "Yes. That's exactly what I intend to do."

She looked now at Seifer. And she wasn't going to be intimidated by some suave guy in a fancy suit trying to pull some con. She almost smiled at the image: a perfect description of Bernard.

"I don't believe you," she said. "Now, what is it that you want?"

He was silent for more than a few moments, again, she felt, appraising her. Then he reached into his attaché case and withdrew a document.

"Do the numbers 4-3-0-8-6-3-7 mean anything to you?"

The way he had stated them, without pause, puzzled her for a moment, but then she realized. "That's my cell phone number."

He held up the document in front of her. She recognized the familiar striped orb of the AT&T logo.

"Marilyn Jarvis's phone bill," he said. "Your number is on it. Several times."

Suddenly frightened, Kay looked, and there it was: the woman's name and a Nebraska address at the top of the bill and, among dozens of other itemized calls: New Croydon, (203) 430-8637 on three consecutive lines.

"That's impossible. I would remember her calling me."

"Look at the date of the phone calls. If you check your own

bill for March 18, you will see you have *her* number on it. When you responded to her calls."

Seeing the confusion on her face and apparently to press his advantage, he withdrew another document from his case. He passed it over to her.

She looked at it and for an instant wondered how he could have obtained her hotel receipt. But then she noted the name. Marilyn Jarvis. A Nebraska address. For a weekend stay at the Englebrook Spa & Inn in Vermont six months ago.

"Look at the dates," he said.

Friday, March 18, and Saturday, March 19.

"Kelley was with the Girl Scouts that weekend, wasn't she?" Seifer said. "And you probably needed a little bit of rest and relaxation, perhaps. To get your head together, perhaps. To come to a decision about your future, perhaps. Yes?"

It was scary, but that was exactly why she had gone to the Englebrook. But what was Marilyn Jarvis doing there at the same time?

He held out his left hand for the receipt, and she passed it back. He immediately put it in a plastic bag that he must have removed from his attaché case while she was studying the receipt. He sealed the bag before placing it in the case. Noticing her look of puzzlement, he said:

"I don't want your fingerprints smudged."

"But you've just held it yourself. And the phone bill, as well."

He shook his head and displayed the fingers of his left hand. "My fingertips were protected by a little transparent piece of plastic that stage magicians use on occasion."

"Well, what would my fingerprints prove, anyway? I didn't stay in that woman's room. I never met her until last month. Besides, I have my own hotel receipt."

"What would it prove?" He shrugged. "I don't know what the police would make of it. It's the hotel receipt of the woman who drove the vehicle that killed your husband. The woman that you undoubtedly told the police you had never previously met. The hotel receipt from the same weekend that you stayed at the hotel. And your fingerprints are on it. I can't imagine it proves anything—*exactly.* But the district attorney might think it means *something.*"

He closed the attaché case and stood up. "Now, I must go to my next appointment. I would like to continue our discussion this evening. Are you aware of a restaurant in Westport called Juno's?"

She nodded, unable to think clearly. Police? District attorney? Fingerprints?

"I've arranged a reservation for eight o'clock. If you're unable to make it, you may reach me here." He handed her a business card. "But, Mrs. Daniels, for all of our sakes, please make it."

He bowed slightly, a gesture from someone not of this country, turned and left. Kay looked at the card. Two centered lines in crimson. NIKOLAS SEIFER. And a telephone number.

She said the name aloud. "Seifer."

Strange, she thought, noting the spelling. He had pronounced it *cipher.*

Chapter Two

"I want to follow her."

Tommy Dixon, chief of the New Croydon police department, rolled his eyes. He was supposed to be running out the clock in this Connecticut burg, but with cops like Frank Sinclair to contend with, his already high blood pressure threatened to go off the charts.

"Frank," he said. "Now why would you want to follow her?"

Detective Frank Sinclair wanted to collar a murderer. And, Kay Daniels, he believed, murdered her husband.

"It smells, Tommy. This rich guy gets killed two months after his wife splits with him. Knocked down while he's out jogging. All because some lousy streetlight was broken? What are the odds?"

"Don't handcuff yourself to that line of reasoning, Frank. Odds are odds. Just because it's a million to one you'll be struck by lightning if you step outside your door, it doesn't mean it's not possible. Unlikely, but possible. Same here. The streetlight was out. The guy was jogging in the dark. It had started to rain. A vehicle happened to make that turn."

"And you're not in any way suspicious that the neighbors say the light was fine the previous evening?"

"Look, Frank. If the driver of the car had been humping the guy, then I'm suspicious. If the two of them had gone to the same college or worked in the same company at some time in the past, then I'm suspicious. But she's from fifteen hundred miles away. Never even *been* in the state before. You determined all this yourself."

But he saw that Sinclair was unconvinced. "What is it, Frank? Where are you going with this?"

Sinclair shook his head. "I don't know. It just seems too damn coincidental. And too damn lucky for the grieving widow. She inherits big bucks and a hefty life insurance policy. And an abusive husband out of the way."

"Sometimes you get lucky. She got lucky. Seems she deserved a bit of luck, I'd say."

"Well, it wouldn't hurt to follow her for a while. To see if she meets anyone interesting."

The chief shook his head. "No. You have plenty of other cases to handle. Let this one drop. It's over."

It's over. No, thought Sinclair, leaving the chief's office. It's not over. He went to his desk and, after prioritizing his half-dozen outstanding cases, opened the top drawer. He glanced at the chief's closed door, then made a decision. He picked up the manila folder with the single word DANIELS on the label and began re-reading the initial interview.

"You first met Mr. Daniels when he interviewed you for a job, is that correct?"

"Yes. He hired me eight years ago."

"Director of Marketing, correct?"

"Detective, clearly you know all of this. So why are you bothering to ask?"

"Do you wish to have an attorney present?"

"I don't believe that was the question I just asked."

"The answer to your question is: Procedure. I was merely implying if you're uncomfortable with this procedure, you may certainly have your attorney present."

"I don't need an attorney. Why should I?"

"Let's continue, then. Your husband's business was a chain of rent-to-own stores?"

"Yes."

"Why did he need this position filled?"

"The business was going well. He was expanding to other cities in the TriState area and he needed marketing expertise. I had worked in Manhattan, at Bloomingdale's, for several years."

"So, the initial relationship was purely business?"

"Purely."

"When did that change?"

"When I discovered that Congress had passed the Telecommunications Act."

"What connection did that have to a chain of rent-to-own stores?"

"It meant that telephone service could be offered by anyone, not just the existing big companies."

"Anyone could offer telephone service? How was that technically possible?"

"Congress wanted to open up the entire field. The Act made it possible for anyone to re-sell telephone services."

"Re-sell? So a company would buy the service from the big providers and re-sell it?"

"Yes, exactly. The customer would be getting the service from the providers but would be paying the smaller company."

"Why would a customer bother to do that? Surely by having to buy and re-sell the service, the cost would be higher for the customer than if he bought it directly?"

"You catch on fast, Detective. The average customer wouldn't bother to do that, of course. But the customer I had in mind was the same one who frequented our stores."

"*You* had in mind?"

"Yes. It was my idea to move into phone service. It seemed a natural progression. We had thousands of credit-challenged customers across the region. Why not offer them phone service in addition to a refrigerator or big-screen TV?"

"Why would people like that have a problem getting phone service from the big providers?"

"The same reason they have a problem buying a kitchen appliance or piece of furniture—they have terrible credit. When you or I apply to a phone company or any company that offers a service—cable TV, utilities—we are, in effect, getting credit extended to us. The company provides the service and sends the bill later. And before they provide the service, they check your credit history so they know you will pay your bill. People with bad credit can't even get phone service from a big provider."

"So you made this suggestion to Mr. Daniels."

"Yes."

"And what was his reaction?"

"He was against it. It was too unproven, he said. The start-up costs would be significant. People, lots of them, would have to be hired to staff a call center. Marketing would have to be expanded beyond just local newspapers and radio. Attorneys—specialized ones who knew the telecommunications industry—would have to be retained to negotiate the contracts with the big providers."

"But he changed his mind?"

"Yes."

"Why?"

"I offered to put my money where my mouth was. I was willing to bet all my savings. I suggested we form a new company, specifically to focus on this. We would own it together."

"That was enough to change his mind?"

"I guess. Yes."

"All right. So you formed a new company. New Croydon

Telecomm. Did your personal relationship develop because of this?"

"Yes. We were spending a great deal of time together getting ready for the launch. There was a tremendous amount that had to be done. And to learn. We worked a great deal, even into the evening. To save time, we would even eat out at restaurants and work on the plans over dinner. One thing led to another. He proposed and I accepted."

"You had been married before?"

"Yes. For eight years. I had a daughter. Then I got divorced. That's probably why I took the job in Connecticut. It promised less stress than the City. And with a toddler to handle, it seemed the right move at the time."

"You have no children by Mr. Daniels?"

"No. He—"

"Mrs. Daniels?"

"Sorry."

"There's a box of Kleenex right behind you."

"Thank you. Sorry."

"Would you like to take a break?"

"No. I'm fine now."

"You were saying about your husband and children."

"He—Mr. Daniels wasn't terribly fond of children."

"He didn't accept your daughter? Kelley?"

"Well, he was . . . *tolerant,* shall we say."

"Did you respond differently to him when you came to realize this?"

"Not at first."

Sinclair stopped reading, then closed the file. *Not at first.* He had missed it during the interview. Someone had come in at that point with an urgent message for the woman. Her daughter had left school early, and no one knew where she had gone.

Not at first.

If not at first, he asked himself, then *when?*

Chapter Three

"You're going out on a date!"

"Forty-one-year-olds don't go out on *dates.*"

Kelley picked up a pearl necklace from Kay's jewelry box and tried it on.

"Then why are you dressing up to go out at night?"

"It's just business," said Kay, looking into the mirror and deciding that lipstick would give Seifer the wrong impression. Her flaxen hair, too, she decided, would have to be tied up.

"And put that down," she said. "I'm leaving it to you in my will, but until then keep your hands off it."

There, she thought, much better. What else? A dowdy pants suit. Yes, that would communicate that she was all business. She turned and looked at herself in profile. But there was nothing she could do about her trim, toned figure. Three years of staying at home meant she had the time—sixty minutes a day, every day—to exercise. Forty-one? Not too bad for a forty-one-year-old.

"You *should* go on a date, you know," Kelley said, ignoring her, and picked up a pair of pearl earrings that seemed to match the necklace. "Your relationship with *him* ended more than a year ago, really, didn't it?"

Dear God, thought Kay. Him. Sure, it had always been hard for Kelley to call him "Dad," but now she wouldn't even refer to Bernard by name?

"I mean," Kelley went on, angling her head in the mirror to

see how the jewelry looked, "I know you were living under the same roof and all, but you two weren't doing it."

Kay stared at her.

"Well," said Kelley, "not that I could hear anyway."

"Did you finish your homework?" Kay asked, vainly hoping the change of subject would change Kelley's train of thought.

"Yep. So, who's this dude you're meeting?" She coughed a phony cough. "For business."

"How do you know it's a 'he'?"

"Puh-leese. If you were meeting a woman, you'd go out in your bathrobe. Unless . . ."

"Unless what?"

"Unless you're looking into the lesbian lifestyle."

"Could you please go find your birth certificate. I just want to verify that you are indeed thirteen years old."

Kelley laughed and punched Kay in the arm. "Good one, Mom!"

Kay smiled. "I have my moments."

"But seriously, who is he?"

"Just a boring business dude, that's all."

"Yeah, right."

Yeah, right, Kay thought as she pulled into the apparently full parking lot in front of Juno's. Nikolas Seifer was the least likely businessman she had ever encountered. Or whatever his "business" was, it was not of any conventional kind that she was aware of. It *had* to be a con of some sort, she had reasoned on the drive to the restaurant. Otherwise it was too preposterous. But what in God's name was that Jarvis woman doing at the Englebrook Inn six months ago? And why did Seifer have her actual receipt—it was clearly not a copy.

Additionally, there was the business with the phone numbers—how had that happened? The first thing Kay had done when she arrived at her house was to go into the home office and rummage through her receipts. Fortunately, that was a period when she was still at home and her contribution to the marriage was not just to take care of the conventional housework but all the household bills. She had filed everything by category, so it was only a matter of minutes to locate the cell phone bill for March.

Incredibly, the number she recalled from Jarvis's bill was among the others listed. Just one occurrence, on March 18, as Seifer had said. But she didn't remember calling the number. It was only for a few cents, it was brief and among dozens of other calls on the listing; she had little time to check through a phone bill and, in any case, had never attained the habit. Why should she call that number, she asked herself? She didn't know Jarvis, and didn't know her number. So someone else did. Could it have been Bernard? But, no, it was listed as taking place at 8:14 P.M. She had arrived in Vermont an hour before. Bernard was five hours behind, at home in Connecticut, scowling no doubt, and whining that he would be alone for the entire weekend.

She pulled into what seemed to be the only vacant parking space, at the rear of the building. For goodness sake, she thought, why was this restaurant so mobbed on a Wednesday night?

She turned off the headlights and the engine, then stared into the dark. She heard the sound of muffled music and when it stopped, immediate applause.

Wait a minute, she thought. Why not just call the hotel and ask to verify if indeed a Marilyn Jarvis had stayed there that weekend? She looked at her watch. It was almost nine. She had called Seifer and told him she would be at least an hour late, that she had to arrange a sitter for Kelley. So she had a few minutes. She turned the cell phone on and dialed Information. When she gave the location, she was transferred to a Vermont operator. Within a minute she had the number and called the hotel.

The receptionist seemed delighted with her company. Perhaps, Kay thought, Vermont is a lonely place in late autumn.

"I'm—" She stopped. No, she couldn't use her own name. They wouldn't give out any information about another guest. "I'm—Marilyn Jarvis. I stayed at the Englebrook last March. I—"

"Oh, that's wonderful," the girl interrupted. "I'm so glad you were part of the Englebrook family, Ms. Jarvis. Are you planning another visit?"

"Maybe next year. But I was just wondering if you could confirm the dates of my last stay. It was a business trip, and there's some issue with my . . . ah, expense report."

God, Kay thought, I'm going to burn in Hell. Since when was she so facile with on-the-fly deceit?

The girl chuckled. "Okay, Ms. Jarvis. Not a problem."

Kay heard a keyboard being clicked, and then the girl was back on the line. "Okay, Ms. Jarvis. Our records show that you stayed March 18 and 19. Does that sound about right?"

"Yes. That seems right."

"Okay. Is there anything else I can help you with this evening?"

"No. Wait, yes. Was I . . . alone?"

There was silence at the other end of the phone. Kay guessed the girl figured she was dealing with some sort of amnesiac idiot.

Again the keyboard clicked. "Yes, Ms. Jarvis," the girl said. "You were booked into a single room, non-smoking."

Kay thanked the girl and turned the phone off. The music had started up again. Some discordant, throbbing sound. Not rock or pop. She had never visited Juno's before but was vaguely aware it had gained some prominence, had even been featured in the *Times* weekend section. The noise, muted as it was, made it difficult for her to think.

"Okay, concentrate," she said aloud. Marilyn Jarvis had evidently stayed at the same hotel as she, six months ago. Jarvis had also phoned Kay's cell number three times, and Kay's phone had evidently been used to call Jarvis back. So how had it happened? Think!

Then she remembered. She had arrived around seven o'clock, exhausted. Exhausted from the driving, from Bernard, from the whole damn trajectory of her life. She had not been hungry, and after depositing her overnight bag in the room, she had decided to treat herself to a massage and sauna. That was what the Englebrook was famous for, anyway—the mountain waters or some such malarkey. She had called Bernard from the phone in the room to confirm her arrival and then gone downstairs. Of course! She had left her pocketbook in the room—she had figured it was a useless encumbrance in the spa and the sauna's moisture might even do damage to the expensive Italian leather.

And the cell phone was in the pocketbook, where she always kept it. She had merely taken the key to the room when she left for the spa. It was an old-fashioned country inn, more large mansion than hotel. They didn't have modern card-keys, just standard door locks and latch keys.

She nodded. So that's how it was done. Jarvis—or Seifer—had picked the lock, found the cell phone, and made the calls. But even so, that was last winter, six months ago. As far back as March, then, this had all—

She felt her heart racing, suddenly frightened at the thought.

This had all been *planned.*

Chapter Four

"Good evening, Mrs. Daniels. I'm glad you finally made it."

Kay realized immediately why he had chosen this place. It wasn't just a restaurant, she now remembered. It was a hot spot for jazz groups on the cusp of recognition. Dark, crowded, and noisy, it was perfect for Seifer to conduct whatever business he was involved in without fear of being overhead. And, as if that wasn't enough, he was sitting at a table on a small balcony at the rear, isolated from the people below.

She mumbled a greeting and sat down.

"I've taken the liberty of ordering for all of us. I'm sure you're famished."

Famished. Another curious word, she thought. Foreign sounding. She was about to disagree, that she had had no appetite since 4:30 that afternoon when she wondered: *all of us?*

Seifer saw the uncertainty and gestured to Kay's right.

"This is an associate of mine. Johanna—meet Mrs. Daniels."

The woman, brunette, petite, and delicate-looking, remained standing. Kay exchanged nods with her.

"Mrs. Daniels," said Seifer. "Would you please accompany Johanna to the ladies' room?"

"*What* did you say?"

"I need to establish if you're wearing a wire."

"A wire?"

"A recording device. From the police."

"But—why would I—?" The thought of contacting the police

had not occurred to her, at least not until she had heard what exactly it was that Seifer wanted from her.

"I'm not wearing any recording devices," she said. "And I'm not going into the ladies' room with her."

Seifer smiled. "Please. Mrs. Daniels. The sooner we get this done, the sooner you can go home and tuck Kelley into bed."

Again it was neither carrot nor stick. But when you possess the whip hand, she realized, perhaps you don't need either. As it had in her office, the casual reference to Kelley unnerved her. No threat was stated or implied. It was simply there—it didn't need to *be* implied.

She stood up and followed the woman who, apparently familiar with the layout of the place, headed directly to the ladies' room. There was no one else present. Fortunately Kay had changed from her business skirt and blouse into the pants suit. The thought of that stranger's hands beneath her skirt . . .

Kay had no knowledge of such things but, mercifully, the woman seemed to have experience of the process. It was all over in a few seconds, the small hands quickly gliding along legs, thighs, and torso. Relieved the ordeal was over almost as soon as it had begun, she tried to find some gallows humor in the situation.

"I suppose I should be grateful you're not a lesbian."

Johanna looked at her for a long moment, then said, "I'm not?"

Kay turned away, even more embarrassed than she thought she already was. Making assumptions—about Seifer, about this woman—was not going to be useful in controlling the situation. Best to look and listen, then make a judgment on how to proceed. That's what she had always told Bernard, but he invariably insisted on roaring bull-headed into any problem, confronting it directly, as if any other alternative would be a diminution of his manhood.

Johanna led her back to Seifer's table, where the food had already been served. And now Kay remembered another reason the restaurant had gained some distinction in the media. Its chef was some young hotshot from Europe with an original taste in his menu.

"Leg of lamb garnished in grilled cocoa," explained Seifer, indicating the plates with both hands. "With cardamom white chocolate demi-glace."

To Kay, it sounded an appalling hodgepodge, but she had to admit the spices led a pungent, appealing aroma to the sliced rosettes of pink meat. She forced herself to eat, and they dined in silence for a few minutes while the quartet on stage played what, to her, seemed some typically unending piece of discordant music. Seifer, evidently, seemed to prefer eating to talking.

Kay, thinking of his concerns with being audiotaped, said, "I'm surprised you just didn't have me followed."

"Oh, I did," Seifer replied, gesturing with his fork to Johanna.

Kate blanched. "Well, then, you must know I didn't go to the police."

He nodded. "Yes, but you could have phoned them. A lot of people entered that office building today. A lot of people carrying all types of briefcases and bags. One of them could have been a police officer."

She put down her flatware. "Mr. Seifer. Let's get right to it, shall we?"

Seifer looked at her, took another helping of the coconut steamed white rice, then, somewhat regretfully it seemed, put down his fork.

"Very well. Let's." He swallowed some red wine, patted his lips with a napkin, then began.

"Mrs. Daniels, I help people in need. Even those who aren't aware they *are* in need. People who, in an unguarded moment, wish they could . . . eliminate their problems but don't have the nerve or the experience to do so themselves."

He leaned closer toward her, apparently enthused with the notion.

"Think about it for a moment, Mrs. Daniels. It's perfect. There is no prior connection between my client and me. You have no foreknowledge of the deed. Therefore you have the perfect alibi. Why do you think I'm so confident? Because I've done it before. It works, Mrs. Daniels! It works!"

"What if the . . . client has buyer's remorse and goes to the police?"

He seemed genuinely puzzled. "That has never happened. Why should it? The client—just as in your situation—is ahead of the game. Do you honestly think if you and your husband were the Ozzie and Harriet of New Croydon that I would get involved? Not a chance. I only concern myself when there is conflict—irreconcilable and clearly terminal."

"Husbands and wives fight all the time. They separate, they get back together."

"True. True. But we conduct research. Look me in the eye and tell me there was ever going to be a reconciliation between you and Bernard Daniels."

Instead of looking at him at all, she took the opportunity to reach for her own glass of wine.

He said, "You do know he and his secretary were fornicating?"

Kay stared at him, disbelieving. Bernard had been having sex with *Linda?* She felt suddenly nauseous. No, she didn't know. She thought that Bernard had lost all interest in intimacy of any kind. But, she realized now, perhaps that was the rationale behind the jogging, the dying of his salt-and-pepper hair, the expensive veneers applied by the "cosmetic dentist to the stars" in L.A.

Apparently aware she didn't know, Seifer went on:

"We don't always deal with husbands and wives, of course. We've had clients who benefited by the early death of a grandparent or a businessman who was glad to see the back of a partner."

"And I take it you don't offer your services to Joe Sixpack or his wife?"

He smiled. "Precisely. This is a costly enterprise. There's a lot of . . . infrastructure. Logistics. Equipment. Palms to grease. Most of all, there is time. Time is the most costly of commodities in my profession."

"And what do people charge in your . . . profession?"

"Fifty percent."

"You can't be serious. Fifty percent of the insurance money?"

"Fifty percent of everything. The estate, insurance money, 401(k)s, everything. Cash only. I'm not interested in automobiles or houses."

"You're insane."

Johanna laughed, then spoke for the first time. "Insanely clever."

Seifer smiled at his associate. "Mrs. Daniels. I have no intention of leaving my clients in penury. Yes, fifty percent is a lot. But one hundred percent of nothing is nothing. And that's what you and so many of my clients are potentially faced with before I make an appearance."

"Not a chance. It's extortion."

"Mrs. Daniels, I don't know why you are putting up obstacles to the resolution of this. I really don't. None of my other clients made such a fuss. They were *delighted* to meet their benefactor and reward him for his foresight."

"I have morals."

"So do I. Expensive ones."

"What's to say you won't show up again in a month's time for the rest of the money? That's what blackmailers do, isn't it?

Bleed the person dry?"

"My dear Mrs. Daniels. First of all, I'm not a blackmailer. I'm a service provider. Perhaps you don't read *The Wall Street Journal* every day. But I do. The United States is no longer an industrial economy. Steel, automobiles, manufacturing—they're history. Now we exist in a service economy. I merely provide a service.

"Second, I'm not a fool. I have no desire to make you penniless. Your husband's estate is valued at $3.8 million. Wills are public documents, as you probably know. If I try to be a pig, you will have nothing, and therefore nothing to lose. I don't want you as an enemy. I want you as a satisfied client. Think about it for a moment. Consider the situation you now find yourself in—thanks to me. An abusive husband is out of your life. You have a business and substantial capital to make it thrive again. Your daughter can grow up healthy in a non-threatening home. And you have me to thank. I really don't see any necessity for debate."

Kay felt exasperated by his reasoning, by his astonishing calm in admitting he was a murderer. She made a flailing gesture with her hands.

"And what if I just refuse to believe any of this?"

He turned to Johanna. "Mrs. Daniels needs convincing that I'm not some sort of charlatan."

Johanna nodded, then reached down under the table and placed an oversized pocketbook on her lap. She removed a buff-colored file folder and handed it to Seifer. Kay wondered where was the attaché case with the keypad but guessed that it would look oddly conspicuous for a man to carry an attaché case to a late-night supper.

Seifer said, "I do understand that you might find my proposal difficult to accept. But perhaps these will establish my credibility."

He handed the folder to her and, after a moment's hesitation, she opened it. There were about a dozen newspaper clippings of several sizes. She flipped through them, a cascade of different typefaces, different cities, different titles. *San Francisco, Denver, Toledo. Chronicle, Sentinel, Courier.* She went back to the first clipping, from a year ago, and read the headline. "Department Store Heiress Dead; Apparent Heart Failure." A forty-five-year-old woman in the wealthy enclave of Lake Forest, outside Chicago. *Cardiac arrhythmia . . . Siblings at odds for months, report neighbors . . . Police discount foul play.*

Kay flipped through the next few clippings, then stopped at one dated six years before the first. "Businessman Drowns in Pool." She skimmed through the initial paragraphs. Some guy in Asbury Heights had been found floating in his swimming pool. The phrases jumped out at her: *Death by misadventure . . . Competing lawsuits . . . Business partner out of country.*

She skipped the next several clippings and selected the last one in the bunch. It was faded, clearly the oldest. Nine years ago. My God, she thought. Nine years. This one remarkably similar to her own situation. But not just an abusive husband. An abusive father. Houston. An oil executive. A two-ton SUV had crashed into the man's convertible. The driver from Minnesota, first time in Texas.

She saw the obvious connections. Seifer had recommenced eating, paying her no attention, evidently allowing her time to consider what she had read. Now she had no doubt. Sure, he could have cut these stories out from papers across the country—accidental deaths happen every day. But the common denominator was not just the untimely deaths, not just the wealth of the deceased. The one thing they all had in common was the enmity between the parties. To say nothing of the lack of suspects, the alibis of the "beneficiaries," and the ostensible absence of foul play. That connection—in conjunction with all the rest—couldn't be explained away so easily.

Dear God, she thought. Poor Bernard. This man sitting across from her had killed her husband. Had Bernard really deserved to die, she wondered? A wife beater, alcoholic, failed husband, reluctant stepfather, and—if Seifer was to be believed—an adulterer. Not the best of male specimens, certainly, but no one else had a right to determine when he should die.

But it was Kelley she now thought of, not Bernard. Her first priority had to be Kelley. Seifer was clearly a man with resources, and not just financial. How had he managed to dispose of all these people without being caught, without any suspicions directed toward him? Yes, she sensed, he had more than resources: he was ruthless, determined, and without conscience.

"All right," she said. "I believe you. But what if I still refuse—for any reason: my religion, my morals, my pig-headedness. What exactly would you do?"

He sat back in his chair, clearly annoyed.

"Very well, Mrs. Daniels. You want a straight answer. I'll give it to you. I'll wash my hands of the entire affair."

He saw the relief move over her face.

"Wait! Hear me out. I'll accept my financial loss, the waste of my time. And I'll move on. But before I do, I'll send the New Croydon Police Department an anonymous package. The hotel receipt and the phone bill. They tie you into Marilyn Jarvis. It's powerful circumstantial evidence, especially as you've no doubt already denied to the police that you knew her. You have an obvious motive. They will assume Jarvis was an accomplice. Maybe the district attorney won't get a conviction. Maybe he will. Personally, I will be beyond caring. I will have lost time and some money, to be sure. You, potentially, could lose your freedom."

"If that *were* to happen, I would tell them about you."

"I don't have a record, Mrs. Daniels. I have nothing to fear. It will be your word against mine. Why do you think I checked you for a recording device?"

He paused, seemed to think of something. "There's one more thing. You realize if you do acquiesce to my terms, there will be only one more meeting between us? There will be no further opportunity to tape me, to argue with me, or to debate me. *This* meeting is your opportunity to come to an understanding. No delays or excuses will be acceptable. I've been in this situation several times. I know how long banks and brokerage firms take to dispense clients' money."

"You've forgotten one thing."

Seifer appeared puzzled, as if he never forgot anything of relevance. "What is that?"

"Marilyn Jarvis. Your entire plan is based on her being in what appears to be an unavoidable accident. If I'm going on trial for murder, then she goes too, as my accomplice."

He seemed bored. "I'm aware of that."

"But—why would she be willing to do such a thing?"

He smiled. "Because, obviously, she won't. She's no longer in this fine country of yours."

Chapter Five

Glioblastoma multiforme.

Frank Sinclair sat in his car outside Juno's restaurant and said the words in his mind once again.

Glioblastoma multiforme.

He looked at the clock on the dashboard. Ten P.M. She had been in there an hour now. Of course he couldn't go in—she could hardly miss him if he showed his face. If this were an official surveillance, he could have had two patrol officers—posing as a couple out for a meal—keep an eye on her and whomever she was meeting. But this was unofficial, extremely unofficial. So he'd have to stay out here and wait, and watch, and follow.

10:01 P.M.

Time. Moving so slowly. But only when you have plenty of it. When you're diagnosed with *glioblastoma multiforme,* you don't have much time. "A common estimate, Mr. Sinclair, is that sixty percent die in the first year, ninety percent die by the second year, and only a few individuals make it past three years."

Time. For kids, they have endless amounts of it. Summers seem to go on forever.

Glioblastoma multiforme.

"No, Mr. Sinclair, that's not possible either. The doses required to eliminate the tumor exceed the radiation tolerance of the brain."

10:03 P.M.

"Maybe I'm one of those 'few individuals,' honey," Alison

had said. "So don't sweat it. God is good."

He had made a *harrumph* sound. "There's no 'maybe' about it. You damn well are one of those."

10:06 P.M.

Eighty-four days later she was gone.

Glioblastoma multiforme. The name was grotesque, he had thought when the doctor first told him and Alison. Even the *sound* of it was grotesque. And yet he could never get the phrase out of his head. Even when driving away from the cemetery, it popped into his mind, tormenting him. That was two years ago. And still the words would not lay dormant.

Initially, he had tried to run, to get away from the words, the memories, the hurt. Oh, that constant hurt that makes you feel as if you're suffocating. He handed in his badge, a ridiculous gesture, he realized, even as he did it. The chief of the Sixty-Third precinct in Brooklyn was no fool. "Forget it, Frank. You're not getting off that easily. Take a vacation. Go away for a week. Two weeks. Just go. The badge will be here on my desk when you get back."

So he had bought a car and drifted south. Drifting. Such a wonderful word. A wonderful feeling. Just to drift, with no thoughts of the present or past or future. Drift, and just let yourself go. It was toward the warmth and life of the sun that he found himself drifting. When he reached the Keys, he stopped and spent his time sitting on the beach staring at the water, at the horizon, at the space just above the horizon. After five days, he got in the car and headed back north.

Driving on I-95 through Connecticut, he had needed gas and took the nearest exit ramp. It was after dark, the directions were poor, there was little streetlight, and he got lost. Then, for the first time in his life, he actually ran out of gas.

He sat against the hood, wondering what to do next. Sleep in the damn car? Wander around and try to find a motel or gas station? Two teenagers turned the corner and walked toward him. They might have been high school basketball players, taller than average, and black. Now what, he thought? A mugging? A fight defending myself? What difference did it make, anyway? He could handle himself, had handled a lot worse than two teenagers. But what was the point? Who cared if he got beaten up? He certainly didn't. Refuse to hand over his wallet because he wanted to be assaulted? Why not?

"You okay, mister?" the one on the left asked.

"Ran out of gas."

"You kiddin' me?"

"Nope."

The kid turned to his silent companion, then back to Sinclair.

"You got a container?"

Container? Was that new street lingo for a wallet? He'd never heard that one before.

"What sort of container?"

The kid shrugged and gestured with his hands. "You know, a container. To hold some gas."

Frank stared at him. "You mean a gas can?"

"Yeah, a container. If you got one, we can go get you some gas. There's a station about a mile from here."

"Why would you do that?"

The kid smiled and pointed to the car. "Beats pushin' it there, don't it?"

Frank smiled, and nodded. "Yeah, I guess you're right. I have something in the trunk." He walked back, opened the trunk and gave the yellow bucket to the kid. Then he handed him a twenty-dollar bill.

"Keep the change."

"Thanks, man. Be right back."

The two turned around and walked away. Frank stared after

them, pushing away the thought that as soon as there was some gas in the tank, they'd carjack him. Thirty minutes later they were back with the gas and directions to the station. He gave them another ten dollars each and they went on their way.

From the attendant he got directions to a motel. When he woke up the following morning, he wondered if he had dreamt the surreal encounter. The motel had complimentary coffee and danish in the lobby. The smell of the coffee was strangely invigorating. After finishing the first cup, he poured another, took one of the danish, and went outside into the sunshine. When he'd finished his breakfast, he returned to the clerk at the receptionist desk and paid for another night. He took a map of the area from a display stand and spent the day driving around.

Not quite horse-and-woods country, he thought, but almost. Certainly no skyscrapers, no apartment blocks, no smog or excessive traffic. He found the Police Department, introduced himself and asked to see the chief. There were no vacancies, but the chief, a ruddy-faced, cheerful man, winked and made a phone call. He then told him the New Croydon police chief wanted to see him. Frank drove the twenty miles immediately, and after an on-the-spot interview with Tommy Dixon was told if his references held up, he could start the following Monday.

The pay was less than New York, but so was the caseload. The cost of living, apart from housing, was more or less the same as Brooklyn, but with the life insurance money he was able to afford a small house. He told himself he wasn't unhappy. He worked longer hours than anyone, solved every one of his cases. There were far fewer murders than in the Sixty-Third and, with his experience, he was the go-to guy, it soon developed. He didn't mind in the slightest, even enjoyed sharing his knowledge with some of the younger men. He didn't smoke, drank nothing more than an occasional beer, and socialized only with colleagues, and even then just on semi-official celebrations—promotions, birthdays, Friday night get-togethers. Everyone knew about his wife—presumably the chief was the source—and everyone refrained from asking questions about her. He wasn't unhappy, he told himself.

10:23 P.M.

The door of the restaurant opened, and a shaft of light fell across the lot, allowing him to recognize her immediately. Damn, he thought. No one with her. He waited until she pulled into the street and then followed, wondering who was the driver of the Cadillac Eldorado, the only car in the entire lot with the silhouette of Lady Liberty on its license plates.

Chapter Six

"You're a . . ." Kay felt silly saying it. ". . . A private eye, right?"

She looked at the man sitting where Nikolas Seifer had sat the previous afternoon. Kelley would probably have used the words "roly poly" to describe Thomas Scanlon. Bald-headed, mustachioed like some archetypal Mexican bandit, and wearing a blue Yankees windbreaker and filthy sneakers that hadn't seen betters days in a decade, he was a sight to behold. This, she marveled, had been the Brooklyn D.A.'s finest detective for ten years?

"A private investigator, Mrs. Daniels."

It was Paul Keating who had recommended him. As soon as Seifer had left yesterday, she had called her lawyer and told him she needed a private detective. Despite the inevitable questions, she had fended Paul off and got Scanlon's number. Keating and the D.A. had attended Columbia together and had kept in touch both personally and professionally. Kay had called Scanlon immediately and told him she was meeting a man she wanted followed and identified. Scanlon didn't seem fazed that his new client needed him to start that very evening. Told of the eight o'clock reservation, he asked her to try and push it back, to give him enough time to find the place. It was Scanlon who suggested the babysitter ploy. Kay was well aware that Kelley didn't need a babysitter but agreed to make the call to Seifer with the excuse. Score one kudo for Mr. Scanlon, she now thought.

"Are you in disguise or something?" she asked.

He laughed. "God, no. I always dress like this. I'm a big Yankees fan. Can't you tell?"

"Oh, I see."

He held up his right hand and wagged it. There was an enormous gold ring on the index finger.

"It's genuine," he said.

"Genuine what?"

He seemed stunned at her ignorance. "World Series ring."

"You were a baseball player?"

To Kay, the only professional activity this man could have done in a baseball stadium was as a hotdog vendor.

He laughed. "God, no. I did a job for a certain Yankee, and he gave me one of his rings. From the '99 World Series."

"Must have been some job."

He laughed again. Kay suspected Mr. Scanlon found much in life to be a joke and laughed a lot.

"Yeah," he said. "I found his wife humping a rock star on a tour bus. That violated the prenup, and saved the guy a million smackers."

"I see. Well, you come highly recommended, as I said on the phone yesterday. How long have you been in the business?"

"I left the D.A.'s office in '95. Decided to hang up my own shingle. I've been able to make a living ever since."

"All right. So, you were in the restaurant last night?"

"Yeah, no prob. You described yourself pretty good and that Seifer guy, too. So it was no big deal to spot him and then you. The brunette I wasn't expecting, but there were so many people in the place, I doubt she made me."

Kay had a sinking feeling that even Helen Keller wouldn't have failed to spot Mr. Scanlon if he showed up alone dressed like that.

"You're sure? You look kind of . . ."

"Conspicuous?" He laughed. "I hear you, Mrs. Daniels. Don't

worry. I was dressed for the occasion, and I had company."

Oops, thought Kay. Score another couple of kudos for Mr. Scanlon. She just had to stop making immediate assumptions about people.

"So, did you learn anything about them?"

"They left the restaurant together but got into separate cars."

"Oh, right. Seifer said she had followed me."

"I figured since the male seems to be calling the shots on this deal, I should follow him."

"And?"

"And—" He looked shamefaced. "And I lost him. He was easy to tail for the first couple of miles—kept a steady pace. I figured maybe he was being careful after having a few brews and didn't want to be pulled over for a possible DWI. But then he stopped suddenly at Route 21. It was just before a crossroads. I couldn't risk stopping, too. It was a narrow country road with no other traffic in sight. So I had to keep going. I decided to take a chance and took the New Canaan turn, but he didn't follow me. When I doubled back, I couldn't tell which choice he had made at the crossroads. He may even have turned right around and headed back toward Juno's if he thought he was being tailed."

"God. Do you really think that's possible? It wasn't just a coincidental stop?"

Scanlon shrugged. "As I drove by, I could see peripherally that he was making a phone call. It's against the law to use a cell phone while driving in Connecticut, so it could have been a lucky break on his part. Then again, if he was smart enough to suspect a tail, it was a perfect excuse to stop and force me to keep going. If I had stopped too, he would have been certain he had made me."

She sighed. "So, where does that leave us? Did you get his license plate?"

"This guy is no dummy. The last two digits had some mud over them."

"Mud?"

Scanlon nodded. "It's an old dodge. Makes it look as if some mud was splashed up on the car. Just covering the last two digits is a nice touch, it's less obvious that it's intentional. And it gets the job done—you need the entire number to identify the registered owner. The DMV can't help with a partial. But it was a Connecticut plate, for what it's worth."

"Sounds like this guy is a handful."

"Sure seems that way. So, Mrs. Daniels, how do you want to proceed? Is it likely you'll be meeting him again? That's the only way I'll be able to get a handle on him."

"I think I will probably have to."

Scanlon rolled the big ring around his finger. "Do you want to tell me now what this man is after?"

What to tell him, she wondered? She knew from Paul that Scanlon was a former New York City police officer before he became a top investigator who had worked on many prominent cases for the district attorney. She wasn't sure if the relationship between her and Mr. Scanlon was as sacrosanct as that between a client and an attorney or doctor, but she felt he could be trusted. Still, she had been reluctant to tell even Paul and was now equally hesitant to reveal too many details to the private investigator.

"Let's just say he's looking for money."

"That he didn't earn."

"You could say that."

"Is he dangerous?"

"What! Why do you ask that?"

Scanlon shrugged. "He looked like a tough hombre. Seemed very fit and toned. Unusual for a man of his age. He might have been wearing a sharp suit, but he seemed like he could take care of himself. Just a guess, you know?"

Kay suspected Mr. Scanlon had met enough "tough hombres" over the years that he didn't need to *guess* about any of them.

"He said last night he would contact me in a couple of days to arrange another meeting."

Actually, she remembered, Seifer had given her three days to think it over. Perhaps he had as much experience in these situations as he'd indicated and knew three days was the optimum time for a victim to come to a final decision and obtain the money. Although, she thought, perhaps the correct word was not "victim," but "collaborator."

"Okay. Well, you have my cell and my office numbers. As soon as you hear from him, let me know where the meeting will be."

He rolled the ring around once more.

"You know, Mrs. Daniels. There's something I always tell my clients at the beginning of every investigation."

That it was going to be expensive, Kay was sure he was about to say.

"What's that, Mr. Scanlon?"

"You could always go to the police."

She stared at him. Wasn't it obvious she couldn't do that? Why did he think she had hired him?

"I'd rather not go to the police."

He laughed yet again. "And that's how all my clients respond."

Chapter Seven

Marilyn Jarvis. She was the key. Seifer's weak link. A mousy, old maid chartered accountant from Nebraska. There was no way this woman would serve time for Seifer. Find out more about her and, Kay was sure, Seifer's whip hand would lose control of its whip. She had given Scanlon as much information about Jarvis as she knew. So while he did what he could in tracking her down, Kay figured she had at least a full day to do her part. And who better to tell her about the mysterious Marilyn other than the police themselves?

While she waited for Detective Frank Sinclair to come out of his office, she thought back to the aftermath of the accident. A week following the funeral, she'd received a phone call at home. Jarvis identified herself and asked if they could meet. Whatever grief Kay had initially felt was gone. She agreed to the request. Kay felt it best if they met at a local coffee shop.

Jarvis, she remembered, hadn't been particularly distinctive. Kay vaguely recalled that the woman was well groomed; her accessories—pocketbook and jewelry—all indicated quality. The woman herself seemed timid, and clearly distraught. She licked her lips constantly, whether from nervousness or a long-acquired habit, Kay couldn't tell. She apologized repeatedly, said she simply didn't see the jogger when she made the turn around the corner. It had started to rain, but the main reason, she insisted, was that it was simply too dark. She wasn't speeding she said, just doing the area limit, but it was a big SUV and Bernard, apparently, was running toward—and not away from—her direction.

"Even the . . . bump didn't seem significant," she'd said. "I thought it might have been an animal or something."

She seemed embarrassed at the image. "Sorry."

Kay shook her head. "It's okay. Go ahead."

Another lick of the colorless lips. "Well, I got out right away and couldn't believe it. He just lay there, not moving. It probably sounds crazy, but I've never been in an accident in my life before. Not even a—what do they call it?—a fender bender. I didn't know what to do. I went to him, naturally, but had no idea how to give him any first-aid. He wasn't moving. I took off my jacket and folded it up, and placed it under his head. Then I went and got my purse and called 911. I went back to him, but he seemed the same. So I ran to the nearest house and banged on the door."

The ambulance arrived within six minutes but Bernard, the police told Kay, was pronounced dead at the scene. Massive internal injuries. A Chevrolet Suburban, all three tons of it, will do that, Kay thought now.

"Mrs. Daniels?"

She looked up. She hadn't heard him approach.

"Oh, hello, Detective. Do you have a few minutes?"

"Why?"

"I just wanted to ask you a couple of questions."

"I think that's what I'm supposed to say."

"Well, I promise it will only be a few minutes."

"All right. Come into my office."

"So," he said, when he had closed the door. "What can I do for you?"

"May I see your report?"

He stared at her. "About your husband?"

"Yes."

"You're kidding, right?"

She was genuinely puzzled. "No. Is there a problem? Doesn't it belong to the taxpayers?"

"Mrs. Daniels, a police investigation into a suspicious death is not . . ." He seemed at a loss by her gall, or her incredible naiveté. "Not the property tax rolls in the Town Hall."

"Oh. Well, can you tell me what's in it?"

"What!"

"Clearly you think there was some foul play. Otherwise, why all the interrogations?"

"They were interviews, not interrogations."

"Ah, no floodlights were in my eyes. That's correct. That makes them 'interviews.' "

Again he stared at her. Did he think she was playing with him, taunting him? A murder suspect wanting to see her own file.

He said, "What exactly do you want to know?"

"I'm interested in this Jarvis woman. What did you find out about her?"

He shrugged. "What you read in the papers. First time in the state. Visiting an old classmate from college who lived in the area. She was on her way to see her that night and—well, you know the rest. It was dark; it was raining; she hit your husband."

"This classmate. You talked to her?"

"Of course. And her husband. They corroborated what Jarvis said."

"So Jarvis has now gone back to Nebraska?"

"No."

"No? She's still here in Connecticut?"

He shook his head. "It seems Ms. Jarvis has gone abroad."

"Abroad?"

"To Europe. On the *QE2*. That's why she was on the East Coast in the first place. To catch the boat in New York. She hadn't seen her friend in years, and it was less than an hour's drive away from her hotel in Manhattan. So she rented the vehicle and drove here intending to spend the weekend before she set sail."

"Will you be able to keep track of her over there?"

He blew out a breath, exasperated. "Mrs. Daniels. It was a traffic accident. You don't drag Interpol into a traffic accident."

But you do badger me repeatedly, she thought, even after my husband is long buried.

He said, "Why are you so interested in this woman now? She reported the accident right away. Allowed herself to be interviewed by us without a lawyer present. She didn't leave the state until we said it was okay for her to go."

Something was bothering Kay, something in what he had just said. What was it? He looked at his watch, and it was obvious he wanted her to notice he was looking at it. Her time was up, she realized. He had other things to do, other cases to solve, other widows to interrogate.

She stood. There was nothing to be learned here, she thought. She forced herself to thank him and turned toward the door. Then she stopped, realizing what was bothering her. She suppressed a smile, thinking of *Columbo.*

"One more thing, Detective."

He looked up from a file folder, clearly not getting the humor. Maybe he was a workaholic and didn't even own a TV.

"Yes?"

"I was just wondering."

"Yes?"

"If you were a woman alone renting a vehicle to travel forty miles, would you choose a three-ton SUV?"

Chapter Eight

"So what did you learn in school today?"

In the passenger seat of the Volvo, Kelley put her right forefinger in front of her open mouth and made a gagging sound.

"Great," said Kay. "I'm paying an arm and a leg for a private school that teaches you how to vomit."

Kelley laughed. "Oh all right. It wasn't that bad. Hey! I met your friend Nik."

"Nik? I don't know any Nik."

"Mom! You went out to dinner with him the other night."

Kay pushed her foot onto the brake and swerved to the side of the road. A Mercedes sedan behind her blared its horn.

"What are you talking about, Kelley? Tell me! What are you saying?"

Kelley stared at her, the color gone from the child's face.

"What's the matter, Mom?"

"Seifer? Did you speak to him today? Where? Tell me!"

Kelley seemed puzzled by the name. "He called himself Nikolas. He spelled it for me. He said I could call him Nik."

Once again, Kay could feel her heart racing. "He came to the school?"

Kelley nodded. "We were waiting for the bus to take us to practice. He walked right over to me. Said he recognized me from your description."

That was a lie, Kay thought. She had never discussed Kelley with him. And yet he now knew her daughter by sight.

"What else did he say?"

"He asked me about school, how I was doing. You know, just chatting. He seemed nice. Then the bus came. He said he wanted me to give you a message."

She reached into the backpack on the floor between her legs and pulled out a small box wrapped in blue and gold paper. A red ribbon sealed the box.

"Jewelry already, Mom! You really must have made an impression. Can I open it?"

"No. Give it here."

Kay placed the box into the left pocket of her jacket, then put the car in gear and drove toward home. When she pulled into the garage, she said, "Go ahead and change. I'll be there in a minute."

"Okay." Kelley got out of the car and let herself into the house with her own key.

Kay waited until the door closed and then reached into her pocket. The paper wrap on the small box felt silky, luxurious. She looked up at the house and saw the lights go on. Then, at the thought of Seifer talking to her daughter, she tore at the paper, ripping it from the box. The box, now uncovered, could have held a wristwatch. She had bought a couple of watches for Bernard over the years, and this box appeared just like those. So was that the "message," she asked herself? That she was running out of time? That she only had until tomorrow to make up her mind?

She flipped open the lid of the box, then screamed. Atop a blue velour base lay the bloody stump of a man's index finger. Around the finger was a thick gold ring inscribed with the words: "World Series 1999."

Chapter Nine

"Please state your name, including middle name if applicable."

"Didn't I do all that already the last time?"

"Mrs. Daniels. This is a second interview. Not a continuation of the first."

"Katherine Marie Daniels."

"Now, Mrs. Daniels. Yesterday, you had to terminate our interview because your daughter left school early and her whereabouts were unknown."

"Yes."

"But you located her?"

"Yes. She had gone to a friend's house."

"Has your daughter ever done this sort of thing before? Run away from school? Or from home?"

"Just once."

"Was your husband physically abusive to her?"

"What?"

"He was abusive to you."

"Not . . . not that I'm aware of."

"Was he molesting her?"

"Detective!"

"Was your husband molesting your daughter? I have to ask."

"No. I don't believe so."

"Well, why do you think your daughter behaved like that?"

"I don't know. Well—we, my husband and I, had been arguing a lot at the time. I think that had an effect on Kelley."

"Arguing about what—the business?"

"Yes."

"Things weren't going well?"

"Not since I'd left."

"Why did you leave?"

"I got pregnant."

"I thought you said earlier that you didn't have any children with Mr. Daniels?"

"I didn't. I had a miscarriage."

"Oh. I'm sorry."

"That's all alright. It happens . . . I guess."

"You didn't return to work after the miscarriage?"

"No. I . . . I guess I needed time to myself. To think. To focus on being with Kelley. I didn't want to miss her growing up. I had been working ten, twelve hours a day. Six days a week. And it looked like I wasn't going to be able to have another child."

"Did your husband resent that you didn't return to the company?"

"Yes. Things started to go downhill. Bills were not being paid. Employees started to quit. Contracts were not renewed in some states. The business we're in requires that every year you have to convince the state agencies that you're maintaining certain approved standards. The process is rigorous because opening up the telecommunications field was so new. No state wanted people ripped off by fly-by-night companies."

"Wasn't your husband a partner? Didn't he run the business, too? Why were all these problems happening?"

"I guess because I was the one really running the company. It had been my idea in the first place, as I mentioned to you the last time. Once we got up and running, and things were going smoothly, he . . . sat back, I guess. It was growing so fast that he even decided to sell his rent-to-own stores. With phone service, there was no inventory to maintain—TVs, furniture, and so on.

We merely sold a service. The big phone companies provided the actual service. So he was involved in all that, meeting with potential buyers, trying to arrange to sell the stores. Then when I remained at home, he had to contend with running New Croydon Telecomm, too."

"So you were having arguments. And they escalated? It that what happened? That's when he became physically abusive."

"Yes. He had also started to drink heavily. Because of the stress, I suppose."

"Mr. Daniels was considerably older than you, wasn't he?"

"Twelve years."

"So. Your husband was being abusive; your business was deteriorating; your daughter felt sufficiently traumatized that she ran away from home. That's about the size of it—how things were for you at that time?"

"Yes."

"It's a miracle you didn't snap."

Chapter Ten

"So you got the message?" Seifer asked Kay.

"You're not going to search me this time?"

Kay didn't care if his woman searched her now. She was past caring. She realized she hadn't even changed from her business skirt. She had come directly from the bank after arranging for the wire transfer from her brokerage account. She didn't care. What did it matter if that woman's hands searched beneath her skirt? She just wanted them both out of her life as quickly as possible. Out of Kelley's life. You can't reason with madness, she had determined. And, certainly, Seifer was mad. So best to pay up, pay them off, and get on with your life.

Seifer shook his head. "No need. You're not wearing a wire."

He glanced at Johanna, who leaned against the hood of a bone-white Jaguar sedan. Seifer had instructed Kay to meet him in a commuter parking lot close to the New Croydon train station. In mid-afternoon during the workweek, the location was deserted. Johanna smirked then shook her head. Kay didn't care. They had won. She admitted it. Face reality, she had told herself. He held the whip hand. He had always held the whip hand. And he was certainly mad. A killer. Ruthless. Whatever word you want to use, she told herself. But the most important word was *dangerous.* Too dangerous to bargain with. Too dangerous to have anywhere near her daughter. Money was merely paper. Kay would gladly have given him all of it if he now demanded it.

"No, Mrs. Daniels," he went on. "Something tells me you haven't gone to the police."

No, she hadn't gone to the police. Initially, though, that had been her first reaction when she had calmed down—with the aid of a straight scotch—after she'd opened the little box. Miraculously, Kelley hadn't heard what Kay thought had to be her ear-splitting scream. Because Kelley, as usual, already had her iPod at full blast. Kay made it to the drinks cabinet and swallowed the whiskey in one gulp. She began to pour a second, then stopped. She realized she would need her senses fully alert if she were to proceed. She picked up the phone and then immediately put it down. No police, she decided. Not yet.

She needed advice. She couldn't manage anymore by herself. She thought of Paul Keating. But then dismissed it. He would only recommend calling 911. Paul had never met Seifer, wouldn't know what the man was capable of. Couldn't know. Besides, Paul was not a criminal lawyer. His expertise was in the arcane world of telecommunications legislation. She walked around the living room, unable to remain standing, trying to come to some solution. Very quickly she realized she was indeed going around in circles. After a while she heard Kelley tramp heavily down the stairs. Then her voice.

"What's for dinner, Mom? Are we going out or something? I don't smell anything in the kitchen."

Kay looked at her watch. Good God, she thought. It was almost six o'clock. She'd been walking around like a mental case for almost an hour.

"I don't feel too great," she explained, when Kelley came into the living room. "I'm going to lie down. Why don't you order a pizza for yourself."

"Cool." Kelley skipped into the kitchen, and Kay heard her talking on the phone.

Kay went upstairs, closed the door of her room, and sat on

the bed, staring into space. After a while, she heard the doorbell chime, a jolly singsong tone that seemed from a time different than the present. Again, she looked at her watch. 6:45 P.M. For God's sake, she said to herself. I can't go on like this. She heard Kelley's voice talking to the deliveryman, then his car driving away. Finally, she made a decision. There was only one person she felt she could trust.

Janet came over within the hour. Kelley, after cleaning up after herself in the kitchen, was in her room talking to her best friend, Carol. She would be on the phone at least until bedtime. Nevertheless, as a precaution, Kay closed the door to the living room before she began explaining to her sister.

Janet, with her customary serenity, stared at Kay while she started at the beginning, when Seifer had first walked into the office. Kay had always felt her sister resembled a nun. It was not just the physical appearance—the short hair, the austere clothes usually in blacks and grays, the lack of much jewelry beyond a pair of small pearl earrings that Kay had given her when Janet had graduated from veterinarian school. It was some inner calm or a sense of balance—whatever it was, a trick or talent, Kay knew she herself lacked it and Janet so effortlessly possessed it. Like a nun, too, Janet forgave easily. She forgave Kay for what she had done—or, more correctly, failed to do—many years before.

Janet remained silent, holding off asking questions until Kay was through. Kay finished by taking out the little box from a bureau drawer, worried that Janet wouldn't believe a word of what she had just been told.

Janet was clearly reluctant to open the lid but realized the necessity of doing so. She grimaced at the contents and, prepared for the sight of the bloody finger, no more than gasped.

"Kay," she said. "You have to go the police."

Kay pressed her lips together, an old habit from childhood

that helped prevent tears, and shook her head.

"I don't think I can. I'm too . . . involved."

"Nonsense. Show them that," Janet said, pointing toward the coffee table where she had placed the small box. "It's evidence."

"You don't know this man. Look what he's capable of."

She reminded Janet of the murders reported in the newspaper clippings. Of the preparations he'd undergone as far back as her stay at the Englebrook last spring.

"Clearly he's got . . . resources. Money. Power. It's hard to describe. He seems so . . . cavalier about all of this. So confident that he can't be touched. I don't think the police would have enough to link him to all these deaths."

"But you have that box. Kelley can tell them this man gave it to her at the school."

Again Kay shook her head. She had already thought it through.

"Kelley never saw me open the box. Seifer would claim it contained a watch or some jewelry. That *I'm* responsible for . . . for Mr. Scanlon. Remember, Scanlon came to see me at my office. My secretary saw him, knows his name. I called his office number from my phone. I'm connected to him. Seifer is not. Just like he's not connected to Bernard or Marilyn Jarvis or, I'm sure, any of those other people he's killed."

There was silence while Janet considered this. Then Kay spoke again:

"Besides, he still has me connected to Jarvis. And to Bernard's death. God, what a mess."

She had made a mess of it, she realized. She should have just gone to the police immediately and called Seifer's bluff. The evidence, at best, was circumstantial. But as always, ever she since she was a teenager—despite the constant reminder from her father that "It's a man's world"—she had foolishly believed she could prevail over anyone who thought she was second best.

So she'd called in Mr. Scanlon, convinced with a professional's help she could bring the matter to a satisfactory conclusion. And look at what happened to that poor man. It was a mess, and she was responsible.

Just as she'd made a mess of her marriage. What had she been thinking? Janet had told her she was crazy to marry a man so much older than herself. But she responded that she saw *something* in Bernard, something she could manage. She explained frequently that he had "the hurting heart of a child." Yes, she had worked for him long enough to realize many of his failings. But, she sensed, his bullying of employees, his short temper, his stinginess with money, were inherited from a youth of being himself bullied and of deprivation. He had been overweight for most of his early years. But in college his intellect more than compensated for physical and fiscal deficiencies, and an MBA from Wharton led to a lucrative sojourn on Wall Street. Several Christmas bonuses were invested shrewdly over the years, and in his late thirties he came up with the idea of the rent-to-own stores. He'd bought out one small chain in Jersey City and, after a few successful years of modest expansion, merged with another larger chain in Trenton. He was wealthy and ambitious. That ambition, of course, had led directly to their initial acquaintance.

And it had all started so well. He had even promised to make an effort with Kelley. But after a year it had begun to go downhill. He was too old, he felt, to become the archetypal father. His interests were those of a middle-age businessman. He didn't have the patience to sit with a three-year-old and watch *Sesame Street,* to push a toddler on a swing-set, to help a child make sandcastles on the beach. Kay had tried to make it work for the three of them, taken on the burden of the actual child rearing. Then she felt the pregnancy would change things, as if somehow because the baby was actually his own, that he would emerge from his cocoon into a classic Dad. But it wasn't to be. Her own body had failed her. Another mess.

"There's only one way out of this," she said finally, her decision already made before Janet had even arrived.

"What?"

"Pay him off. Give him what he wants."

"Kay! It's blackmail. Robbery, even. We need to get the police involved."

Kay made a dismissive gesture with her right hand.

"Even if I was successful in persuading them I'm not involved, the situation has changed. Look at what this man did to Mr. Scanlon. He's hardly the type to forgive and forget. If it was just me, I could handle it. I think. But I can't take the risk with Kelley. I just can't. That was the *message* he was sending by having Kelley bring me the box. So, no police."

"No," she said to Seifer. "I didn't call the police."

She handed the canvas overnight bag to him. "Now, take it and go."

He opened the zipper and removed some bundles of $1,000 notes. After flicking through them and checking inside the bag, he was evidently satisfied. He closed the zipper and gave the bag to Johanna.

"I have something for *you,*" he said.

He removed an envelope from his jacket pocket and passed it to her.

"What's this?"

"Open it."

She was surprised to see the envelope contained Jarvis's receipt from the hotel and the telephone bill.

He said, "See, Mrs. Daniels? I'm a man of my word. I *always* do what I say I'll do. You should have listened. You really shouldn't have brought the late Mr. Scanlon into this."

Kay stifled a gasp. She had held the hope—forlorn, she sensed—that Scanlon was still alive, but now it seemed that hope was dashed.

Seifer went on, "There was no need to get anyone else involved. We could have concluded our little business deal with no muss or fuss. But I can't tolerate anyone, *anyone,* prying into my affairs. So you have the guilt of Mr. Scanlon's death on your conscience. I hope you can live with that."

She looked down, ashamed and close to tears.

"I spend a great deal of time and effort and money setting up these deals. I do that to prevent *disorder.* Because disorder attracts police attention, and I don't want police attention. Mr. Scanlon's appearance forced a change of plans."

He nodded to Johanna, who went to the car and sat in the passenger seat.

"I'll take my leave of you now, Mrs. Daniels." He turned and walked toward the car.

"It's in the bag," she called out to him. "At the bottom. Beneath the money."

He stopped and faced her, clearly puzzled. "What is?"

"Mr. Scanlon's . . ."

He smiled. "Ah! I thought you would have burned that by now. Or disposed of it in the nearest river."

"I burnt the box. It had my fingerprints on it."

He nodded. "That's right. You're learning, Mrs. Daniels. You're learning."

He got into the Jaguar, then pulled out of the parking lot without a further look at her. You're a good teacher, she thought, as the vehicle took the man called Seifer out of her life.

Whoever you are.

Chapter Eleven

The man who called himself Nikolas Seifer—a private joke—was born John MacBride in Belfast on July 24, 1960.

His true life, he would come to believe, had begun proper on January 30, 1972, an unremarkable date to the rest of the world, but forever known to all in Northern Ireland more infamously as Bloody Sunday.

He was eleven years old and, incredible as it seems now, he was not the only youngster among the ten thousand marchers demonstrating against the policy of internment without trial. Perhaps it was a more innocent time, although the "Troubles" had been in full swing for the previous four years. But innocence surely died that day. When the soldiers from the 1st Battalion Parachute Regiment opened fire with their 7.62 millimeter SLR assault rifles, like everybody else, he dropped instinctively to the ground. The disciplined *crack, crack, crack* of the rifle fire became distant and unreal to him, not at all like the cowboy or war films he loved to see with his mates. When the firing stopped and the screaming began, he raised his head and saw only the woman next to him: a stranger, with her lifeless eyes staring at nothing.

Weeks later, he was witness to more carnage. A car bomb went off outside a department store on a Saturday afternoon. He heard the noise from several streets away while playing football. The entire group of boys ceased playing and ran to the scene. He saw a man with his right leg blown off—the leg, a bloody stump, lay on the road a dozen yards away. The man alternately looked at the leg and then back at his own body from which blood dripped quickly to the ground. MacBride expected him to be sobbing or something, but there was no sound from the man. A baby carriage was on its side, a baby screaming for its mother who lay lifeless next to it. The smell of smoke and vomit surrounded him. And again, he felt somehow detached, as if it was all unreal. He went to the baby carriage and set it upright on its wheels. Thinking back to that moment, he would always believe that was the first adult thing he had ever done in his life.

Two months later, with the relentless tit-for-tat bombings and shootings beginning to plague Belfast, his parents sent him away from the city to an uncle's farm in the country. The excitement of new surroundings, the tractors and the tilling machines, the mystery of the big barns and haylofts with their numerous secret places, and all the different animals, made his homesickness disappear after a few days. His uncle even gave him chores to do, and because he paid him a few shillings a week, referred to them as "his job." He was happy, as he never could recall being happy.

His parents frequently visited, but he was told he would be staying at the farm for some time. It was too dangerous to go back home. So for the next five years, he remained with his uncle, going to a local school and helping on the farm before and after classes as well as on weekends. He felt his body grow stronger with the sustained physical labor; his muscles became hard, his stamina increased daily.

One summer evening, shortly after his sixteenth birthday, he went for a walk with his dog through the darkening fields. The evening was his favorite part of the day. The work was done; the forced requirement to interact with other people was past. His body was pleasantly tired after the day's exertions. Now he could let his mind wander in the almost silent countryside. The air was still and mild. Then the dog suddenly ran off into a copse of trees, chasing some small animal. He called it to heel but it wouldn't obey. Irritated, he followed it into the woods, finally coming across the dog barking at a rodent that had made it to safety on a lower branch of an oak tree. MacBride called the dog to heel but it was too excited by the chase and the proximity of the cornered rodent and continued to bark and claw against the tree trunk. MacBride picked up a piece of broken branch and hit the dog on the rump. The dog yelped, turned on its haunches, and bared its teeth. MacBride suddenly lashed out with his boot, catching the dog in the side of its head. It went down, dazed. MacBride knelt quickly and placed his hands around the throat of the dog and squeezed. He hadn't realized how strong he had become. He sensed, felt, the life draining from the animal. But still it struggled, kicking with its feet, squirming with its body. But after a minute, perhaps it knew there was no escape from the unwavering grip of those hands, and the struggle began to cease. Even after the animal was dead, MacBride continued to grasp its throat, flushed with excitement, a sense of power surging in him that he had never before experienced. All his life he had been buffeted by others, by events, by the clock, by directives of one kind or another. Here, alone in the woods, surrounded by the indifference that he knew was the land and its creatures, he sensed, for the first time, freedom. He also sensed his dominance to his surroundings. He could survive because he could kill.

A few months later, his uncle, who felt he was becoming too old for the continuing rigors of the farm, decided to retire and sold out to a neighbor. MacBride returned to his family's small flat on the Shankhill Road.

After a month, his parents were killed, not by a bomb or a bullet, but, almost unbelievably in that near-war zone, in a stupid bus accident. After the funeral, he offered his services to the IRA. It was not, he realized even then, for patriotism or any of the typical motives. He wanted excitement, an escape from the tedium that he saw lay ahead of them all—Patty, Bill, and his other friends. The jobs they were going to get—even if they *could* get jobs—would be stupid and menial and boring. He didn't care if the IRA paid him anything. As long as they gave him shelter, a bed, some food, he could survive.

A week shy of his twentieth birthday, after two years of sniper training, he murdered his first British soldier. The pimply-faced youth in the crosshairs—a private in the Eighth Infantry Brigade on sentry duty at a border checkpoint—probably wasn't older than MacBride. But the real difference was *he* was going to die and MacBride was going to live. MacBride was surprised by his complete absence of sympathy. He felt no hostility to the boy in the uniform two hundred yards away. He knew the soldier almost certainly didn't want to be there and had probably joined the army because he couldn't find work. Suddenly, he hardened his heart. *Choice,* he thought. The soldier had chosen to do what he was doing. And *he* had made his own choice. Now the soldier's spotty face was no more unique to him than one of the many goats and pigs he had killed during his training. He smiled to himself at the thought: He felt nothing because he felt nothing. He pulled the trigger and the boy's forehead was smashed by the explosive impact of the single bullet. MacBride didn't wait to view the body but, as he'd been instructed, quickly turned away and jogged down the hill to the waiting car. But with the other kills that followed, he did linger a few moments, examining with interest the result of his handiwork.

There would be scores more over the next dozen years. Not all of them would be from the comforting distance of several hundred yards with the aid of a sniper's rifle. Changing tactics by the Brits made the easy shots of the past a pleasant memory only. He was given different assignments. He was dispatched to England as the bodyguard to the bomb teams that blew up pubs and restaurants in Liverpool, Manchester, and London. He executed informers with a pistol-shot to the head when they were caught. He tortured the occasional soldier they managed to capture.

After the cease-fire in 1993, he knew he couldn't go to London. There was little at home to interest him, and he knew he was useless at foreign languages. London would have been the ideal location. But the Underworld there would consider him an outsider, he suspected, and wouldn't tolerate him on their patch. An ex-IRA man could only bring heat down on them. He decided to try the States.

But that meant Canada, first, of course. From there, it was easy to get across the border. It meant a hike through the isolated terrain of Manning Provincial Park, the northern terminus of the Pacific Crest Trail, but equipped with the right gear from a camping store in Vancouver, he made his made way into Washington State three days after arriving in Montreal.

He settled in New York and considered the best course of action. He had savings stashed in a money-belt beneath his shirt. As a participant in some of the numerous bank robberies across the country in the '80s that partly financed the IRA campaign, he had always helped himself to a portion of the loot. They all did it, so nobody minded. But he knew that in six to nine months he would need to start acquiring income. He decided against hitting banks. There was no equivalent in Northern Ireland to the FBI, but he was well aware of the reach of that organization and had no intention of having them on his tail. He decided to specialize in burglary.

The bedroom communities of Westchester County where the ambitious and, as yet, childless wives worked in the city along with their husbands, had the optimum set of conditions for his requirements.

He had learned the fine art of breaking-and-entering from the experts themselves back in the IRA. His first haul consisted of jewelry, two ladies' watches, a fur coat, and collectibles.

His original intention had been to take money and jewelry only. But, he realized almost immediately as he prowled through the dozen rooms of the property, American homeowners, unlike those in the British Isles, kept little actual cash around the house. So he had snatched the fur coat when he had seen it in the huge walk-in closet and then the figurines in the étagère that he suspected must be of some value. But now what, he asked himself, as he looked at the disparate items tossed on his bed? He needed cash, not a fur coat.

He talked to one of the men at the Irish bar in Queens where he went for meals most nights. The man recommended an establishment in Brooklyn. MacBride visited the place the next day. The neighborhood, on 15th Avenue, was one of small residential buildings, with some storefronts on the ground floors. He checked the address again, then opened the barred door. It may claim to be a pawnshop, but he knew from his contact's own activities, it was surely a lot more. He told the proprietor the name of the man who had recommended him, showed him the jewelry, and said he had "other merchandise" that he wanted to sell.

The man held a pearl necklace up to the light, squinting with his right eye.

"Nice," he said, finally. "Where'd ya get it?"

MacBride knew enough not to bullshit these people and sensed that straight talk from the get-go would only grease the wheels.

"I stole it."

Perhaps the man was not accustomed to honesty. He laughed and said, "Is that right?"

He nodded at a side door. "Come on back."

He unlocked the door from the inside and stood aside as MacBride entered the room. The door was then locked again. In the middle of the small room, three men sat at a card table playing gin rummy and smoking with a fury that suggested cigarette prohibition was imminent. All three looked up but, just as quickly, returned their attention to the cards.

The proprietor, a small, tough-looking man who walked with a slight limp, said to MacBride, "You wired?"

He was momentarily at a loss—this was the first time in his life that he had been considered a member of law enforcement. Then he shook his head. Realizing almost immediately that Hell would freeze over before these people would accept the word of a stranger, he removed his jacket, then unbuttoned his shirt.

The man kneeled in front of him. "You don't mind, do you?"

MacBride shook his head. The man ran his hands up along his legs and thighs, then stood, apparently satisfied.

"All right. Let's deal."

MacBride was shocked at the percentage that was offered. But the man explained that ten percent of the retail value was fair. After all, he said, he had to make a profit in turn.

Knowing there was little alternative—the stuff was stolen, for Christ's sake, he told himself, as he drove home—he had agreed. When he returned the following day with the other items, the man smiled warmly and again nodded to the side door.

"You know the drill."

MacBride entered the room. The same three men were in the same chairs as the previous day. One of them nodded in greeting. The proprietor made a curious wagging gesture with his fingers at MacBride's body.

He was genuinely baffled. "What?"

"Your shirt."

He could hardly believe it. Didn't they trust him? But it

quickly dawned on him that these people had remained in business precisely because they trusted no one outside of their own. He sighed and again removed his jacket and shirt. To convey his irritation, he loosened his belt and dropped his pants.

"Okay?"

The man shrugged. "Hey, you look in great shape. Just like an FBI man. I've got to check."

The others laughed without malice. It was just business, they all implied.

They concluded the transaction and the man, who finally introduced himself as Tippy-Toe Joe, invited MacBride to sit and have a glass of wine. The cards were put away and a bottle of red wine appeared. They toasted each other's health and drank to continued prosperity. MacBride was told they would take whatever he brought in.

One of the others laughed. "Tippy-Toe Joe took in a load of frozen shrimp last week. If he'll take frozen shrimp, he'll take anything."

The others roared, even Joe. MacBride couldn't help smiling.

"Frozen shrimp?" he asked. "How do you dispose of that?"

Joe shrugged. "Any idea how many restaurants there are in Manhattan?"

MacBride nodded. "Got it."

For the next six months, after every burglary, he went directly to Joe's, not even bothering to go home first. It was three months before they stopped making him strip. They had all done time in prison and none wanted to repeat the experience. He became friendly with them and ate with them once or twice a week in a trattoria around the corner. Then, one afternoon in July, they were playing cards when Joe came in, clearly agitated.

MacBride had never seen the usually jovial face so grim.

"What is it, Joe?" one of the others asked.

"It's that fuck, Donaghue."

"Our cop?"

"Yeah."

"What's the matter with him?"

"He's squeezing me. He's not getting enough, he says. He has a wife and a girlfriend to keep, he says. He has kids to send to college, he says."

"How much does he want?"

"Twenty-five percent."

"Twenty-five percent! That's insane."

"Twenty-five percent. Or he's not going to look the other way anymore."

MacBride glanced at the others. He saw the seriousness on their faces and wondered why were they not discussing the obvious solution to their problem.

He turned to Joe. "Kill him."

Joe snorted. "Can't. Cops and judges can't be killed."

"Or children," said one of the others.

MacBride said, "This one seems to deserve to die."

Joe nodded. "I can't argue with that."

MacBride took a breath, made a decision. "I'll do it."

There was silence, save for the labored drone of the ancient air conditioner in the solitary window. Perhaps, MacBride thought, the smoke-filled air had finally brought it to its knees.

Joe said, "Johnny, I told you. We can't kill cops."

"I can. I'm not a member of your Family."

MacBride had given it a great deal of thought these past few months. It occurred to him that successful burglary was a business with diminishing returns. The spate of robberies in the Westchester area had alerted local police and residents to the dangers to their homes. All in all, he decided, he needed a different line of work. The Mob, he knew, was one possible source of that work.

He looked at Tippy-Toe Joe. Despite the ridiculous nickname

and the warm embrace he'd given to "his favorite ace burglar," he knew from his Irish contacts that the man was a killer, as were the others in the room. None of them would hesitate to shoot, stab, or pummel to death a driver of a hijacked truck who put up resistance to being deprived of his load. None of them would hesitate to kill an informer who threatened to land them in prison. None of them would hesitate to lash out if they received even the slightest of personal insults. MacBride realized that if he wanted the ultimate in credibility with these men—beyond the fencing of stolen goods—he would have to kill someone.

"Consider it a favor. Since there will be no payment, there will be no connection with you."

Two months to the day, there was a knock on his apartment door. He looked through the peephole and saw Joe. He opened the door.

The joviality had returned to Joe's face. "Special delivery!"

When MacBride closed the door, Joe hugged him, an action that made him uncomfortable, but fortunately it was momentary. Joe then reached into a side pocket of his jacket, removed a thick buff-colored envelope, and gave it to MacBride.

He opened it. It was full of $100 bills. There must have been at least two hundred of them.

MacBride felt uncomfortable. "I said it was a favor."

"Those who do favors for us get favors in return. Relax, Johnny. You deserve it. Just think of the small fortune you've saved me with that fucker out of the picture."

MacBride decided not to argue, sensing any further hesitation might be construed as insulting. He nodded.

"Okay," said Joe. "Now, come down to the store tomorrow at lunch. We'll have some pasta all'amatriciana that my wife makes the way it's supposed to be made—with guanciale. Then we'll talk some business. And you'll give me a chance to win some of that money back—we're gonna have to raise the stakes, a dollar a point. Whad'ya say?"

"I'll be there."

MacBride found there was demand for his services. Joe acted as a broker, vouching for his discretion and expertise, securing jobs, preparing everything and pointing in the direction of the target, then rendering the increasingly lucrative payments. He was even loaned out to other families when an especially critical task, such as eliminating a witness scheduled to testify in a trial, was deemed too sensitive to be handled by local associates.

Things began to change as he approached his thirty-fifth birthday. The FBI was pursuing the Five Families in New York with renewed vigor. Armed with the RICO statute—with its wide net of thirty-five assorted crimes and its draconian mandatory sentences, including the confiscation of the guilty party's assets—together with improved surveillance technology and turncoat mobsters, the Bureau was making inroads, sustained and deep, into all the Families. The mob's glory days, MacBride sensed, were clearly behind them. When Vincent Delacroce, the brother of the head of Joe's Family, was indicted following the audiotaping with a Bureau infiltrator, MacBride began to wonder if he had sufficient savings to consider retiring.

One mid-winter afternoon, he was sitting with the others in the back room of the pawnshop when Joe let out a whoop of delight.

"Would you believe this?" he said, pointing to the newspaper he held in his hands. "I'm tellin' ya—even the suburbs are becoming dangerous nowadays."

Joe was the son of immigrant parents who had moved to Bensonhurt from Napoli. Italian was the only language spoken at home until Joe was fourteen and the old man died. Reading *Il Mattino* was a habit he had never been able to break.

"What is it, Joe?" someone asked.

"This rich guy was killed walking his dog! Some idiot knocked him down. He didn't see the guy in the dark. Can you believe that? Holy fuck."

He turned to MacBride and punched him lightly on the arm.

"Who needs the services of Johnny Mac when the neighbors are as dangerous as this?"

MacBride listened to Joe read the article aloud and shared Joe's bemusement at the absurd incident but thought nothing further about it until a week later. There was a follow-up story in another issue. After an investigation, the local prosecutor had decided not to press charges against the driver of the vehicle. The man had no alcohol or drugs in his system. He had called for an ambulance immediately and, despite being residents of the same affluent suburb, there was no connection between the two men. It was "regrettable," the prosecutor said, but "clearly an unfortunate accident." The early evening darkness and the terrible misfortune of a street lamp malfunctioning contributed to the bizarre death.

MacBride glanced at the others as they began to play gin rummy with their typical noisy exuberance. *Who needs the services of Johnny Mac when the neighbors are as dangerous as this?* He was confident none of them noticed the smile that appeared on his lips.

Chapter Twelve

Sometimes it's better to be a spectator rather than a participant, Sinclair thought as he watched Kay Daniels answer questions put by Detective Mo Lipinski of the Eighty-First Precinct in Brooklyn.

This would have surprised most of the people he had encountered in his life. He was what his grandfather called a *doer.* When he was seventeen he bought a ten-year-old junked-up Trans Am and, with the aid of a friend, several reference manuals, and his innate technical ability, repaired it. A year later, he sold it for enough money to pay his first year's tuition at Columbia. In college, he excelled in sports and, therefore, made many friends. After college, he joined the Navy because, as he said with glee to every incredulous friend, he "wanted to see the world." After two four-year stints doing exactly that, he returned to New York and, enthralled by *Serpico,* decided that being a detective would be his ideal career—it would combine decision-making and a results-oriented occupation with considerable independence of movement in daily life.

It was, he admitted at the time, the least rational decision-making he'd ever undertaken, but it . . . *felt* right. His degree, his experience commanding men in the Service, and his test results put him on the fast track. He made detective after four years on the force.

So it was unusual for him to sit back and just listen and observe, not to be the one asking questions. But he had asked this woman so many questions already, it might prove useful now to watch her react to an interview by Mo Lipinski.

Detective-Sergeant Mary-Jo Lipinski looked to be in her mid-thirties. She wore a black pants suit of the type favored by female agents in the FBI. Her auburn hair was tied back in a bun, making her makeup-free face seem surprisingly stark. But if the intent was to hide her natural prettiness—high cheekbones, full lips, bright blue eyes—she had failed. Sinclair suspected Lipinski engaged—or believed she was engaged—in a daily struggle to prove herself to her colleagues in the Eighty-First. Hence the less-than-feminine contraction of her simply-too-cute first name. In any event, she was good at her job, as Sinclair discovered when he made a few inquiries following Lipinski's phone call.

"It's a missing persons case," she explained. "A P.I. called Thomas Scanlon. Someone in your backyard hired him shortly before he disappeared. A Mrs. Kay Daniels of Ridgewood Court. Just a courtesy call to let you know I'll be in your neck-of-the-woods tomorrow."

Lipinski paused and added without much sincerity: "You're welcome to sit in, if you'd like."

Sinclair smiled. "I'd be delighted to sit it and hear what Mrs. Daniels has to say about this man."

As usual, Sinclair thought, she was maddeningly cool, vaguely irritated at being questioned, as if she was pure as the driven snow. In his experience, such reaction to a police interview meant a clear conscience or a very clever criminal. He'd seen enough scumbags in his career defeat a polygraph; a "wrong" answer merely reflects anxiety at that particular question but provides no real reason as to why the person is anxious. Anybody who doesn't feel guilt was going to easily pass a polygraph. Either she was innocent or so desensitized she was incapable of feeling guilt.

"Yes," she had responded to Lipinski's initial question, "I hired Mr. Scanlon."

Lipinski had begun by telling her Scanlon had not been seen for a month and a search of his office and phone records had turned up her name, number, and location.

"Why did you hire a private investigator from out-of-state?"

"My attorney recommended him."

"And why did you need a private investigator?"

She then gave Lipinski the runaround. Her explanation was some bullshit about the business she was in. Credit-challenged people, she said, are, by nature, poor people. And some poor people get angry when they feel threatened by collection agencies sending them nasty notices. They get angry and lash out. She gestured toward Sinclair himself.

"Last year we had to call 911 when a customer showed up at our office and kicked in a glass door."

Lipinski had turned to Sinclair, who nodded. He had looked into it during his initial investigation of Bernard Daniels's death. Some idiot from Jersey City took exception to being asked to pay his telephone bill and made the trip all the way to Connecticut to let the company know he wasn't intimidated by the collection agency that New Croydon Telecomm used to go after delinquent customers. He'd been arrested, fined, and given probation.

Now she was explaining to Lipinski: "I thought it prudent to hire Mr. Scanlon to look into a number of phone calls I was personally receiving from the New York area."

Sinclair looked at Lipinski. Was she buying any of this crap? Who the hell hires a P.I. to look into malicious phone calls? But Lipinski seemed charmed by her. She was nodding as Daniels spoke. Sinclair watched Daniels closely. She seemed different since he'd last met with her more than a month ago, more assured, more collected. *Hardened* was the word that popped into his head.

"Were the calls threatening?" Lipinski asked.

"Not in so many words. I figured this man was angry about the collection agency, like the others, but I didn't want to take any chances. You see, Sergeant Lipinski, I'm a widow. My husband had recently passed away."

Dammit, thought Sinclair. He shouldn't have tried to be so cute with Lipinski. He should have forewarned her. The Brooklyn detective, he saw, was buying into her act. A look of concern appeared on her face.

"I'm sorry to hear that, Mrs. Daniels."

Lipinski then glanced down at the notepad on her knee. Christ, thought Sinclair. I thought you were experienced, woman? What are you doing—looking for the next question to ask!

"And what did Mr. Scanlon discover about these phone calls?"

Daniels shrugged. "I don't know. He came to my office. We discussed the situation and then he left. I assumed he'd get back to me with some sort of report. But I never heard from him again."

"And you never thought to call his office to get an update?"

Another shrug. "Well, I was just so busy. As I mentioned, my husband was gone and I was occupied full-time with the business. In any case, the phone calls stopped."

I bet they did, Sinclair thought. Again Lipinski, he saw, was looking down at her notepad. That was it? Sinclair thought. Nothing else to ask this woman?

Daniels evidently thought the pause was some concluding break in the interview for she said:

"May I ask a question now, Sergeant?"

Lipinski looked up, surprised. "Eh, yeah. Sure."

"What's happened to Mr. Scanlon?"

"We . . . don't know. We haven't been able to find him. None of his family or clients have heard from him since the middle of November."

"You've searched his house?"

"Of course. There was no evidence of a break-in or any struggle of any kind."

"Did you locate his car?"

Sinclair stared at Lipinski. Didn't she catch it? *Locate* Scanlon's car? Why would she use that particular word?

Lipinski stared at her. "Excuse me, Mrs. Daniels?"

"Yes?"

"Why did you say *locate* Mr. Scanlon's car?"

For the first time, Daniels looked unsure, almost nervous.

"I . . . don't know. Is there something wrong with that word?"

Lipinski *was* good, thought Sinclair. She didn't respond immediately. She sensed something odd and was letting Daniels stew, hoping she would blunder on in the silence that now lay between them, hoping that in doing so she would reveal more of whatever it was she was withholding.

It seemed to work. Daniels went on, "I just . . . assumed he had taken off in his car. Didn't he?"

Lipinski waited a little more before replying. "Yes. But I hadn't mentioned that specifically. I only told you he was missing. I didn't tell you he even had a car. Not many people in Manhattan bother getting cars because of the expense involved."

"Well, I don't know. I figured his job would require traveling around by car."

"Yes. But if someone who owns a car goes missing, it doesn't automatically mean they went missing while driving that car."

Daniels seemed to get her equilibrium back because she said, "Well, in any event, did the car show up?"

"No. That's vanished, too."

Chapter Thirteen

It was six months before Kay stopped checking the rearview mirror every few seconds when she drove her car. It was twelve months before she allowed Kelley to take the school bus. Every morning she drove her daughter to Hanover Hall and, despite the embarrassed protests, walked her into the building. Every afternoon, irrespective of business commitments, Kay was there waiting to escort Kelley to the car and drive her home.

She bought a Heckler & Koch P7K3, the classic "ladies' gun"—small enough to fit into a pocketbook, powerful enough to bring down an adult male—and took shooting lessons twice a week until the instructor told her she "was as good a shot as she was ever likely to be." She took a course in self-defense taught by a street cop moonlighting from the Bridgeport force. She installed a security system in the house.

But after a year she finally felt things were as normal as they appeared. Over lunch with Janet one Sunday afternoon, she smiled an embarrassed smile.

"All the precautions now seem like a waste of effort," she said.

It was the first time she had brought up the subject since the night Janet came over and learned about Seifer. Once Kay had returned from handing over the money and said, "It's done. He's gone," her sister never asked any further questions.

Janet made a face and put down her coffee cup.

"Until the cash runs out. Then he'll be back."

"I don't think so. He was right about one thing. He doesn't want me as a penniless enemy. Much better for him if I'm a satisfied *client.* Besides, the country is probably full of other clients, more willing than I was to comply with his tempting offer."

"Well, let's hope so."

Kay put all her other energies building the business into what it was before Bernard had begun wrecking it. She re-established relationships, secured financing to expand throughout the Northeast, recruited top technical and marketing talent with above-average compensation packages. She spurned offers of a buyout from a similar company in the Southeast and felt confident enough of New Croydon Telecomm's future that she offered to buy *them* out. She felt it was time for the company to expand their services by offering cell phones, Internet access, and, after her own recent experience, residential security systems.

She took little vacation for herself, only managing some time off during the summer to be with Kelley. She gave no thought to romantic relationships. Her life was her daughter and her business. That, she told herself, was all she needed.

Except it wasn't. Eighteen months had now passed. She disliked the word and tried never to use it herself, but she admitted that she needed *closure.* Or perhaps it was something more elemental—there was an unsolved mystery in her life, and it was human nature to want to solve any mystery.

It was the second summer following that horrible autumn, and Kelley was with her best friend's family in London. Kay would have loved to have gone, but she simply couldn't afford to take two weeks away during a period when she was in negotiations about a possible merger with a company from California. The opportunity to expand further into the world's sixth largest economy was too tempting even for a visit to

Europe to forego. So she had urged Kelley to make the trip with Carol and her parents. Perhaps Kelley was growing up, for she didn't protest too much at Kay's decision.

It was London that made Kay think of Marilyn Jarvis. Wasn't England where Jarvis was supposed to be heading on the *QE2* before she had so conveniently shown up in New Croydon that rainy October night? Kay had always felt that Jarvis was the key to the solution of the Seifer mystery. But she had had little time or motivation to pursue the issue. Then two days after Kelley had arrived in London, the investment banker handling the merger with the California company phoned. The deal was off. The owners were selling out to one of the bigger phone companies who had become interested in that sector of the market they had heretofore ignored.

Kay was disappointed but knew the overall market in the country was still considerable—the credit-challenged, she had long ago discovered while researching the feasibility of establishing a company like New Croydon Telecomm, was a permanent underclass. The future looked rosy for her and Kelley. But as she sat in her office after hanging up the phone, she realized she now had something that was previously in short supply in her recent life: Time. She called in Mike Bishop, her number two, hijacked a year ago from AT&T where he'd been a well-regarded vice-president of operations for the Northeast region.

"Mike, I'm going to be in and out of the office for the next week or so," she told him after explaining the collapse of the deal.

"Vacation?"

"Yes and no. There are some personal things I have to handle. I'll be available by cell, and I'll check E-mail frequently. But for the next couple of weeks, you're essentially in charge."

"You can depend on me."

She smiled. "Yes, I know. That's why I hired you."

Where to start, she asked herself? Marilyn Jarvis? No, not right away. Let's go back further, she thought. Back to the beginning. She sat at the desk in her home office and looked down at the blank sheet of notepaper. She tried to recall the meeting in Juno's, to picture in her mind the newspaper clippings in the folder. Oh why, she scolded herself, didn't she actually *read* the damn things? She recalled she had merely skimmed through the pieces of newspaper, focusing only momentarily on a sentence here, a photograph there.

She wrote down the meager details that had stuck with her. Then she turned to the computer and logged on to LexisNexis. Using her credit card, within five minutes she had opened an account that entitled her to explore databases containing the contents of virtually every major news publication in the world.

She typed in the search keywords: "swimming pool," "Asbury Heights," "drowning," and the date range. In moments, several links appeared to different newspaper stories on different days of the same year. She selected each individually and read the contents of them all. The *San Francisco Chronicle* had the most detail, as she expected, given its size and proximity to the location of the incident. Some of the links were follow-up stories. An idea occurred to her, and she did a new search with the same criteria but changed the date to the following year. There were no hits. And none for the year following. So there had been no further police activity; clearly the death was considered an accident.

She re-read the articles from the *Chronicle*. An owner of a chain of Nissan car dealerships in the state had drowned in his swimming pool. There was a mention of the man's business partner, a Jeff Reynolds, who happened to be in Tokyo on business and clearly had a perfect alibi. Each of the partners has filed lawsuits against the other in the previous months; charges of embezzlement by both parties. She opened a new window on her Web browser and went to the Standard & Poor's Web site. She typed in the name of the dealership chain and up came the company profile. Sole owner and proprietor: Jeffrey Reynolds. Annual revenue range: $2–3 million.

"Mmm," she said aloud. "So, Jeff, did you eagerly embrace Mr. Seifer when he came calling?"

How was it done, she wondered? Not much detail of the condition of the body was given. All the stories merely referred to it as a "drowning." So there must not have been any suspicious marks on the body. Clearly, she thought, the poor man had not been hit over the head and tossed into the water. Drugs, perhaps? Would the medical examiner do an autopsy on what appeared to be a domestic accident? And if he did, would the immersion in water over a seventy-two-hour period—the incident had occurred during a holiday weekend—have contributed somehow to the breakdown or elimination of drugs in the system? She made a note to check into that possibility.

She cleared the screen and began again, this time typing in "Lake Forest," "heart failure," "siblings," and the date range. That was all she could remember and, given the paucity of detail, expected to have dozens of hits. But to her surprise, there were only a few results. Lake Forest, she thought, must indeed by a tiny community. The *Chicago Tribune* gave the story a lot of column inches, presumably because of the players and the exclusive location. Two sisters had been feuding about the will left by their father upon his death a year previously. No way to ascertain dollar amounts, Kay saw, but reading between the lines, the family fortune, derived from a department store chain in the Midwest, was considerable. Charges flew back and forth about a last-minute alteration in the will by the old man, who had incipient Alzheimer's. The estate was in limbo until the lawsuits could be resolved. The younger sister was at a restaurant with her attorney when she complained of shortness of breath and nausea; then she fainted. An ambulance rushed her to the hospital, but she was dead within half an hour. The other sister was in New York with her husband, attending an opera at Lincoln Center. Despite the bitter relations between the women, the police made no arrests. The determination of the cause of death by the doctors at the hospital was cardiac arrhythmia. There was no autopsy. The surviving sister got the entire estate. The story was then buried in the graveyard of yesterday's news.

Cardiac arrhythmia, thought Kay. That didn't seem like the work of Seifer. How could he have pulled it off? It occurred in the most public of places and the woman's dinner companion—a sixty-seven-year-old man, a dean of Chicago attorneys, according to the *Tribune*—was above suspicion. So again Kay asked herself: How did Seifer do it?

She looked at her notes. The earliest clipping in Seifer's folder, she recalled, was about a guy in Houston, a traffic accident, the ever-popular SUV, the driver from out-of-state. Again, using just these key words and the approximate year, Nexis provided the correct links. She scanned quickly through the stories. This had been the oldest death among Seifer's clippings. So presumably it was his first. After all, she reasoned, why wouldn't he retain *all* articles relating to his handiwork to convince—or coerce—his next client? With experience came expertise. So if there were flaws in his methodology, she rationalized, it would be in this incident. Now, where would it be, she wondered? And *what* would it be?

She read the stories several times but saw no obvious anomalies. The circumstances were remarkably similar to Bernard's—nighttime, rain, a stranger to the state, substantial wealth. The only difference was that the victim was at the wheel of another vehicle when the SUV slammed into him: a Mazda Miata.

She smiled. Just before she became pregnant with Kelley, she had come close to buying a Miata; had even taken a "Hunter Green" model out for a test drive. But when she found out about the pregnancy, she quickly realized that luxuries would be things of the past once the baby was born. She remembered, though, how frail she thought the vehicle was once she was behind the wheel. Even her husband, while drooling at the streamlined sports car, was apprehensive about her driving such a fragile-looking thing on the highway. No wonder it—and its occupant—was crushed by the SUV.

Curious to see pictures of what the little car looked like after the impact—the Nexis articles were text-only and Seifer's newspaper clipping was from some other newspaper—she opened another browser window and went to the *Houston Journal*'s Web site. She searched through the archives and quickly located the issue that first reported the accident. In the Metro section, as expected, she saw a photograph of the crushed vehicle did indeed accompany the article. It actually headed all three columns of the story. Then her eye caught another, smaller photo, further down the page. It was a headshot of the driver of the SUV. According to the caption, she was from Minnesota, identified as Mary Ellis, visiting a friend in Houston. The hair was different, Kay noted. Different color, different cut. But the face was undeniably the same.

Johanna.

Chapter Fourteen

The woman was pleasant. "Yes?" she said, smiling. "May I help you?"

Something was wrong, Kay thought, staring at the thirtyish person who had just opened the door of 38 Primrose Lane. This can't be Marilyn Jarvis's college friend. She's way too young, at least twenty years younger than Jarvis. But, Kay realized, perhaps it was the woman's daughter, in New Croydon on a visit.

"I hope so," she replied with a smile equally as warm as the woman's. "I was looking to meet with the owner. I live on Ridgewood Court, a couple of blocks away, and understand we have a mutual friend—Marilyn. Marilyn Jarvis."

The young woman continued to smile but seemed confused.

"Oh? I'm sorry. I don't know any Marilyn Jarvis."

"You're the owner? *You* live here?"

"Absolutely! For the last sixteen months. We love it! My husband and I think it's a great neighborhood to raise kids."

She tapped her enlarged belly. "I'm due in October. Do you have kids?"

Kay stared at her, could only nod. The woman opened the door wider.

"Would you like to come in? Have a cup of tea?"

"Eh, yes. Thank you."

The woman, who identified herself as Marge Haynes, must have been desperate for company, thought Kay. She was a regular Chatty Cathy and hardly gave Kay a chance to get a word in while she made the tea. It was only when the woman put the cup to her mouth that Kay quickly said:

"So you moved in sixteen months ago?"

"Yes. We got a *fabulous* deal. Our realtor said it was an absolute *steal.* In fact, she said it was such a bargain, so below the going market rate for a property like this, she was even thinking of buying it herself as an investment. Thank God she didn't!"

"Do you find out why it was such a bargain?"

Marge nodded. "They were moving out-of-state. The husband was being transferred by his company. Insurance, he said."

"You met the sellers?"

"Yes. A *lovely* couple. But . . ." She seemed a bit disapproving.

"Yes?"

She leaned toward Kay and said in a lowered voice, "No kids."

Kay was puzzled by the couple's behavior. They left sixteen months ago, just a couple of months after Bernard's accident. Why?

Marge was talking again. "It's funny, though."

"What? What's funny?"

"I told Peter—my husband. I told him, Mr. Johnson didn't *seem* like an insurance type. I have a nose for this sort of thing—I took psychology as a minor in college. I would have said he was more of an Army man."

Kay stared at her. "*What* did you say?"

"You know—military."

"Hey! I thought you were on vacation?"

Kay ignored her secretary as she rushed into her office and shut the door. She went to the small safe that Bernard had built into the floor and removed a large brown envelope. She sat down at her desk, then emptied out the contents of the envelope.

The pictures were black-and-white and blurry. The security video camera in the lobby of New Croydon Telecomm was low-resolution. Bernard had it installed shortly after the disgruntled customer kicked in the glass door in the foyer. Naturally, it was the cheapest model he could find. So the quality of the stills taken from the video was poor. But, she saw, the photos were most definitely Seifer, taken when he'd entered the building.

Kay had remembered the camera a couple of days after handing over the money. She realized the tapes were recycled every seven days and quickly alerted the security company that she wanted stills taken from the grainy video. *Why* she wanted them, she probably couldn't answer herself. But, somehow, she acknowledged, she couldn't let Seifer just walk away scot-free.

She dropped the photos onto the desk. It had been at least a year since she had last looked at them. At the time, she had anticipated that she had not heard the last of Seifer and wanted some sort of weapon to repel him, even if it was only a photo. But now, she asked herself, what *really* were her intentions? She shook her head. She didn't know but she felt obligated to at least confirm who Marilyn Jarvis was visiting that night. She put the photos in the envelope and headed back to see Marge Haynes.

"So you're *not* looking to sell your property?" Dorothy Kramer asked.

"No," Kay replied.

"Oh," said the realtor, clearly disappointed at the loss of such a potential juicy commission.

Kay went on quickly, "But if I do put my house on the market, you will definitely get the listing."

That cheered the woman up. "Wonderful!"

"So if you could just tell me a little bit about the Johnsons I'd be very grateful."

Kay had given Kramer the same spiel about a "mutual friend" as she'd given Marge. There was no doubt in Marge's mind the photos were of the man who identified himself as Johnson—"Peter always tells me I have a photographic memory," she explained.

"Well, Mrs. Daniels," said Kramer, "there's not much to tell. The listing for Primrose Lane had appeared for a couple of hours when I got a call from Mr. Johnson. He asked if he could see the house right away. I told him we'd be having an open house the following Sunday, but he insisted on seeing it immediately. I wasn't going to argue—so few houses become available in your wonderful neighborhood, as I'm sure you know."

Kramer paused, waiting presumably for Kay to acknowledge the status of her neighborhood. But as Kay merely nodded, the realtor continued:

"Well, he and his wife were already waiting at the house when I drove up for the appointment. I showed them around. They seemed interested, but I figured they'd get back to me for a second look before making an offer. Everyone does. But Mr. Johnson said they'd take it. The strange thing was—"

Kramer was in her late fifties and Kay guessed she'd been in the business for many years. If she noticed something strange, it would be strange indeed.

"Yes? What was so strange?"

Kramer smiled, seemed a bit embarrassed to be talking about clients this way.

"Well, most men discuss these things with their wives. Actually, in my experience, men usually *ask* their wives, *What do you think?* And what they really mean is, *What shall we do?* Mr. and Mrs. Johnson didn't seem to discuss it at all. I wasn't eavesdropping, of course—God forbid. I was waiting by my car, and they were on the walkway. But it looked as if . . . as if he was *telling* his wife they were going to take the house."

I bet he was, thought Kay. She said, "And were you surprised when they decided to sell so quickly, after what—nine months?"

Kramer shrugged. "I've seen people sell out after just a few months. Unforeseen things happen. Problems on Wall Street, couples getting divorced. But, yes, it was a bit unusual."

She didn't seem particularly interested, and Kay guessed the reason: It would mean yet another commission if she was selected as the selling realtor.

"And they were in a hurry to sell, is that right?"

"Yes. Mr. Johnson said he'd received a big promotion and was willing to sell even if it meant a loss. Just so long as the sale could go through quickly."

Kay wondered if she could get anything else out of this woman. But quickly decided even if Kramer was amenable, there was little to be really gleaned. As the realtor, she merely facilitated the sale of the property. She would not have been present at the closing, would not have been privy to the banks where funds would have been deposited. And even if Kay had such information, what could she do with it?

She could only think of one final thing to ask.

"Did they say where they were headed?"

"North Carolina, I think."

"North Carolina?" Kay repeated, in the forlorn hope that Kramer would remember the particular city.

"Or South Carolina." The realtor made a dismissive wave with a manicured hand. "One of those types of places."

Janet looked at her sister. "So that's how it was done. All the time, they were just a few minutes away."

Kay nodded. Seifer and Johanna had been living at 38 Primrose Lane for six months prior to the accident. Jarvis's rationale for being in Connecticut, for driving in that neighborhood, Kay realized, had to be airtight.

"The police would only interview her friends to verify her story. They would hardly check into the *background* of the friends. It was even unlikely they'd search the background of Jarvis as far back as college as soon as they identified her and confirmed she was an upright citizen."

"And I bet even if they did, there would be a student who attended that college at that time with whatever maiden name Johanna would have given the police."

"Yes. Assuming the police even asked."

"Right. So, are you going to the police with this?"

"Why? It really doesn't prove anything. People move into houses and move out again all the time. There's still no proof that Jarvis wasn't doing what she claimed she was doing—merely visiting an old friend."

No, thought Kay, it didn't prove anything. But it did confirm Seifer's ingenuity. And his thoroughness. And his patience.

"I'm telling you, Janet, this guy is something else. Can you imagine? That he would sit quietly in a Connecticut suburb for six months, keeping his head down, waiting. Waiting for the opportune time to strike."

"Best to let sleeping dogs lie, then."

Kay didn't answer. She felt at a dead end. Seifer could have gone to North or South Carolina, but what difference did it make? Even if he told the truth to Kramer, that was sixteen months ago. He could easily have moved on by now. And even if he was in one of the Carolinas, where could she even begin to start looking?

Janet must have been worried by Kay's lack of response. She said, "No? You're not going to try and find Jarvis in Nebraska?"

"No. She's obviously a conspirator, part of the gang. Despite the convincing performance she gave me after the accident."

“Well, what then? What are your plans? What *do* you want?”

Indeed, Kay thought, what did she want? To retaliate, she felt like responding. But it wasn’t just that, she suspected. Something else. But not now, that was clear. She was in no position to pursue Seifer. Maybe, she thought, when Kelley was grown and graduated from college, a self-supporting adult. Maybe, then, she could go after Seifer. For Bernard. For Mr. Scanlon. For the extortion.

She looked at Janet and shrugged. “Justice?”

Chapter Fifteen

"Hey, Frankie! It's Mo."

Sinclair smiled. Every time Mary-Jo Lipinski called, she referred to herself the same way, but seemed completely unaware of how ridiculous it sounded. But perhaps the Brooklyn detective was too young to be familiar with the Stooges.

"Hi, Mo. What have you got?"

"Fuck all. What about you?"

"The same." He sighed. "I never thought I'd say this but I'm ready to give up."

"Shit, no, Frankie. They're connected. You *know* they're connected. You're the one who convinced me, remember?"

Yes, Sinclair remembered. After they'd interviewed the Daniels woman more than a year ago, they'd adjourned to the Anchor Bar & Grill for a burger and a Rolling Rock. Sinclair shared everything he'd learned about the accident. It was self-serving, he admitted to himself. Lipinski could do more in her own territory tracking down the whereabouts of the missing P.I. the Daniels woman had hired just a month after her husband so conveniently died. And he wanted Lipinski to share with him whatever she did find. So he felt it less like professional courtesy and more like expediency to pool resources.

"It's been eighteen months, Mo," he said. "She doesn't go out. She doesn't date. Doesn't see anybody. Maybe everything happened exactly as she says it happened."

"Fuck, no!"

Sinclair grimaced. Despite an overexposure to foul language during his two hitches in the Navy, he still found the casual profanity from as pretty a woman as Lipinski startling. She had restrained herself during the interview with Daniels, but at the Anchor, her every second word seemed to be "fuck." Sinclair wondered, not for the first time, if it was part of her armor in the daily battle for respect she waged with her colleagues.

She went on, "If there wasn't four million dollars involved, I'd agree. Nah. There are too many loose ends with this case, Frankie. A private dick she hires a month after the accident disappears and not a peep about his whereabouts ever since. Completely gone from the face of the earth. What are the odds? And this Jarvis woman. You told me yourself: Why the hell would she rent a motherfuckin' monster SUV just to drive forty miles?"

Sinclair chuckled. "Remember, Mo, it was Daniels herself who pointed that out. Why would she do that if she was in bed with Jarvis?"

"Because they're connected! That's my point."

Sinclair laughed. "Mo, you know we can't take that to the DA. That's not evidence."

"Well, we'll get evidence. We'll go to Nebraska and check into this woman."

"Mo, your chief is like my chief. He's not going to finance a trip to the Midwest to look into the background of a woman who had a traffic accident. The case is closed—that's what they're both going to say."

"The Scanlon case is not closed. Not by a long shot."

"No, but Jarvis isn't a part of the Scanlon case. Besides, I checked her out, you know that. I even contacted the cops in Lincoln, gave them the lowdown and after they did some checking, they faxed me a report about her. I sent you a copy, remember?"

Lipinski made a *blow-it-out-your-ass* sound. Sinclair sensed he was winning the argument. He went on:

"I even used my contacts at the phone company to look into their phone records—Daniels's and Jarvis's. Their numbers weren't on their bills for the preceding twelve months."

"They could have used cell phones."

"I checked. Nothing. Even if they were using those phones with the pre-paid minutes. The calls would still be routed through the cellular networks of the major companies. And *they* keep records. There's no connection between Daniels and Jarvis. Or Jarvis and Scanlon."

"No *obvious* connection."

Sinclair caught it immediately. Lipinski had something. That's why she was calling, her first phone call in over a month.

"What is it, Mo? I thought you said you had nothing new. You found something?"

"Maybe. Possibly." She let out a sigh of exasperation. "Oh, I don't know. Could be nothing. Maybe just a coincidence."

"What is it, for Chrissake, Mo?"

"Well, I went to a wake last week."

"A *wake?*" Where the hell was Lipinski going with this?

"Yep. Billy Brewster died. A good guy. Loved being a cop. Retired five years ago. Anyway, I was chatting with one of his buddies at the wake. Swapping war stories, you know how it is. He's retired and working as a P.I. I'm thinking along the same lines myself when I'm eligible to go. Anyway, that made me think of Scanlon, and I mentioned the Daniels woman and the husband's accident. Well . . ."

"Yes? Well what?"

"Well, before this guy moved to the Eighty-First, he was on the force out on Long Island. He told me about a case he worked on nine or ten years ago. It was open-and-shut, he said, but it bothered him for a long time before he became convinced it was what it appeared to be—a traffic accident. You see, a guy was knocked down outside his house in Glen Cove. It was nighttime, it was raining, and the guy who knocked him down was a complete stranger. And he was driving an SUV. And the dead guy was wealthy."

"Jesus. You're not telling me the Daniels woman—"

"No. No connection with our lady friend. I've been looking into it for the past week. It really does seem to be a freak accident. But I couldn't help thinking."

"Yes?"

"What if the next time an accident like that happened, it was a carbon copy of the first time it happened?"

Chapter Sixteen

Don't forget the condoms, he had been told. And he hadn't. Though it had been mortifying to place the box of Trojans on the counter in front of the snotty-nosed teenage cashier in the supermarket. Henry Pierce hadn't bought condoms since before he was married. And that was more than twenty years ago. But nowadays, he understood, there was no stigma attached to the transaction. And indeed, the teenager barely paid attention, merely scooping up the box and swiping it against the scanner like the other items.

God, thought Henry, how different he must seem from the Henry Pierce of two decades ago. Here he was, a purchaser of condoms, an attendee at a Catholic mass. And a man about to commit murder.

The priest was leading the congregation in a prayer. Shortly, Henry knew, he would conclude with the refrain "Peace be with you," everyone in the church would repeat the phrase and shake hands with their nearest neighbors. Henry knew nothing of such ceremonies prior to meeting Mr. Seifer. It was Mr. Seifer who had instructed him. It was Mr. Seifer who counseled him to attend several masses until he was comfortable with the entire ceremony. It was Mr. Seifer who had provided the small, green bottle. And it was Mr. Seifer who had given him the reminder not to forget to buy the condoms.

"It will act as a sheath," he'd explained to Henry. "Your gloves will be sufficient but if it will ease your mind, use the condom for added protection. Together they will protect your skin from contact with the liquid."

Mr. Seifer always seemed to have the expertise; always seemed to have the wisdom; always seemed to *know.* Mr. Seifer even seemed to have the answers to Henry's questions even before Henry would ask the question.

"Kill Elizabeth Carlisle and for the rest of your life you will be free, Henry. With all that money to enjoy. All that freedom. And the only thing you have to do is shake her hand."

"But—but she will collapse right in front of me. Everyone in the church will know."

Mr. Seifer had shaken his head. "Henry. Would I place you in such a predicament? It will be at least ten minutes. Maybe more. But at least ten minutes, I guarantee it. Besides, she will still be alive. It will be as if she fainted. She won't be dead for another half hour."

"But when I do it, she'll smell the almond scent. Everyone will. I've looked into it. It's famous for the almond smell."

"Dimethyl sulfoxide, Henry."

"What?"

"It will disguise the almond smell."

Mr. Seifer made it sound so easy. And after Henry had attended a dozen masses at St. Patrick's Cathedral on Fifth Avenue over a three-week period, he had to agree it didn't seem that difficult. Like clockwork, the priest would say the phrase and like puppets the congregation would mimic him and do the hand-shaking. Henry practiced it several times, without the liquid, of course. Then he bought a small bottle of water and practiced opening it with his left hand in his overcoat pocket. His dexterity—after the inevitable first couple of fumbled failures—surprised him, and he was pleased with the swiftness and sureness of his fingers as they uncapped the bottle. Equally dexterous, he then dipped his index finger into the water and managed to re-cap the bottle. He could do this, he convinced himself after managing the feat without flaw several times. He *would* do this. And then he would be free. A single man, wealthy, with all that money, all that freedom. He was only fifty-seven. He had lots of good years left.

Poor Elizabeth Carlisle, he thought, staring at the back of her silver-haired head. Do you even know I am sitting right behind you? Did you have any inkling when you woke up this morning, you would not see the evening? And all because of a couple of drops of liquid. He opened the bottle now and confident—because of Mr. Seifer's assurance—that the condom and the glove would protect him, dipped his finger into the liquid, then capped the bottle.

"It's hardly possible," he had said to Mr. Seifer. "So little?"

"Six drops of sodium cyanide, Henry. Dissolved in dimethyl sulfoxide to open the skin pores. It never fails. Trust me."

". . . Peace be with you."

Oh God, thought Henry. The priest had finished, he was saying it. You idiot, he chastised himself. Why weren't you paying attention? Why was your mind wandering? You should have been preparing yourself!

Everyone had begun shaking hands, the echoing hiss of *Peace be with you* throughout the entire building. He repeated the phrase to the man on his right and shook his hand, although his eyes were staring at Elizabeth Carlisle, waiting for her to turn. She was shaking the hand of a man in front of her. Henry felt something touch his left arm, and he jumped. It was the woman on his left offering her hand and smiling. He nodded, mumbled the phrase, and shook her hand.

Then he became alarmed. Elizabeth Carlisle hadn't turned around! She had shaken hands with the man on her right and the woman on her left and the couple in front of her. But she hadn't turned around! Oh God, now she was sitting down.

What was he going to do? Peripherally, he saw groups of people starting to sit back down. It was almost too late. He had to act.

He touched the woman on the shoulder. She turned around, and he quickly said "Peace be with you" and extended his right hand. She nodded and clasped his hand. Then, as some people do to emphasize a handshake, he placed his left hand against the back of her hand, allowing him to brush his index finger against the portion of her wrist exposed beyond her glove. He couldn't smell the almond smell—the incense in the air also helped, he suddenly noticed—and guessed that she was unaware also.

They released themselves from the clasp; she turned around and sat down. She didn't move, didn't make any reaction. Henry wanted to look at his watch but, fearful that the action would be noticed and remembered, contented himself with counting to five hundred. He had determined that would be sufficient time. At that point he would leave.

He had done it. Elizabeth Carlisle was going to die. And he—finally—was going to *live.*

Chapter Seventeen

"Who's next?"

Seifer smiled. "*Always* so greedy. We haven't even counted the money from Mr. Carlisle and you're ready to go to work again."

Johanna smiled and did the thing she knew all the men in her life loved. She moved her top lip over the bottom and stared at him, not saying a word.

Seifer laughed. She always used such gestures to soften him up—God, did she think he was stupid?—to get her way. But it only worked if he was in the mood to give it to her.

"I can't help it," she said finally when he wouldn't respond. "I have . . . *needs.*"

She reached over and ran her right palm over his crotch. Despite the immediate, inevitable quiver in his cock, he decided to make her wait. Make her aware who would determine when they'd fuck. Make her suffer.

He remained silent, and the silence forced her to speak again. She said, "Money makes me horny."

He picked up two bundles of $500 bills from the table where he was counting and tossed them at her. "And lots of money makes you very horny."

Laughing, she picked up the bundles and, laying back on the bed, rubbed them between her legs. "Oh, yes!"

She closed her eyes and rubbed harder. "Mmm. Who needs *you* anyway? President McKinley is really my type of guy."

She kissed each bundle. "Mmm. Who knew I'd go for older men?"

He shook his head. She'd been like that from the time he'd first met her. He hadn't been sure initially if she wasn't on drugs of some sort. He had stopped by Tippy-Toe Joe's because he had something substantial to sell. The previous night, a man he'd killed had pleaded for his life, offering him a gold bar to let him go free. MacBride had been intrigued at the offer. He'd never seen an actual gold bar in his life and more out of curiosity than agreeing to the man's offer, asked to look at it. The man—a stockbroker who had reneged on a legitimate deal with the head of the Family—had said it was in a safe, built into the floor. MacBride had told him to go ahead and get it. The man had pulled the oriental rug aside and eagerly punched in the combination on a keypad. As he opened the little door, his body tensed. MacBride immediately shot him in the head. He knelt and looked inside the safe. On top of the thick slab of gold was a brand-new Ruger P97.

Joe wasn't at his usual station behind the wire-mesh, so he rang the bell. The side door opened, and Joe's head popped out around it. He motioned MacBride to come in. That's when MacBride saw the girl. She was standing by a table on which lay a great deal of jewelry, so much, in fact, it was a tangled mess of pearl necklaces, gold bracelets inlaid with gleaming stones, and Rolex watches. He thought at first perhaps she was buying the jewelry, but quickly became aware she was the one who had brought it in.

She saw him staring at the jewelry, then reached down among the pile and pulled out a pair of ruby earrings.

"Here," she said, offering them to him. "They'll go with your eyes."

Joe laughed. "Ain't she something? Best thief on the Island."

"And biggest mouth, I bet," MacBride said.

She smiled. "Big enough to handle your little dick."

Joe said: "You better skidaddle, girl, before you get him mad."

He took an envelope out of a drawer and handed it to her. She put it in her bag without opening it and walked toward the door. As she passed MacBride, she punched him lightly on the arm.

"Call me if you need more abuse. Joe has my number."

He hadn't known what to make of her. He had never shown much interest in anything like a relationship with any woman. He satisfied his basic needs with any of the numerous women who associated with the Family, those who were accustomed to saying "yes" to anything their men demanded. Many of them wanted more from him, offered to move in with him and take care of the domestic routines that any man would require. But he'd always declined. The price to pay for not using a vacuum cleaner wasn't worth it. He could handle his domestic chores for himself.

But she was different, and he didn't know why. After a day had passed, he called Joe and got her number. He waited another two days before calling her. It was as if she had been waiting by the phone for him to call. She picked up immediately and said: "Is that you?"

He was too surprised by the greeting to reply. She said:

"Mr. Earrings, right? Hello, hello?"

He told her the name he went by. She gave him directions to her apartment and half an hour later, he rang the bell. She opened the door, completely naked.

"Come on, let's screw first," she said. "Then we can get something to eat."

He watched her on the bed, believing she was mocking him, making him jealous. If he had thought he was going to get to know her better, he had been mistaken. She mentioned things, places, some names—all stops on a journey, not a cohesive narrative of a life: a broken home, a scholarship to a college in the Midwest, a marriage that lasted two years, hitchhiking from city to city for another two, dancing in a upscale gentleman's club in Vegas, having affairs with some of the married men that frequented the place, a little blackmail, just enough to have them pay, not enough to make them go to the police, then meeting a burglar who admitted what he did while she performed a lap dance. He was a pro, and she used him to learn the ropes; then after three years, she went out on her own throughout the Southwest. And then Long Island.

She lost some of her cocky self-assurance when she realized MacBride was something other than a thief, that his visit to Joe's was not a regular occurrence. He didn't tell her what he did, but she suspected and she used some source—perhaps somebody at the pawnshop—to confirm it. Instead of being afraid, she'd said:

"Take me out on your next job."

He thought about it for a few moments, then said: "You drive. That's it."

When he came back to the car, there was blood on his hands and the cuffs of his shirt. She had been strangely thrilled at the sight of it. A man who woke up this morning unaware that this was the last day of his life had just died. What must have gone through his head as MacBride had plunged the knife into his chest again and again? Was the steel cold? Was the pain severe or did the shock and realization somehow numb the actual pain of the metal cutting the flesh? What was it like to die? What was it like to kill?

"Let me watch next time," she asked.

The next time was three weeks later. Again, because the target was in a residential neighborhood, he chose the knife rather than the gun. It occurred to him that she should ring the doorbell; that she would allay, if only momentarily, the fears of the man who would answer the door. He bought her a good blond wig, one made from human hair, and she wore plain-lens glasses and a navy blue suit appropriate for a businesswoman. It was as unlike her normal appearance as his own. The man opened the door. And at the sight of the two bespectacled, well-groomed individuals with briefcases, he relaxed. That was his mistake. As arranged, she had stepped aside slightly, allowing MacBride to throw his bulk against the door. The man fell back with the force of the blow. MacBride was inside in a moment, Johanna only a step behind, closing the door quickly.

MacBride dragged the man by his shirt collar into the living room and propped him onto a couch. She expected a speech, at least some remarks, a demand perhaps. But MacBride unsheathed the knife and thrust it into the man's chest. The man gasped. MacBride thrust the knife in again, pushing upward toward the rib cage and the heart.

She went over to the couch and said: "Let me."

She was breathing hard, he saw, and her eyes were wide with anticipation and excitement. He gave her the knife, and she buried it to the hilt in the man's chest, then turned it left and then right. The man made a long, sighing sound and then became still.

MacBride touched her hand that still held the knife. It was rigid, clasped tightly around the handle. He unclasped the fingers with difficulty and removed the knife from the body.

She looked at him, with a bright smile. "The family that slays together, stays together."

That had been ten years ago, he realized. And they *had* stayed together. He knew he didn't really need her. Yes, she was useful in gaining entree to certain places and diminishing the fears of those that he might be stalking: a team of a man and woman was the one factor a target seldom took into account. So, yes, she had been useful on occasion. But no, he didn't need her.

He was sure of that. He didn't need her.

He stood up from the table and went over to the bed. Her eyes were still closed, and she was still moaning, but he knew she was aware that he was standing over her. He waited for her to stop, and after a few moments, she did. She opened her eyes and looked up at him, then instinctively spread her legs. He lifted her skirt, reached his hand under one side of her panties and suddenly ripped a fistful of the silk fabric away from her body.

He put two fingers inside her. Of course she was already wet, she always was, always needed so little external stimulation. He cupped his hand and stroked the top of her vagina. Then he coaxed a third finger inside her. Initially his stroking was rhythmic, insistent, but not rapid. She began to moan, to breathe noisily. As he felt her vagina expand, he pushed a fourth finger inside her.

"Oh! That hurts."

"It's supposed to hurt."

She hit her hand against his left arm, trying to make him stop but he was pressing down on her shoulder while he continued. She stopped hitting him, aware, given her prone position, of the futility of resistance.

She began to whimper, tears ran down her cheeks. He ignored her. Her breathing had intensified, the pleasure overcoming the pain. Her chest rose, her lower torso arched. She let out a moan, a gasp that was half-pain, half-joyful. He stopped, withdrew his fingers.

She wiped her eyes with the back of her hand.

"Bastard," she said, in a weak voice.

He placed his right hand, fingers extended, in front of her mouth and stared into her eyes. After a moment, she closed her mouth over his fingers.

When he was satisfied by her docility, he went to the

bathroom and washed his hands. He opened the bottom drawer of the bureau and withdrew the brown attaché case. He entered the combination, opened the case, and removed two folders.

"Clean up," he said. "We're going to work."

"Where?"

He looked at her, then smiled.

"I'll let *you* choose this time."

He tossed the folders onto the bed.

Chapter Eighteen

It always sounds more fun than it ends up being, Kay thought. *Las Vegas.* Her secretary had squealed with delight as if she was the one going. *"You'll have a great time, Kay!"* she had said.

And Janet was just as bad. *"Sin City! Don't worry, I'll come over to your house and stay with Kelley. You go commit some sins!"*

It was a ridiculous place to hold a convention, Kay felt, as she walked around the floor of the casino. Yes, she knew there was a vast acreage of convention space in the city, but a dozen other—more sober, more respectable—places could have been chosen by the Telecommunications Association for their annual get-together. When she heard that Vegas had been selected, her first reaction was to avoid attending. But then she recalled last year's convention in New York where she'd met many new contacts, established new relationships, and, as she admitted to Janet, "networked my ass off." It had helped New Croydon Telecomm, she couldn't deny, and she finally decided she had more to lose by staying home.

So she convinced herself she would stick with business, keep to herself, and when the day's work was done, she'd avoid like the plague the noise and the crowds. She had no interest in gambling, and beyond the mindlessness of the slot machines, had no knowledge of the various table games. Nevertheless, on the second night of her stay, around eleven P.M., she became restless. She couldn't sleep. Maybe it was the strange bed, maybe it was the vulgar neon lighting the night outside of her window, or maybe it was just the . . . *essence* of the entire environment. She got up, threw on a pair of jeans and a blouse, and went down to the casino.

She wandered around, amazed by the noise, the lights, the shrillness, the seemingly endless rat-a-tat tinkling of the slot machines, and most of all by the sheer number of people wandering around. Spring Break for adults, she had heard someone describe Vegas. And that was hardly inaccurate, she thought, marveling at the middle-aged men in shorts, the shuffling retired couples, women of all shapes and ages in flimsy halter tops and tight jeans—virtually all of them clasping a drink in their right hand and a plastic cup of coins in their left. She shook her head and, despite the absurdity of the hour—she'd have been already asleep had she been home in Ridgewood Court—decided a drink seemed like a good idea.

She went to one of the huge, circular bars, manned by three busy bartenders. Sitting down on a stool, she ordered a screwdriver. A television set above the bar displayed CNN but the sound was turned down and she couldn't make out what the news anchor was saying. She sighed. People, she realized, didn't come to casinos to watch TV. She contented herself with reading the crawl at the bottom of the screen, deciding she'd finish the drink, hopeful the alcohol would make her drowsy, then head back to her room.

"Hello, Kay."

She had peripherally been aware of someone sitting on the stool next to her. She turned to her left.

"Long time, no see," said Johanna. "Two years, at least, wouldn't you say?"

Kay stood up and backed away a couple of paces.

"Shusssh," said Johanna, as if to a child. "Don't cause a scene. Sit down. I'm not going to bite."

Kay continued to stand and to stare. This woman was the

last person she expected to see.

Johanna spoke again, this time with more urgency. *"Sit."*

Kay looked around but the bar was full of people who had eyes only for each other. No one paid them any attention. She sat down but still could not find any words to say.

"No," said Johanna, with what seemed her perpetual smirk. "It's not a coincidence."

"What—what do you want?"

"He'd like to see you." She gestured toward the ceiling. "Upstairs."

An image of the Heckler & Koch laying on the bed linen in the top drawer of her bureau at home came to Kay. She had—eventually—stopped carrying it in her pocketbook. But given the rigors of airport security, there would have been no way for her to bring it on the plane to Nevada. And even if she had it with her now, though, she realized, what would she do with it?

"Why?"

Johanna stood. "Let's go up to the room and see."

What to do, Kay asked herself? If Seifer and his woman were both here, it meant that Kelley, thousands of miles away, was safe from them. Her first reaction, therefore, was to tell Johanna to go to hell. But, as always, she reminded herself of Seifer's resources, his reach, his resolve. If he wanted Kay to talk to him, he would hardly take no for an answer. Besides, she reassured herself, they surely wouldn't consider doing her harm in a hotel room in the middle of Las Vegas. Further, she realized, there was a final reason why she was reluctant to dismiss Johanna's request. She *wanted* to see Seifer again. For two years he had been merely a memory, however harrowing. She had simply been unprepared for the man, his methods, his casual cruelty. After two years of living with the memory of her humiliation, she felt she could face him again with equanimity.

She got to her feet. Johanna turned around, and apparently

confident that Kay would follow, headed toward the elevators. Minutes later, Kay was again face-to-face with Nikolas Seifer.

He was less formally dressed this time. No suit, pressed white shirt, or silk tie. Nevertheless, even in the casual clothes—a navy polo shirt and pearl-colored pants—he had the unhurried look of the carefree affluent.

The room was a suite, more than three times the size of her own room. Naturally, she thought, looking around at the plasma television, the creamy, leather couches, the huge king-size bed, my money is paying for it.

She decided attack was the best form of defense and eschewed a greeting.

"So you're back for the rest of the money, right?"

He appeared surprised. Then he shook his head.

"No, Mrs. Daniels. I have plenty of money."

"Well, then, what is it that you want?"

"I need you to do something for me." He picked up a manila folder, bulky with materials, and held it toward her.

Kay shook her head. "I'm not touching that."

He laughed. "Ah. Of course. You're worried about fingerprints. That's not an issue, I assure you. But I'll humor you. Come over here."

He walked to a large cherry-wood dining table in a separate alcove and, opening the folder, spread out the contents. Kay hesitated, then went and stood next to the table.

Seifer picked up a color snapshot of a middle-aged male.

"This is Eugene Fanning," he said and held up the photo in front of her.

The name and the face meant nothing to Kay. She shrugged. "So?"

"I want you to kill him."

She thought she had become accustomed to outrageous statements from Seifer but this was beyond belief.

"What on earth are you talking about?"

"As I just said: I want you to kill this man. I will provide you with the means and the opportunity. It will be straightforward. There will be no danger to you. And then you will be free of me once and for all."

From the first minutes with Seifer, she had been always apprehensive, at times terrified even, but now, she realized, she was simply bemused.

"Mr. Seifer—if that's your real name. I don't know what the hell you're talking about. I don't know who this person is, but if you think I'm getting involved in any way with this, you're out of your mind."

He put the photo down on the table.

"Mrs. Daniels. Let me explain my methodology. The essence of my . . . system is that *I*," he pointed to himself, "kill no one."

"You killed my husband. And all those other people in the clippings you showed me."

Johanna said, "She still doesn't get it."

Kay looked at her. Get what? What were they trying to say?

Seifer nodded. "Indeed. Mrs. Daniels, I didn't kill your husband. Marilyn Jarvis did. And do you think *I* killed Marilyn's mother?"

Kay stared at him. *Marilyn's mother?* Jarvis's mother had been killed?

"You've lost me. What are you saying?"

"Marilyn's domineering, controlling bitch of a mother died of cardiac arrhythmia four years ago. I arranged for that to occur. Marilyn was very grateful to be free. Free to live her own life after a childhood—and adulthood—of oppression from a very nasty individual. Free to travel. Free to meet other people. People of the same sex. Free to establish a relationship with one of those people. And free to spend the money that her mother had controlled for many years since Marilyn's father passed away and left Marilyn rather dependent on the kindness of her mother. Well, free to spend half of it. The other half she was very happy to give to me for being her benefactor."

Kay shook her head. It's not possible, she thought. It couldn't be possible. Seifer saw her indecision.

He nodded again. "Oh yes, Mrs. Daniels. I was *her* benefactor, too. And Marilyn was happy to do a final favor for me. To drive an SUV on a fall evening in a small town in Connecticut and knock down another very nasty individual."

Kay felt dizzy. She reached out to one of the chairs and sat down.

"Would you like a beverage, Mrs. Daniels? Johanna, something for Mrs. Daniels."

Johanna went to a bureau that contained numerous bottles of liquor and Waterford Crystal glasses. She returned with a tumbler of amber liquid.

"You enjoy a drop of scotch, I believe," said Seifer.

Kay continued to stare at him, still dazed by the monstrousness of what he had revealed.

"Now I think she's getting it," said Johanna, placing the glass on the table in front of Kay.

"I certainly hope so," said Seifer.

Kay looked at the glass of scotch, needing to focus on something, anything other than Seifer's smug, self-satisfied face, beginning to understand. It was monstrous, she thought. It couldn't happen. Surely, it couldn't be possible? Almost despite herself, she saw her hand reach out to the drink. She lifted it to her mouth and swallowed half of it.

"Ah, that's better," said Seifer. "Yes, you are beginning to understand, I think. The man who killed Marilyn's mother was, of course, another individual for whom I was a benefactor. Two years prior to that event. He was very grateful to be free, and to be rich. And had no compunction in disposing of Mrs. Jarvis at my request. For what it's worth, Marilyn was initially a bit squeamish about driving the SUV, but she soon came around when I shared details of your husband's personality and behavior."

Kay said, almost to herself, "And all the others. All of the people in the clippings. Each person committed the murder of the next."

She looked up at Seifer, almost dazed at the ingenuity of it. "And all strangers. They were strangers to the victims. No connections, no relationships. The police would have so little to go on because there would be no obvious motive."

Seifer nodded, but remained silent, waiting for her to fully work it out.

She said, "Except the very first one. The man in Houston in the sports car. That's why *she* was driving the SUV." Kay pointed at Johanna.

Seifer seemed impressed. "My, we've done our homework, haven't we?"

"And all accidents. Staged by you. Even less reason for the police to be suspicious. No—wait. You said something about cardiac arrhythmia."

She remembered the woman in Lake Forest who collapsed in a restaurant. Didn't she, too, die from cardiac arrhythmia?

Seifer explained, "The automobile accident was the original conception. And it worked beautifully several times. But I decided I needed variation. I couldn't have an ongoing series of accidents involving wealthy people. Even if they occurred in different states, years apart—another vital component of my system, by the way—the authorities would be bound somehow, sometime, to eventually make connections."

He reached into a pants pocket and withdrew a small, green bottle.

"So with the aid of a little liquid, I introduced variety into my system."

"But Bernard—you chose to stage an accident. Why?"

"Your husband, Mrs. Daniels, was a strangely aloof man. Very hard to approach. He attended few public functions, had little interaction with strangers. His few friends socialized in each other's homes. He even chose not to eat out at lunch—saving money, perhaps? In short, he was—as you are probably well aware—very difficult to get close to. Close enough, in any event, to utilize my little friend here." Seifer held up the green bottle.

"Poison? That seems very . . . risky, doesn't it?"

He shook his head, assured as always.

"At an autopsy, the contents of the stomach are routinely examined. If no poison is found, the authorities look for other reasons for cause of death. Occam's Razor. Whatever seems the simplest explanation, usually is—the shortness of breath, the nausea, the fainting. Few people, even expert medical examiners, think of poison as something that can be administered externally. Sodium cyanide is one of the few poisons that do not need to be ingested to do its deadly work. As long as the pores of the skin are open, it can be very effective, with no need to introduce it into the victim's internal system."

Kay thought it through. Now it was all so obvious. No wonder he had been able to get away with it for so long. Eleven years, she recalled, since that first victim in Houston.

"But how did you persuade them all to do it?" she asked.

"Mrs. Daniels, it's incredible how little *persuading* I had to do. You have to realize these individuals were very unhappy until I came along. As I said to you many months ago, if you and your husband were a happy couple, do you really believe I would show up and do what you know now I am capable of doing? To be sure, some of my clients have been initially dubious, but, like you, I show them irrefutable proof. And they nearly all cooperate in the end."

And what about those who refuse to cooperate, Kay wanted to ask, but was afraid to.

He placed the little green bottle on the table next to the folder and its contents. "Now," he said, "it's your turn."

CHAPTER NINETEEN

There was no way she was going to kill this man, Kay thought, staring at the photograph of Eugene Fanning in her hand. It was past two A.M. and if she couldn't sleep before, she knew certainly she would not sleep this night.

She was back in her room, trying to absorb all that Seifer had disclosed. It was incredible, yes, but, she acknowledged, it was all true. It all made some sense out of what had initially seemed a senseless event. Perverted, yes. Even . . . evil, but it was all true.

"I don't want to know anything about it," she had said and got up from the table with its ghastly debris.

"You really have no choice, Mrs. Daniels," Seifer had replied. His didn't raise his voice, didn't make any threatening gestures. Naturally, she thought. He felt he didn't need to. Because he believed, once again, that he held the whip hand. But not this time, she determined.

"I'll go to the police. I'll take my chances. They'll investigate you. They'd have to."

Seifer shook his head. "Don't waste your time, Mrs. Daniels. I've told you before—I have no record. It will be your word against mine. And whom will they believe? I have no connection with Bernard Daniels."

"Jarvis," she had replied. "I'll involve her. And the others. All of the others."

"They're all incriminated. They're not going to testify for

you. Or against me. They'd bring themselves down. There would be everything to lose and nothing to gain. You continue to misunderstand the fundamental essence of what I actually do—I've been a *genuine benefactor* to each of them. I've given them what they most wanted—freedom, money, the opportunity to change their lives. Don't you understand? None of these people *hate* me."

She gestured toward the folder and the bottle of poison.

"Those. They incriminate *you.*"

"Not in the least. You could have procured the poison—you're a wealthy woman. Money will buy anything in this country. You travel, you have the opportunity. As for the materials in the folder—they're in the public domain. Anyone could have assembled them."

She folded her arms against her chest, trying to fight him, to combat him with some weapon, even if it was only silence. She suddenly felt very tired. And alone.

He took her silence for further resistance. He picked up the green bottle and walked over to her. After removing the cap, he held the bottle up to her face. She caught a sharp scent and backed away quickly.

He said, "Do you realize what just a few drops of this liquid will do in a child's lunchbox?"

She gasped.

He poured out a couple of drops of clear liquid onto the carpet between them.

"Do you realize what just a few drops of this will do if touched on a child's neck while she was at the movies?"

Kay started to cry. "Oh God."

Seeing his advantage, he stood just inches in front of her. And the look in his face and the tone of his voice was immediately different, she saw. Now she realized the manners, the polished demeanor, his accent, were as much a mask as the charcoal suit and silk tie he wore at their first meeting. This was the real Seifer.

"What are you going to do—pull her out of school, go through life with her attached to you like a Siamese twin?"

Again Kay felt dizzy. She had to sit down. She went to one of the couches and put her head in her hands.

But he followed her, again standing over her.

"And you're missing the most fundamental point. Eugene Fanning is a very bad man. He's going to divorce his wife, leave her with nothing. Take his two children away from their mother. Not because she's a bad woman, but because he's ruthless. Ruthless in business, ruthless as a person. He'll not be missed. His family will be glad to see him gone. His employees will dance on this grave. As for you, the actual procedure is ridiculously easy. You merely have to bump into him in the lobby of a crowded theater. That's it, and you're done. Free to go on with your life. The only real issue you confront is your *guilt.* But why, Kay? Why feel guilty?

"I'm not capable of murder, dammit."

"You would be surprised what people, very ordinary people like yourself, are truly capable of. If you were at war, for instance, you would feel no compunction about killing."

"I'm not at *war!*"

"But you are, Kay. You are. You're at war for your freedom and for the life of your child. Isn't that worth killing for?"

"You're mad."

"Even if I were, does that change the position you are in?"

He went over to the dining table and gathered the scattered documents. Then he returned and dropped the folder onto the coffee table in front of her.

"Study the folder," he said. "Get to know him. Get to know your target."

★ ★ ★ ★ ★

Good God, she thought, flipping through the documents in her room. Had Marilyn Jarvis been provided with a folder on Bernard such as this? Profiles of their company. A newspaper clipping from the real estate section summarizing the purchase of their house. A typed schedule of his daily habits. Photographs of the hairpin turn at Munson and Deepdale, taken both at night and in the daytime. It was incredible. No wonder an average citizen would be an easy target for an assassin, if that assassin were equally average, differing only in the preparation supplied by Seifer and backed by the ruthlessness and focus of such a man.

She read through the several newspaper stories of Eugene Fanning and his rise to prominence in the Boston area. To her amusement, she realized these were not actually clippings but printouts from Nexis. Was that how Seifer found his *clients?* Was it as simple as merely scouring the newspaper databases to locate affluent couples with ongoing conflict and mutual hostility? In the back of her mind, she had vaguely assumed that Seifer was the archetypal mastermind at the center of a web of criminals, all of them busy searching the country for the next perfect victim. But now that Jarvis was revealed to be another client and not a co-conspirator, it was clear to Kay that Seifer and his woman constituted the entire extent of this "organization" and that armed, as she had been, with the keys to the treasure trove of the Nexis databases, they could locate their victims with just a few keystrokes.

That presumably was how they had located Eugene Fanning. Although there were not many articles about what appeared to be a very discreet man. That must have been why Seifer had provided the color photo. The few pictures of him in the newspaper clipping were black-and-white and of a much younger man, one of them in a cop's uniform. After graduating from college he had entered the Police Academy and then, a few years later, attended night school to earn his law degree. A brief sojourn in the district attorney's office to acquire some experience was followed by a decade-long stint in a prominent Boston law firm. That, inevitably, led to marriage to one of the partner's daughter, a residence in Beacon Hill, and two delightful children. Then Fanning got the urge to go out on his own and took several of the firm's clients with him. Five years later, his firm's prominence was greater than his father-in-law's. Perhaps that was the beginning of the hostility between Fanning and his wife. Perhaps she felt her family had been betrayed. There were reports—in the gossip columns—of a separation, quickly followed by a reconciliation. One story concerned a "domestic disturbance" at the home that required a police cruiser dispatched to the Fanning home, but no arrests were made or charges brought. The local reporters tried to dig deep into the events, but everyone was tight-lipped and details were few. As his wealth grew, Fanning apparently felt he should socialize more, and his name appeared on the boards of several charities and cultural institutions, including the Biltmore Theater. That was where Kay was supposed to rendezvous with her target.

Seifer had given her not just the means and the methods, but also the location and the date. December 15. Before she could ask how he could be so precise, he had explained. The fall season of the Biltmore was to conclude with a gala performance of a new play by a Boston local. A major Broadway star was to play the lead. In the folder, Kay found a ticket to the performance already purchased by Seifer. She examined it. Eight P.M. on Saturday, December 15. Then she picked up the color snapshot of Fanning.

Sixty minutes after the curtain first rose, the intermission would begin. You, Mr. Fanning, she thought, staring at the photo, will go into the bar for a drink and to chat with friends.

On your way back to your seat, a woman will bump into you and pretend to know you and shake your hand. Thirty minutes later, before the end of the play's second act, you will be dead.

Chapter Twenty

Mo said it had to be a coincidence, Sinclair thought. But only because she couldn't connect the Daniels woman to any of the players involved in the Long Island accident. But what if there was indeed no connection between the two accidents, but it was still not merely a coincidence? When are two apparently contradictory events not, in fact, contradictory? When they're both true.

He re-read the copy of the report that Mo had sent to him. It was, in fact, a copy of a copy. Mo had secured *her* copy from the Glen Cove police. The similarities between the two accidents were striking, Sinclair noticed. An early fall evening, a man out alone in his own neighborhood, a stranger from out-of-state driving an SUV on his way to visit some friends. Even the wealth of the deceased was amazingly similar, as was the widow—squeaky clean with no record, who inherits a princely sum from her Wall Street banker husband. And there was an even more astounding similarity: the husband was seen threatening his wife at a party some months before the accident. Police investigators had uncovered that the man was a heavy drinker and after the wife had refused to allow him to drive their car home after the party, he had grabbed her by the throat, nearly throttling her. Among the guests were the mayor and a federal judge. No charges were filed. The couple continued as before. Until the accident.

Sinclair blew out a breath. Too many similarities, he thought, shaking his head. It can't be a coincidence. The only real difference between the two accidents, in fact, was that the man killed in Long Island was not out jogging but taking his dog for a walk. Jesus! thought Sinclair, changing his mind again. It was so ridiculous it had to be genuine. He was out of his mind. This was no murder. And, as he had indicated to Lipinksi, he was seriously beginning to doubt there was any—as Kay Daniels would say—*foul play* in the death of Bernard Daniels. Who arranges to murder someone who is walking his dog or out jogging? It was preposterous. It was also . . . inelegant. Anyone seriously contemplating bumping off their spouse would come up with a more rigorous plan that this. There was so much that could go wrong. Besides, the driver of both vehicles had no connections to the dead men and no obvious connections to the widows. Both accidents *had* to be flukes, he reasoned. It was one-in-a-million. Now if it were to happen a third time, that would be a different story.

"Holy crap!" he said aloud. Why: if it *were* to happen? What if it *had* happened a third time? Somewhere other than the TriState area? The relative closeness of the two towns from each other—just twenty miles across Long Island Sound—was the prime reason he and Lipinski thought there might be some connection. But what if this scam had been pulled in other towns, other states?

He picked up the phone and called the Eighty-First Precinct in Brooklyn.

Chapter Twenty-One

There were only three options, Kay thought. She was sitting in a window seat of the first-class section of an American Airlines flight from Vegas to Bradley Airport in Hartford. The man in the adjacent seat had tried to chat even before the plane had begun to taxi—"Any luck at the tables?"—but she had shaken her head, put on earphones, dialed in to a classical channel, and stared out the window. He got the message and didn't bother her again. She propped a notepad on her lap and tried to come up with a plan.

The first option was to go to the police. But she reiterated Seifer's arguments why that was not a real option. She had no proof that he had done any of the things he had said he'd done. Additionally, assuming he was not lying, he had no record. The police would undoubtedly investigate him, but unless any of his former clients would testify, it was all circumstantial and ultimately it would come down to her preposterous allegations. And, she realized quickly, none of the other clients *would* testify. Each of them had committed murder. She was crazy if she thought any of them would corroborate her claims about Seifer. And, as he had pointed out, why would they? They were all wealthy, thanks to him, and free to live the lives previously denied them by their domestic or business partners.

Going to the police would undoubtedly protect Eugene Fanning from harm, but what about Kelley? And what about Kay herself? How could she expect to run a business and carry on a normal life if Seifer and Johanna were out there somewhere? He had proved he had patience. He had waited for six months in a Connecticut suburb where he truly did not belong in order to fulfill his plan. He had waited two years to approach her before entangling her in the Eugene Fanning affair. He had the financial and other resources to simply wait. Wait for the police to pull any protective surveillance from Kay's home and workplace, and then he would strike. And what about Kelley? As he had indicated, how was Kelley supposed to live a conventional life—attend school, go to college, pursue a career, get married? Always there would be the threat of an admitted killer.

The second option, she felt, was to kill Seifer. It had immediately occurred to her when next she met the man, she could simply remove the Heckler & Koch from her pocket and shoot him. But the thought was fleeting and useless, she acknowledged. He had told her in the hotel room they would not meet again. Kill Fanning and their arrangement was done. There was no reason for another meeting, he had pointed out. Seifer thinks of everything, she thought. But why not? He had been doing this for more than a decade. Even if he suspected what she was capable of, he had left her without the possibility of any type of direct physical action. And indeed, if she did as he wished and killed Fanning, there would be no further need for them to meet.

The third and final option was to kill Eugene Fanning. She was surprised that she wasn't shocked at the thought. This was what Seifer had brought her to: genuinely weighing the pros and cons of murdering a stranger. Seifer had made it sound so easy. He had demonstrated—using his index finger dipped in water—how simple it was to transfer the poison to an unknowing victim. She had been stunned at the demonstration. She'd barely felt the moistness on her wrist. In a crowded theater, full of noise and bustle, it would be an unusual person who would be aware of what had just transpired. And even if he did, what could he do about it?

So, Eugene Fanning would die and she—and Kelley—would live. Free to live their lives. But how *could* she live with killing another human being? This man Fanning, she suspected, was no monster, just as Bernard, with all his flaws, was no monster. She knew nothing about the others—Marilyn Jarvis's mother, the woman in the Lake Forest restaurant, the Houston oil executive, any of them. Maybe they *were* all monsters. But equally likely, maybe they were just flawed individuals whose deaths benefited others, and with Seifer's interference, those others had themselves been entangled and had no choice but to adhere to his demands.

Oh God, she realized, suddenly despairing at the thought. Even if she did as Seifer demanded, there would be others to follow her. More people would die. The chain of death would continue. She would be merely another link, the newspaper clippings of Bernard's accident and Fanning's cardiac arrhythmia just additional material to buttress Seifer's folder. The man had to be stopped. He *had* to be.

For the rest of the flight, she stared out the window pondering the question and when finally the plane taxied to a halt at Bradley, she looked down at the single word written on the notepad: *How?*

Chapter Twenty-Two

"Is this a date?" Sinclair asked. "I don't do dates."

Mo made an unladylike snorting noise. "Who the fuck would want to date an old fart like you?"

"My twelve years as a detective tell me this is a Saturday afternoon. And that we're sitting in a restaurant next to a tranquil lake. And you're dressed to the nines. This sure seems like a date to me."

"It's not a date. I'm not that desperate. I have men chasing me every day. Every guy in the Eighty-First wants to get into my pants. This is just business."

Sinclair stared at her. "Well, then, why are you wearing a skirt?" It was the first time he had seen her wear something other than the figure-killing pants suit. "And you've wearing lipstick."

"It's not lipstick, asshole. It's lip gloss."

"Well, whatever. It's not . . . you."

She looked at him, seemed hurt at the remark. "Do you prefer the other . . . me?"

He looked away, then snatched up a menu. He was genuinely uncomfortable. He liked Mo, but he had been startled when he'd picked her up in Westport station twenty minutes previously. The pumps, her stockinged long legs, the short skirt, and the creamy white blouse. He almost didn't recognize her. Until she greeted him.

"What the fuck are you staring at?" she'd said.

It was Mo all right. She'd called him at home that morning and suggested they meet. She had some developments she wanted to share. Other than his usual weekend chores, Sinclair had no plans, so he had quickly agreed. But he hadn't expected her like this.

Now, in response to her question, he merely said, "Let's order something. So we can concentrate on the Daniels business."

She picked up her own menu, and while she studied it, he thought about her question. Did he prefer the "other" Mo? In truth, he acknowledged, he'd hardly taken into account her femininity. He had dealt with sufficient female colleagues—subordinates as well as supervisors—in his time not to think of them as other than *colleagues.* Hell, in the Navy he had been a shipmate with a score of women. But he had never been romantically involved with a female colleague in either the Service or on the Force.

"All right," he said, after the waitress took their orders. "Let's hear it. What have you got?"

She removed a folder from her attaché case.

"The guy who was driving the SUV, Jeffrey Reynolds. I had a friend at the FBI run his name through ACS."

Sinclair knew the Bureau's Automated Case Support system, a collection of databases of investigative files and their indexes, was the most comprehensive nationwide collection of criminal records available to law enforcement. But the circumstances for access by conventional police departments were strict. He guessed that Mo had indicated to her "friend" that given the cross-state ramifications of the Reynolds incident, it was a no-brainer to get access to the ACS.

"And?" he asked.

"Clean as a whistle."

"Dammit. They sure it's the same Reynolds?"

She nodded. "The Glen Cove file had all his vitals, even his

Social Security number."

"Well, so much for that theory."

"Except for one small item."

"What's that?"

"He was questioned by Interpol two years before the Glen Cove accident."

"*Interpol?* Give me a break." His derision was undisguised. After sixteen years on the Force, the number of people he knew that Interpol had interviewed could be counted on the fingers of his left hand. Interpol, he was fully aware, was not an investigatory agency. It was little more than an assemblage of computer databases available to law enforcement worldwide.

"Hey, don't fuck with the messenger." She held up the file. "That's what it says here."

"Why would Interpol be interested in this guy?"

"Actually it was the Tokyo police who did the questioning. It was a routine interview following a request by Interpol. And *they* were responding to a request by San Francisco P.D. This guy's partner drowned in his swimming pool while Reynolds was in Japan."

"Why didn't San Francisco P.D. just wait until he came home for the funeral?"

"Reynolds had a girlfriend in Tokyo. That's part of the reason he was over there. He was getting married. And he wasn't giving up his honeymoon for his partner's funeral. Especially after what they had been through with each other."

"What's that supposed to mean?"

"Dueling lawsuits. Accusing each other of embezzlement."

"Holy crap. So, let me get this straight. These two have a falling out and were suing each other. One of them gets drowned in his swimming pool while the other one happens to be abroad. Then, two years later, the same world traveler happens to kill a man on the other side of the country in an auto accident."

She shrugged. "What do you think?"

"I think I have a headache." His life had been so uncomplicated until Kay Daniels and Mo Lipinski had come into it. Now things were getting complicated. He wished Kay Daniels and all her baggage would go away. And he surprised himself by his wish that he could simply sit here with Mo and bullshit about anything other than work. Maybe I *am* an old fart, he thought.

She said, "Alibis don't come any better than being out of the country while the deed gets done."

"Well, that means only one thing."

"What?"

"If the drowning wasn't an accident, someone else committed murder for Reynolds. And to find out who, all we need to do is just one thing: follow the money."

"Why?"

"Come on, Lipinski. You're supposed to be good. Think."

"I'm not an old fart, Frankie, so I don't know all that you know." She winked at him.

He couldn't deny it, but he liked the way she called him "Frankie." No one had ever altered his name like that, even as a kid. It was always a brisk, sharp *Frank*. All sharp edges, he thought, that was Frank Sinclair.

He explained, "It doesn't appear likely sex was the motivating issue. And people don't murder people as a favor. So—follow the money."

She made a face. "There isn't a prayer his bank would give us information about his accounts."

"Not us. But how about San Francisco P.D.? We'll trade."

"Trade?"

"Just as we didn't know about Interpol and the guy in the swimming pool, the case officer in Frisco wouldn't know about

Glen Cove—why should he? It happened two years after the drowning."

"You're not actually going out there?"

He hadn't thought it through to that extent. A couple of phone calls surely would be sufficient. "No. But I will if I have to."

She was silent for a few moments while he started to eat.

"Hey, Frankie."

"What?"

"If you're really going to San Francisco . . ."

"Yes?" He guessed what she about to say: *Be careful.*

"Wear some flowers in your hair." She winked again.

He stared at her. There was something else about Mo Lipinski that he liked. He really liked the way she winked.

Chapter Twenty-Three

She had been wrong. There was, Kay thought, a fourth option. Marilyn Jarvis. Visit Jarvis and convince her to testify. Kay had—thanks to the Nexis databases—the names of other Seifer clients, but with Jarvis, she had a psychological hold—the woman, after all, had murdered Kay's husband. Of course, she realized, Jarvis would be putting her own neck on the line. But Kay suspected the woman had been under the same duress and implied coercion as Seifer had put *her*. All Kay had to do was—somehow—convince her to come forward and Seifer could be stopped in his tracks. Surely, Kay thought, there could be plea bargains that would get Jarvis off the hook if she helped the authorities bring a killer like Seifer to justice?

It was a tall order though, she acknowledged to herself as the cab approached the office building where Jarvis worked. And, making things even more difficult, there was precious little time to accomplish it. It was the Friday after Thanksgiving already. Was that yet another crucial facet of Seifer's planning—to give the victim so little time to formulate any kind of plan to resist him? She had only a couple of days after returning from Vegas to get her affairs in order before she left for Boston and her rendezvous with Eugene Fanning. She had alerted Mike Bishop that he was in charge of running New Croydon Telecomm while she had "issues" to handle. She told Janet the truth despite some initial hesitation about getting her in any way involved, but realized quickly Janet was the only one that she could trust to take care of Kelley. Janet, stolid as ever, agreed to look after Kelley at Kay's house. Realizing she couldn't get the Heckler & Koch through airport security, Kay gave it to Janet who seemed aghast at the weapon. Kay gave her a quick lesson, but realized it was for psychological reasons only. She then took the next immediate flight to Lincoln, Nebraska, arriving late on Thursday afternoon. As she unpacked the single suitcase in her room at the Coburg Hotel, it occurred to her that if Jarvis's name wasn't in the phone book, she was screwed. She had no idea how else to track her down. But she remembered that the police detective, Sinclair, had said Jarvis ran a chartered accountancy business. So she went through the Yellow Pages of the phone book and quickly found the prominent box ad for "Jarvis & Associates. Chartered Accountants."

It was almost six o'clock but if Jarvis were as dedicated a business owner as Kay, she would not be a nine-to-fiver and would certainly be still at her desk. And she was. Kay almost didn't recognize the voice; it was definitely less mousy than she remembered. Perhaps it was Jarvis's business voice and not the real Marilyn. Kay identified herself, told the woman she was in Lincoln, and asked to meet with her. She sensed the reluctance, but when she said, "Our mutual friend in Primrose Lane has contacted me again, and I'd like your advice," Jarvis agreed to meet first thing on Friday morning. She gave Kay directions, and they both hung up.

Kay had little appetite for food and none for company, but realizing the necessity for some nourishment, compromised by ordering a Caesar salad from room service. After picking at it for ten minutes, she abandoned it, then sat in the exceptionally comfortable leather armchair and marshaled the arguments that would, she hoped, convince Jarvis to give herself up to the police.

But very quickly, Kay became despondent. There were few "pros" and too many damn "cons" as to why Jarvis would remain silent. To begin with, if Seifer was telling the truth about the woman's controlling mother, Jarvis was now free to live her own life. She had money; she had her business. Why would she consider giving all that up and gamble with jail time? That was the devilish ingenuity of Seifer's system, Kay realized. It was not just giving up one's freedom, it was willfully abandoning the wealth and lifestyle that had been bequeathed to each of them. And for what? To punish Seifer? To prevent further killings? Who among them had the conscience to trade *their* future for the life of some stranger?

And, Kay realized now, there was a further consideration. What if one of them *did* come forward but Seifer, with his wealth and access to high-powered defense attorneys, got off? Would he then go after his accuser, seeking vengeance? Each of his clients well knew what the man was capable of.

Or, what if Seifer declined even that route and simply disappeared as soon as the police confronted him with any sort of allegations? With the money he had surely accumulated over the years, he could go to ground or simply move abroad. There were a thousand-and-one places that would act as a bolt hole for someone with his resources. And he was not stupid. He almost certainly had some contingency plans for just such an eventuality.

It was impossible, she thought, suddenly kicking the ottoman in frustration. Impossible and foolish. None of them would allow themselves to be persuaded. Even Jarvis. Had Seifer told the truth about her? Had she really been under the control of a domineering parent for much of her life? It was, thought Kay, surprisingly ironic. Not only did she and Jarvis have Seifer in common, they each shared a miserable childhood, apparently.

Kay hardly remembered her own mother. To her credit, her mother stood up to her husband after years of abuse. But in the end, he didn't need force to defeat her. He had the law on his side. When she took off with Kay and Janet, both toddlers, their father called the police and the errant wife was quickly located. A particularly uncivilized judge gave full custody to the father. For the two girls, the abuse that followed was not physical, nor was it sexual. It was the complete absence of love or tolerance. Before her tenth birthday, Kay was accustomed to cleaning the house, handling the laundry, and taking care of a dozen other household chores that her father's frequent girlfriends declined to do. Her father referred to Kay and Janet as "my girls" but not in the daughterly sense of the typical parent, but as mirror images to his women. Kay, initially, refused to run. She heard her father say frequently, "It's a man's world" to his lovers, but Kay was determined to show . . . somebody . . . that it was not, that she could survive and prosper in that world. So she would not run. At least until she was seventeen. She woke up one Saturday night around midnight. Her father was sitting on the bed and his hand was inside her pajama bottom. She could smell the drink, sense his bulk even in the darkness. She knew it was useless to fight. He worked with his hands in construction, and he was a big man. And it was useless to scream, even if he allowed it—their house was isolated from its nearest neighbor by several hundred yards. So she pretended to sleep and endured it.

The next day she met her boyfriend after school and told him she was moving away. Kevin was a year older and had been working in the paper mill since he'd graduated from high school the previous spring. He didn't want to let her go and before either of them knew what they were doing, they had eloped. It was ridiculous, she knew even then, as they drove away in his ancient pick-up. Their entire belongings were packed into two cheap suitcases. She had no high school diploma, and he had no real skills. Their plan was doomed, she felt. And yet, strangely, it had worked. They landed on their feet in La Jolla.

He managed to get a job in a factory; she waited on tables in a diner until her eighteenth birthday, then, legally an adult, enrolled in the local high school. She got her diploma and entered the University of California at La Jolla. Sensing the need for something other than a liberal arts degree, she focused on accounting and marketing.

Following her graduation, she worked for an aerospace company for several years, then told Kevin she wanted to return to school for her MBA. But he was reluctant. Initially she thought the reasons were financial, but then quickly realized it was something even more mundane: envy. He was still in the factory; she was moving further along in a genuine career, and the graduate degree threatened to leave him far behind. She stuck to her guns—the money wasn't really an issue as she intended to work part-time at her old job—and gradually they drifted apart. She had less time for him. He simply lost interest. Kelley came along after she graduated, but the baby was probably the final straw. The divorce went through six months later.

She was frightened of being genuinely alone for the first time in her life, but she forced herself to confront her fears because, she felt, Kelley depended on her. And she was determined Kelley would not have a childhood as barren as her own had been.

The taxi pulled to a stop outside a large building, all-glass and modern looking. And, she thought, she was certainly not going to have Nikolas Seifer threaten her daughter's future if there was anything she could do about it.

Only six companies shared the Majestic Financial Building, Kay saw by the index in the lobby. Jarvis & Associates had the entire fourth floor all to itself. "Who knew there were big bucks in chartered accountancy?" she thought, as she took the elevator.

"I have an appointment with Marilyn Jarvis," she told the receptionist. The professionally dressed woman seemed as sleek, efficient, and . . . *new* as the rest of her surroundings. Kay had expected some tattered carpeting, poor lighting, and ancient wooden desks. Instead the entire floor oozed gleaming glass, bright lights, computer terminals, and a young staff bustling to and fro.

The girl spoke to someone on the phone and then directed Kay to the end of the hall. She was met by yet another polished woman who introduced herself as Jarvis's secretary. Without having to wait, Kay was escorted directly into Jarvis's office.

"Hello again, Mrs. Daniels," Jarvis said, getting up from the large teak desk and extending her hand.

"Hello," said Kay, startled by the firmness of Jarvis's grip. The woman's clothes, too, were a surprise—expensive, silk, and clearly not manufactured in any city in the Midwest. She suspected Versace. Jarvis herself looked different: the hair was colored a strawberry blond and cut fashionably short. The few pieces of jewelry were, Kay thought, unostentatious and well chosen. This was a different woman that the one Kay had met in a New Croydon coffee shop two years before.

"Are you wearing any surveillance devices?" Jarvis asked.

Kay stared at her. It was the one thing of a thousand things she did not expect Jarvis to ask. Out of agitation, frustration, perhaps fear, at what she had been going through since Las Vegas, she burst out laughing.

"You can't be serious," she replied.

Jarvis looked anything but frivolous.

"Yes, I am serious. Are you wearing any such devices?"

Kay sighed aloud, then, past caring about embarrassment, immediately lifted up her blouse. How things change, she thought with some amusement.

"Shall I take off my skirt, too?" she asked.

Jarvis shook her head. "No, have a seat." She went to her own leather chair behind the desk.

Kay sat down. "You're not going to help me, are you?"

"What sort of help do you need?"

"To put him away where he belongs."

"I can't do that."

"Sure you could. All you have to do is testify."

"And end up with a rope around my neck, too?"

"It doesn't have to be like that. Not if all the circumstances were known."

"Who would believe us?"

Kay felt some slight relief that Jarvis had used the word "us." Maybe there was still some hope.

"They'd have to believe us. With your confession. My testimony. I have the poison. That's enough evidence to get them started investigating him. Maybe they could set up a sting of some sort. Maybe they—"

"Stop it!" Jarvis said, hitting the desk with the palm of her right hand.

Kay was startled into silence.

"It's hopeless," Jarvis went on. "Don't you think I went through what you're going through? You can't fight him. He's done this before. Many times. He works it all out beforehand. He does research. He's aware of your routines. Your strengths and your weaknesses. He . . . controls you."

Kay looked down, feeling defeated. She couldn't do it alone. She was dependent upon Jarvis, and it was obvious Jarvis was not going to help. Now she was really alone. She had been alone for so long, even married to Bernard, to Kevin. Neither had pulled their weight. She had made the marriages work, at least as much as they *had* worked. She had pulled her weight and more than her weight. But she couldn't do it anymore. She couldn't fight a man like Seifer by herself, she acknowledged.

"It's time for your murder, I take it?" Jarvis asked.

Kay was struck by the odd phrase. Then she replied, "Yes. Some poor man in Boston."

"Don't tell me. I don't want to know."

"How did you do it? How did you eventually face up to doing it?"

"He told me about your husband. Showed me newspaper articles. Told me about Kelley."

Kay gasped.

Jarvis acknowledged the reaction with a nod. "I told you—he prepares. He even suggested that your husband would abuse your daughter next. He said that was the typical pattern of such men. He was . . . authoritative. Seemed to know about these things. But it was not just that, of course. You probably know about my . . . my mother."

Kay nodded.

Jarvis went on, "I was implicated. Or, rather, he implicated me. I had a perfect alibi when my mother collapsed and died. I was on the other side of the state, auditing the books of an electronics manufacturer. Seifer plans well. He looks out for you, makes sure the murder takes place when you can't possibly be in the same location. After all, if you're in prison, you can't give him half of your assets. And yet, he makes sure of contingencies. He had my fingerprints on the bottle of poison from when he first approached me two years previously. He'd explained how my mother had really died and handed me the bottle to inspect. Like a fool, I took it without thinking."

She laughed, without much humor. "The devil and the deep blue sea. There was no way back. And only one way forward. Besides . . ."

"Yes?"

"Besides, Mrs. Daniels. I was *glad* my mother was dead. Seifer certainly does tell the truth. He *was* my benefactor. My life was . . . actually, I didn't have a life. My father had money, but my mother had good attorneys. I had to work all my life—this company was in my mother's name originally and although I ran it and expanded it, all I made was a modest salary. I'm not strong, Mrs. Daniels. At least, I wasn't strong enough to confront my mother. I was . . . ashamed of my sexual preference. I was lonely, miserable. I'm not embarrassed to tell you I thought of suicide on more than one occasion. Seifer gave me back my life. It was worth the money I had to pay him." Another mirthless laugh. "I would have given even more if he wanted it. I didn't realize later, of course, why he didn't demand it all."

"Why not?"

Jarvis gestured toward her. "The same reason you're here. He extracts the rest of his payment in kind. He gave me a dossier about your husband, and told me what he expected me to do."

Kay was silent for a moment, then said, "Something I've never figured out. How did you know I was going to the Englebrook Inn in Vermont?"

Jarvis was puzzled. "I don't know what you're referring to."

When Kay explained, Jarvis said, "I've never been to Vermont."

"So it must have been Johanna who registered in your name. And the phone call that was on my bill—you obviously didn't make it."

A memory occurred to Jarvis. "I see he repeated his little trick with the phone bill. My number was on your bill, right? And your number was on what was supposedly my bill?"

"Yes, that's right. But *supposedly?* You don't mean—"

Jarvis nodded. "He explained it to me later. Like most tricks, it's pretty simple when it's revealed. The bill was a fake."

"What!"

"It's a variation of a basic street con. Show the victim something genuine, then when you show her something similar but fake, it gains authenticity by its proximity to the authentic article. Your own bill with 'my' number on it was obviously genuine—as you suspected, they got into your hotel room and simply made a call to their cell phone. But because you knew your own bill was authentic, you made the understandable leap that the bill with your number on it was equally real."

"Oh, Christ. No wonder he gave me the bill and the receipt. They were worthless as evidence."

"But you weren't to know that. Nor the police. That's why they found no obvious connection between us. Your number wasn't on my *real* bill, and my real number wasn't on yours."

"Damn him." Kay put her left hand to her forehead. She could feel tears approach, tears of rage, of frustration, of fear.

A phone on Jarvis's desk buzzed. She picked it up and after a moment listening, said, "I'll be right there."

She put the phone down. "I have to go." The tone of her voice changed: quieter, more friendly. "Mrs. Daniels—Kay, I'm sorry about your husband. I really am. But it seemed at the time there was no choice. You came to ask for my help. So let me help by giving you a piece of advice."

Kay looked at her. "Yes?"

"Do it. Do what he wants. Don't blame yourself. Think about the future. Yours and Kelley's. Do it and put it behind you."

Jarvis stood up and went to the door. She held it open, waiting for Kay.

So, thought Kay, not four options. Three. And then she corrected herself. No, not even three. There were never three. There was never more than one. Just the one, single, solitary option.

Kill Eugene Fanning.

Chapter Twenty-Four

Their luck, if they had had any in the first place, ran out immediately. Captain of Detectives Harry Niles of the San Francisco Police Department was now ex–Captain of Detectives Harry Niles of Portland, Oregon, a retiree after twenty-five years of exemplary service. An administrator in Records, following Sinclair's faxed request, gave them Niles's last known phone number.

"Sure, Frank, I remember working that case."

Sinclair was surprised at the man's easy familiarity with a stranger on the other end of the line. But, he guessed, that was how you behave when you were in retirement mode.

"Why?" he asked. "It was deemed an accident, wasn't it?"

A friendly chuckle. "Yes. But what happened two years later made it memorable."

Sinclair looked at Mo, who was listening on an extension, and mouthed: *Glen Cove?*

"What was that, Harry?" Niles had insisted that Frank call him by his first name.

"Reynolds's wife killed herself."

"What!"

"Yep. Poor woman. We talked to her sister. Aoki, I think her name was. Reynolds managed to bring her over from Japan to keep his wife company. According to Aoki, her sister felt 'great shame' at what her husband had done."

"You mean Reynolds's wife believed he had killed his partner?"

"No. That he killed a man in a traffic accident. On Long Island."

Sinclair blew out a breath. Now they had nothing to trade, even if Niles had been in a position to give anything in a trade.

"So you knew about that?"

"Not until Aoki told us. We went out to the house to check on the wife. She had taken an overdose. Left no note. I guess what she had told Aoki was her note."

"What did Aoki say?"

"Well, she didn't speak English very well. We located a translator, but the story was still confusing. The problem was not just Aoki, but her sister was so distraught that *she* was confusing. The gist of it seemed to be that Mrs. Reynolds believed her husband had killed the man deliberately. That was ridiculous, of course. They were complete strangers. Reynolds happened to be visiting an old college friend while he was on the East Coast on business. But it stuck in my head. Soon as you mentioned the swimming pool, I remembered right away."

"You questioned Reynolds about this? And what Aoki was claiming?"

"Naturally. But there was nothing to go on. He was distraught at what his wife had done. I made a call to the Chief in Glen Cove, but he seemed perfectly satisfied it was just an accident."

Mo silently said, *Fuck!* Sinclair agreed. The police report from Glen Cove had made no mention about the inquiry from San Francisco. But, he quickly realized, why should it? A courtesy call from another department, even from a distant state, would hardly be considered official unless it had some real bearing on the case and actually led somewhere.

He said, "But Harry, clearly something was out of kilter with all of this."

"Accidents happen, Frank. Accidents happen."

"What about the drowning. You're happy that was an accident, too?"

"Ah, that was an unfortunate one, I grant you. The damn thing was, the body was in the water for three straight days. Any evidence of drugs or poisoning was shot to hell in a hand basket. Plus the fact that Reynolds was half-a-world away at the time. He was the only logical suspect, the only one with anything to gain. The victim had no known enemies. None of the neighbors had seen or heard anything suspicious. We just couldn't get any traction on the case and had to go with the medical examiner's verdict: Death by misadventure. To my nose, it smelled. But again, accidents happen."

They chatted for another ten minutes, but try as Sinclair did, Niles assured him it would be impossible to get S.F.P.D. to reopen the case. The link to the accident in New Croydon was too tentative to force a busy, undermanned detective squad to open an eight-year-old case that one of its best officers had conceded was an accident.

They exchanged goodbyes, Niles cheerily insisting Sinclair "look him up" if he ever visited Portland.

"Well, that was a bummer," said Sinclair, putting down the phone.

"It was a long shot, at best." Mo hit him on the arm. "Anyway, I'm glad you don't have to go out there. You might have returned as a gay man."

Sinclair made a face.

"Come on, cheer up," she said. "Let's go out. I'll buy you a drink."

He nodded. "Okay. I've got some more ideas we can hash over."

She seemed disappointed. "I thought we could have a drink and take the time to get to know each other."

"What's there to know? I'm ten years older than you. End of story."

"Your cock hasn't fallen off, has it?"

He could only stare at her.

When he didn't reply, she said, "So, then, what's the problem?"

What *was* the problem? He asked himself. Alison was dead. In her final days, she told him he had to go on. He was still in the prime of his life, she said. It would never diminish what they had together, what they were. *Don't sweat it,* she had said, *God is good.* Her favorite phrase. It covered every eventuality, it seemed; even her replacement.

Mo had remained quiet, staring away from him. Unnerved by the absence of her usual volubility, he tried to explain.

"Mo, it's . . . It's just . . ." But then realized he couldn't explain it. Because he didn't know the reason himself.

She turned toward him. He was startled to see tears running down her cheeks.

"Frankie, a life lived in grief is not a life worth living."

He could only continue to stare at her.

She added, "I should know."

Chapter Twenty-Five

She would do it in the theater bar, Kay decided, rather than in the lobby, as Seifer had instructed. The moment the curtains began to close on the first act, therefore, she stood and went quickly up the aisle. But already, thirsty patrons from seats further back were beginning to clog the passageway. She turned her head around, searching for Fanning.

She had easily located him when he'd first taken his seat, an hour ago. She made sure she was one of the first to enter the theater and, after finding her place, oriented herself to where Fanning would sit. Seifer's dossier had provided the seat number and, sure enough, the man from the color snapshot showed up about ten minutes before curtain time. He was dressed in a tuxedo, with the at-ease elegance of one born for the role. The photo must have been taken quite recently because even the man's hair seemed hardly longer or shorter. He was accompanied by an attractive raven-haired woman, about his own age. She wore an expensive-looking cream dress that matched her pearl necklace. Given his stature, Kay had vaguely assumed there would be some sort of retinue, but it was clear the couple were attending the event alone. They chatted together as the seats around them filled up, and neither acknowledged any of their neighbors. Everyone was dressed for the occasion—tuxedos for the men, evening gowns for their female companions. Jewelry, silver hair, and perfect winter tans were much in evidence. This, surely, Kay thought, was the cream of Boston society.

She suddenly became alarmed. Fanning's wife was still in her seat. Kay easily recognized the distinctive hair and the cream colored dress. What if the couple didn't feel like socializing and remained in their seats? But then she realized the place next to Mrs. Fanning was vacant. Kay stood on her toes and looked further down the aisle. When she saw him making his way slowly through the mob, she let out a breath of relief.

The bar already had three lines of people. She had no intention of drinking and stood against a rear wall, allowing the crowd to gradually swell around here. Within minutes, the room was full. She saw Fanning enter and take a place in a line. While she debated how best to approach, she noticed his appreciative look at a young man who walked away from the bar carrying a drink. Was that the cause of tension in the marriage, she wondered? Some latent homosexuality tendencies he had begun to display? But she forced herself to discard that thought and focus on the man himself. The line hardly seemed to move. He looked at his watch and then left the line, heading toward a side door. She realized it had to be an access to the rest rooms.

This was a stroke of luck, she thought. She hurried after him and closed the door behind her. He was walking down a short corridor and had almost reached the door labeled "Gentlemen," when she called out, "Mr. Fanning."

He stopped and turned around. "Yes? Can I help you?"

There was no one else in the corridor. She could hear the muted buzz of conversation from the bar. She walked quickly up to him. He was about a foot taller than her. His black hair had flecks of gray, his eyes were brown, and his lips formed a polite smile. She smelled some sort of aftershave, something not quite masculine.

"You *are* Eugene Fanning?" she asked.

He nodded. "Yes. Do I know you?"

She leaned closer to him and said in a low voice, "Mr. Fanning, you're in great danger."

"I beg your pardon?"

"Please. Mr. Fanning. You can't go back to your seat."

He stared at her, looking at her up and down. Because she had anticipated his reaction, she had dressed for the occasion—the evening gown, ruby earrings, and carefully coiffed hair would hardly indicate that she was some mental case in off the street.

"I'll explain," she said, "but not here. There's a side exit onto Nassau Place. I've checked. We can leave that way."

He didn't respond, merely continued to stare.

"Mr. Fanning. Please! What's the worst that can happen if I'm not telling the truth? You'll be inconvenienced, maybe embarrassed. But if I'm telling the truth, that will be a small price to pay."

She had one final card to play. It wasn't much, but she hoped it would be sufficient to convince him. She reached into her pocket book and withdrew her driver's license.

"Look," she said, handing it to him. "Verify the picture. You can keep it, if you like, and show the police."

She saw him look closely at the license, clearly matching it to the woman in front of him. She felt close to tears.

"I'm trying to help you. Won't you listen?"

The woman-in-distress mode must have helped make up his mind.

"All right. Where are we going?"

She shook her head. God, she was so stupid. She hadn't even thought it through. She had anticipated that convincing a stranger that he was in danger was so huge an obstacle that she had focused solely on that. That was why she had decided to confront Fanning in the bar rather than in the lobby. She had realized that Seifer or Johanna could be in the theater, even in the balcony. But the bar area was smaller and she had assumed it would be easier to spot either of them there rather than in a crowded lobby. But now that she had apparently succeeded in convincing Fanning to accompany her, she had no idea where to go.

"I . . . don't know. My hotel room, I guess."

"Your hotel room!"

"We can't hang around on the street. We might be seen by . . . by the person who means you harm."

"Miss . . ." He glanced at the card. "Miss Daniels. I can't go to your hotel room."

He saw the anguished look on her face, then sighed. "Very well. I have a better idea. There's a company apartment, here in town, for clients and associates. It's available right now."

She nodded.

He said, "I'll have to get my wife. Wait here."

"No! You need to leave now."

"But my wife—"

"She's not in any danger. *You're* the target. She won't be harmed by these people."

It was clear he was on the verge of changing his mind, and she thought, who could blame him—having to leave his wife abruptly. Naturally the woman would be alarmed.

Kay said, "We can get a cab, and you can call the theater from your cell phone. Tell them it's an emergency. You know the seat number. Have the manager bring her to the phone, and she can meet us at the apartment."

Again, he hesitated and then said. "All right."

He pointed further down the corridor.

"That seems to be an exit."

They walked quickly down the corridor and pushed the door open. Although mid-December, the air was still mild and Nassau Place was busy with people on their way to area bars and clubs. Kay and Fanning walked toward the front of the theater, but then they spotted a cab with a "Vacant" sign alight. They hailed it and Fanning said to the driver, "Cumberland Avenue."

"You got it," replied the driver.

Fanning then called Information, obtained the number of the theater, and asked to speak to the manager. Kay wondered if the second act of the play had begun but realized intermission was probably still on. Very quickly, it seemed, Mrs. Fanning was on the line. Her husband said, "It's an emergency. I'm going to the apartment on Cumberland. Take a cab there right away. I'll explain when you get there."

He spoke reassuringly for a few moments longer, then turned off the connection. He said to Kay, "At least, *you'll* explain, I hope."

He put the cell phone back in his pocket and stared out the window. Kay was glad of the silence. She had done it. It was the only way, she reassured herself. She couldn't—wouldn't—commit murder and she couldn't let this man be unaware that Seifer had him on his hit list. So she had determined on the plane from Lincoln to Boston that she would warn him. But she quickly realized that she couldn't warn him in advance. Seifer—or someone in his employ—might be watching her. Or Fanning. She had reasoned that this was how they had located her in Vegas and probably how they detected Mr. Scanlon so quickly. And, she guessed, this was also how they knew she was at the Englebrook Inn. Either she had been followed there or palms had been greased at the travel agency that had arranged the trip. So she had decided she would allow herself to be seen attending the theater, put them at their ease, and maximize the time she had to foil their plan.

"Here we go," said the cabbie, pulling into a parking space outside a large apartment building. There was a long canopy from the entrance to the street. She could see a doorman inside the well-lit lobby.

Fanning paid the driver, and they walked through the lobby toward a bank of elevators. A minute later, they exited onto the eleventh floor.

"It's 1108," he said, pointing to the right.

They walked to the door and Fanning took a key from his pocket. That's odd, Kay thought, as he unlocked the door and held it open for her—that he would be carrying the key to the company apartment on a night out at the theater.

She walked into the living room where Seifer, sitting in a leather armchair, said "Ah, Kay. Always so predictable."

Chapter Twenty-Six

Tears on Mo Lipinski's cheeks, Sinclair thought, seemed as strange as the blouse and skirt she had worn at the lakeside restaurant. He felt an impulse to move to her and brush them away, but then consciously restrained himself.

Mo looked away, and he guessed she was trying to disguise the weakness that all of her colleagues looked for each day.

"Hey," he said, "it's all right. Come on. Let's go get that drink."

"I never wanted to be a cop. Does that surprise you?"

Yes, it did surprise him. Her evident toughness, her rapid succession of promotions, and her much better-than-average conviction rate seemed the essence of those who were born to be cops and who loved what they did.

"What *did* you want to be? With that mouth, you would have given George Carlin a run for his money."

She smiled, brushed away the dark streaks on her face.

"Fucker." Then she took a deep breath, to steady herself, it seemed, and began.

"I was happy to be a wife. That's all I wanted. To be a wife and a mother. My husband's name was Billy. William Lipinski, his parents call him. But everybody else called him Billy. He was a lieutenant in the Jefferson Avenue firehouse in Brooklyn. He had just been promoted, one of the youngest ever to reach that rank. A week after the ceremony, there was a fire in a warehouse."

She sighed, an acceptance of despair. “Billy never came home. Two of his men were killed. The experts soon figured out it was arson. An insurance scam. But nobody went to jail. Nobody was arrested. Nobody paid for Billy and his men.”

Tears flowed again. And again Sinclair, despite a forgotten sense of life beginning to stir within, forced himself to remain still.

“How come?” he asked.

“Not enough evidence. Clearly the owner of the warehouse benefited. But he had an alibi. His house and car were inspected—you know trace evidence of the explosive used in such devices leaves residue that can be picked up by sensors. But he was clean. Nobody on the street had any tips. Informants knew nothing. A detective from the Eighty-First told me that a pro from out-of-state must have been hired to do the job. The bottom line was that one man got wealthy, and four people died.”

“Four? I thought you said—”

“I lost my baby. A miscarriage. I wasn’t strong then. Too much stress. Too much sadness. Too much fear at suddenly being alone.” She smiled, without any humor. “You think it’s easy being a hardnosed bitch? It wasn’t easy—at first. But when I got the runaround from the city, from the bureaucrats, from the lawyers, I found it very easy. Nobody would do anything, even though they *knew*. I thought becoming a cop would be one way of getting to the truth.”

“And did it?”

She shook her head. “He disappeared a few months after the fire. Went abroad, maybe.”

Sinclair was lost. Too full of his own self-pity, he now realized, to connect with anybody else. Too blind to see any pain but his own.

“Mo, I don’t know what to say.”

"Don't *say* anything, Frankie. Do."

He went to her and held her until the tears, like his guilt, ebbed to less than a memory.

Chapter Twenty-Seven

"What—what's going on?" Kay asked. She was confused. Fanning was somehow involved with Seifer?

"Kay, when are you going to stop regarding me as a fool? I *know* you, Kay. I've studied you. What do you think I was doing in that Connecticut suburb for six months? Don't you realize I know about you and Bernard? How the business was *your* idea. How that stupid man was ruining a perfectly nice set-up. I *prepare*, Kay. Do you really imagine I just jump into these things without foresight, without meticulous planning? I know you. And I knew you wouldn't do it. That's why I had my friend here take you for a test run."

"He's not Eugene Fanning?"

"Of course not. Meet Gentleman Jimmy Doyle. Looks the part of a rich man, doesn't he? He's fooled a lot of people in his time."

"But—but I could have given him the poison."

Seifer's laugh was derisive. "It was scented water. I didn't trust you. There was no way I was going to give you that poison until I was absolutely sure you would do my bidding."

As she always did when encountering Seifer, Kay felt tired and worn out. She went to the couch that faced Seifer's chair and sat down.

Seifer picked up an envelope from the coffee table and handed it to the man.

"All right, Jimmy. Good job. There's the rest of it. Make sure you give my regards to Susan."

Jimmy nodded and without even a glance at Kay, turned and left the apartment.

Kay said, "So Fanning was never actually in the theater?"

"Oh yes. He was in the front row."

Kay nodded to herself. "So that was why there were no recent photos of him in the folder. And why you gave me the snapshot."

"That's right."

She sighed. "Now what?"

"Now you bear the consequences."

"The consequences?"

"The consequences of interfering with my system. I told you once—I don't like the police looking into my affairs."

"I didn't go to the police."

"If that was the real Eugene Fanning, what do you think his first reaction would be when you told him his life was in danger? Of course he would involve the police."

"I hadn't—I hadn't thought about that.

"What's the matter with me?" Kay asked herself. Seifer was right. Of course Fanning would want to call the police. Anybody would. God, she was so stupid. Seifer knew her better than she knew herself, she realized.

"Well, I did think about it. I have to think of every contingency. And I knew how you'd react, especially after the reluctance you displayed in the hotel room in Vegas. And I already am prepared for the next contingency."

"Meaning?"

"Meaning that you now carry out my instructions as I've already indicated. I will give you photos of the real Eugene Fanning. The other materials in the dossier are authentic."

She was almost in tears. "Don't you *see?* I can't do it. I just can't. I could never do what you want."

He reached into his jacket pocket and removed a cell phone.

After pressing some numbers, he handed it to her.

She raised the phone to her ear, puzzled. "Hello?"

"Kay, Kay, Kay," said Johanna's voice. "You've disappointed me. I have to admit I'm surprised. I had bet that you *would* go ahead with it. But I should realize never to make a bet with our mutual friend."

Kay looked at Seifer, still puzzled as to why she was holding a phone, talking to Johanna. She gestured with her free hand toward him.

Seifer reached for the phone, then placed it to his ear.

"Told you," he said.

Kay heard something that could have been Johanna's laugh.

"You know what to do." He hit the power button without saying "Goodbye" and returned the phone into his pocket.

Kay asked, "What was that all about?"

"I was sending Johanna a message."

"What message?"

"That she was to proceed with her visit to your daughter."

Chapter Twenty-Eight

No, thought Johanna after she pocketed her phone, it's never a good idea to make a bet with MacBride. He'd said Daniels would try something, would probably refuse to go ahead with it, maybe even warn the target. And he was right. Christ, this woman was a pain. Why was MacBride persevering with her? Yes, yes, she knew how he'd respond—it was his *system.* Him and his damn systems. Everything had to be so precise, so organized.

He hadn't always been like that, she recalled. He'd changed in the dozen years since they'd met. Or was it the big money that had changed him? His payments from the Family had been lucrative enough, but he had never considered himself rich until the money started to roll in when the system started to work as he said it would. That, then, surely, was the rationale behind the fancy clothes, the fancy food, the fancy diction. Christ, he'd even hired a vocal coach to eliminate the harsh nasal twang of the typical Northern Ireland accent he hated so much. And that, presumably, was the rationale behind the name change. He had done some investigating and determined the name of the first man he'd killed, a British soldier. The man's last name was perfect. For the first name, he settled on a simple change of letters from the original Nicholas.

She'd laughed at him when he took the diction lessons, the lessons in how to eat, how to set a table, where the forks went. How it was proper etiquette to wipe your mouth with your napkin before drinking from your glass at dinner. But he didn't care. "It's America," he'd explained. "These people feel they have an obligation to reinvent themselves."

But it was all ultimately ridiculous, she felt. No amount of fine clothes or airs-and-graces could change the reality—he was a hired killer. That's what he was when they'd first met, and that's what he'd always be. Oh, sure, strictly speaking, his *system* now meant others did the actual killing. But he was always the puppet-master, dangling their strings. Besides, he certainly had no compunction about handling the blade himself when necessary. He didn't hesitate to dispose of that fat detective who poked his nose into their affairs. Christ, the woman was so naive. Didn't she realize how long they'd been doing this? Didn't she realize they could foresee people's clumsy reactions? They were all so predictable, all so gullible. And running to find a private dick instead of contacting the police was a common response. They knew how lucky they had been, and none of them ever went to the police. "It's not because they don't want to," MacBride had explained. "It's because they choose not to. Because they worry they will somehow be deprived of their newfound wealth—even if they had nothing to do with the death of their spouse."

It was greed, of course. That, she knew, was the fundamental issue. That's why they always overcame the initial horror at what MacBride had done. That's why they always overcame their scruples when the time arrived for them to fulfill the final part of MacBride's bargain. Because the typical two-year waiting period was not just to minimize the time between the death of their partner and their involvement with a stranger's demise. It was, as MacBride planned, to give them time to adjust to their new life, their new freedom, their new wealth. After two years, none of them ever acquired the courage to say "No." And that's why this Daniels woman was such a fucking pain. Why couldn't she just do the deed? Why was she forcing them to go to these lengths?

Johanna sighed. No point in going over it again. She had been through it several times with MacBride, and he had insisted that Kay Daniels had to be the one to deal with Fanning. It was not just the system, he had pointed out. It was a practical matter. There was no one else available. Neither he nor Johanna could be associated in any way with Fanning. That, of course, was the essence of the system. She smiled. Even if any of the beneficiaries had the balls to contact the police, there could never be any connection established between the deceased and either MacBride or her. So that was why the Daniels woman had to dispose of Eugene Fanning. And now that she had blocked them yet again, there was only one sure way to persuade her to do as they wished.

Johanna didn't need MacBride to teach her how to disengage a household lock. Nor did she need instructions in rendering a standard alarm system useless. She had performed these little chores—for that was how they were considered by experienced burglars—dozens of times throughout the Northeast during her career prior to meeting MacBride. The only thing she worried about, as did all burglars, was the possible presence of a dog. She had been watching Janet Neville and her niece for three days now and not once had either of them taken a mutt out for a walk. That, of course, didn't mean there wasn't one in the house, but Johanna felt reasonably comfortable as she walked to the rear of the Ridgewood Court house the afternoon following her directive from MacBride.

Twenty-fours previously, when the girl was in school and her aunt was at her veterinarian clinic, Johanna had visited Kay Daniels's large home on Ridgewood Court. There was little risk, she knew from experience. The most successful burglaries occur between two P.M. and three P.M. And being a petite female, she had long ago discovered, was the perfect persona for a visit to a potential target. Especially if you simply breezed up to the door and rang the bell. Even if a neighbor notices you, the better dressed you are the less suspicion you arouse. At worst, people assume you're a Jehovah's Witness or Mormon, especially if you carry the requisite bullshit file folders. At best, people assume you have every right to be there. To further assuage any suspicion, she utilized one of her old tricks: a sign of a national realtor affixed to the door of her minivan. So after a moment waiting for a response, she had simply walked around the back of the house, checking the entry points and, after looking into the windows, determined the most likely location of the alarm console. Two minutes later, she was back in her vehicle.

Now she was again at the rear of the house. With a piece of mica—about half the length of a child's ruler—and a screwdriver, she could trip all standard five-tumbler locks. Quickly, she opened the rear door and moved inside, expecting the usual annoying beep from the alarm console that served notice to the owner to deactivate the alarm.

But there was no sound. That was a first, she thought, puzzled. It was a requisite part of every alarm system. So the only reason the alert had not sounded meant that Kay's idiot sister or her daughter had neglected to turn the system on when they'd left that morning. Johanna shook her head at the thought: a million-dollar home unguarded against potential burglars.

She looked at her watch. Now she would just have to wait half an hour before the kid came home from school. For the past three days, like clockwork, the school bus had braked to a stop outside 14 Ridgewood Court at 3:20 P.M., and the kid had walked down the long driveway and let herself in. Johanna estimated, therefore, that within forty-five minutes of entering the house, she would be on her way with the girl stashed in the back of the minivan. So for the next thirty minutes, she could relax and take it easy.

"Don't move!"

Johanna whirled around. Janet Neville was standing in the doorway, holding an automatic with both hands.

Jesus Christ, thought Johanna. Why hadn't she looked in the garage! She had assumed the woman had done what she had done for the three previous days and driven to her clinic. She was wearing a robe and her hair was tousled. Had she just got out of bed? Was she home, sick? Could that be the idiotic reason she was here now instead of at work?

"Who are you?" Neville asked. "What do you want?"

Of course Janet Neville didn't know her. Even if her sister had described Johanna, the odds of this woman putting two and two together were remote. In order to gain some time, she decided it was best to simply admit the obvious.

She shrugged. "What does it look like? Burglary."

Neville was looking around. "Are you alone?"

"Yes."

"Put that weapon down. Drop it on the floor."

Weapon? Then Johanna understood. The screwdriver. Already having made her decision—she was going to have to do it, she realized, she was going to have to kill her—Johanna decided she had only one chance to get her left hand into her jacket pocket. She turned her right side slightly toward the woman.

"This? This isn't a weapon." She held the screwdriver up and—it was the natural reaction—the woman's eyes followed the motion. "It's just a screwdriver."

"I don't care. Drop it on the floor."

Johanna tossed it onto the floor between them, knowing it was now too late for Janet Neville. Her left hand was already in her pocket, unscrewing the cap of the bottle.

"Take your hand out of your pocket!"

"I'm just getting my medicine."

"I said, take your hand out of your pocket!"

Johanna dipped her gloved index finger into the bottle and then re-capped it. She took the bottle out of her pocket and held it up.

"See. Just medicine."

"Put it on the table."

"I need it. I have a condition." Johanna moved toward her.

"Stay where you are."

Johanna had done it enough times to know the turmoil civilians were in at such a moment. She had already established that the woman was unmarried. Neville was now alone, and despite holding the gun, Johanna felt that she was unlikely to be comfortable with it. The intruder was a petite female without any obvious weapon. So it was a gamble, but a well-calculated one, to approach her. The gamble was that Neville would pull the trigger before Johanna could reach her. But it was a gamble that had to be taken: there was no way that Johanna was going back to prison.

So she continued to move, albeit slowly, toward the woman, holding up the bottle and repeating the refrain: "It's only medicine."

It happened too quickly for Neville to appreciate what had occurred. Johanna, now holding the bottle in both hands, thrust it at her and said, "Just check it out." Neville took the bottle with obvious reluctance and backed away, but it was too late. Johanna had swiped her finger across the top of the woman's left hand.

Satisfied, Johanna put up her arms. "I guess now you're going to call the police."

The poison usually took about ten minutes, sometimes less. So Johanna had to stall her from picking up the phone. And there was only one possible way to do that: divulge the mission that Kay was undertaking in Boston.

"Yes," replied Neville. "They'll be here soon." She glanced at the bottle, then put it down on the countertop.

Johanna smiled. "Yes. It will all be over pretty soon."

Chapter Twenty-Nine

"Fuck it!"

Johanna hadn't seen MacBride so angry in years.

"What's the matter? We have the kid. It doesn't stop the plan going forward."

Killing Kay's sister had not been part of the plan, she knew. It was supposed to be a straightforward snatch job. She was then supposed to call Janet and tell her not to contact the police. A second call to MacBride would then result in him having Kay contact her sister to ensure her cooperation. At that point, Daniels would have no option but to carry out their plan to kill Fanning. But they hadn't reckoned on the woman being at home when Johanna had broken into the house.

"Of course it does. It's her sister. She's got to show up at her funeral. It would be too suspicious otherwise."

"Her daughter not showing up for school is going to be suspicious."

"That was an acceptable risk. It was only going to be for a few days, anyway—until Daniels killed Fanning. But this is different. She knows too many people for them not to ask where she was when her sister was being buried. And we need her there to ensure the body gets cremated. No, it's too risky. I had to let her go home."

"Well, she's going to have come right back if she wants to see her daughter again."

Seifer let out a heavy breath.

"I told her a week. I want her back next Tuesday. She kills Fanning on Wednesday."

Chapter Thirty

Kay hauled the suitcase down the stairs and left it by the front door. A single case should be enough, she thought. If Seifer was monitoring her movements, he would be suspicious if she carried more than one bag. She was only going to Boston for a couple of nights, after all.

She looked around. What else? She was pretty certain she'd thought of everything—leaving Mike Bishop with instructions on what to do at New Croydon Telecomm while she was away, paying any outstanding bills, removing food that might turn bad after a few weeks from the refrigerator. Yes, she was sure, she'd taken care of everything. Just turn on the security system as she left, toss the suitcase into the car, and begin the journey to Eugene Fanning.

She had had the best part of a week to come up with a plan. Janet's death was devastating, and for two days Kay had been numb with grief. That Kelley was in their hands was the only thing that made her hold herself together. As the coffin moved into the incinerator, Kay only had one thought: She had failed Janet as a child and now she had failed her again as a grown woman. She had run from her father's home and left Janet behind. Whatever had occurred in the years prior to Janet's own escape made her retreat into herself, her inability to love transferred to the care of the animals that needed her help. Kay had tried to compensate by paying for Janet's tuition at veterinarian school. But it was never enough, despite Janet assuring her that she had no reason to feel any guilt. She knew that Johanna had to have used the poison—the death had been ruled from natural causes, cardiac arrhythmia. She had neglected to impress upon Janet the threat of the sodium cyanide. So Janet had been unprepared. And it was Kay's fault.

When the door of the incinerator closed and the sickening *whoosh* of the device did its work, Kay decided for an instant that she would do it, she would return to Boston the following week and kill Eugene Fanning. But almost immediately decided against it. That would mean that she had failed Janet one more time. And that was something she would not so. So, she was going to retrieve her daughter and she was going to avenge her sister.

The doorbell rang. Kay gasped, then told herself: Calm down! It wouldn't be Seifer. He wouldn't dare show himself in this neighborhood again. Besides, he had Kelley. He didn't need any extra weapons of coercion. Probably another neighbor, coming over to offer sympathy. But the funeral was yesterday. No one she knew should be calling at this time. Still uncertain what to do, she heard the doorbell again, this time a longer, sustained ring. Realizing she had to get started on the trip if the plan was going to work, she decided she had to stop this nonsense and just open the damn door.

"Good morning, Mrs. Daniels."

It had been about two years since she'd seen Detective Frank Sinclair. Had he changed? She could barely tell. His usual morose face seemed less strained. There was still no humor or friendliness, but there seemed to be less . . . sorrow.

She nodded. "Detective." Offer the minimum, she decided. She couldn't let this man delay her. Kelley needed her. Every second was vital.

"May I come in?"

"Why?"

He seemed surprised. "I'd like to ask you some questions."

"About what?"

"About your sister's death."

"What about it?"

Again a look of surprise on his face. Was it her aggressive stance, the tone of her voice? Maybe he was here to offer condolences. But no, he said he had "questions."

"I was at the funeral."

"I didn't see you."

"Well, actually I wasn't in the building. I was in my car, outside."

"And?"

"I was wondering why I didn't see your daughter. Kelley, her name is, isn't it?"

"I don't believe it's any of your business, Detective. But if you must know, she was staying with my . . . my father. In California."

"Your father?"

"Kelley was very close to Janet, my sister. And I thought it best if she could just get away from it all."

Sinclair stared at her. Did he believe any of it? Would he ask for her father's address or phone number and attempt to contact Kelley? But why would he be interested in talking to Kelley? She didn't find the body. They had snatched her after they'd killed Janet, and the body wasn't discovered until Janet's office assistant—unable to contact her—phoned the police.

He finally said, "Your sister. She was very young to die of arrhythmia."

Kay shrugged. "What can I say? No one knew. She was a workaholic. Cared more about her animals' health than her own. She hadn't had a physical in years."

"I'm sorry." A change of tone in his voice, a different look on his face. Unless he was a world-class actor, he appeared sincere.

Her facade softened. She nodded. "Thank you."

"Why did you have her cremated?"

The bastard! A surge of anger shot through her. Affect sympathy, then put the knife in. That was his game, was it? She forced herself to take a breath, then another. The quicker she could get rid of this man, the sooner she could get to Boston and get Kelley released.

"It was her wish. She had lost her faith a long time ago."

He nodded. But how could he know what she meant? Only three people knew what had occurred in her father's house, and two of them were now dead.

"And how about you?" he asked. "Are you holding up?"

"Yes. I'm fine."

"Taking a trip? Going out to visit your father?"

"What?" She stared at him. What was that supposed to mean?

Sinclair pointed at the suitcase.

Oh Christ, she thought. "No. It's just some of my sister's things. She stayed with us occasionally and kept some clothes here. I'm taking them to the Good Will."

Was he now going to demand she open the suitcase and inspect the contents? No, he didn't have the authority for that. In fact, she realized, he had no authority to do anything regarding her or her family.

She said, "Is there anything else, Detective?"

He shook his head, then, as if remembering something, he said, "Thomas Scanlon. The private investigator you hired. You still haven't heard from him again, by any chance?"

"No."

"All right. Well then, I'll let you go."

Was that some taunt, she wondered? *Let you go.* As if he had her under his thumb and deigned to let her roam free for only as long as he desired. He turned and walked to his car. But perhaps not, she thought. Perhaps it was merely a saying, spoken a thousand times every day, a phrase that carried meaning only for those who believed themselves truly guilty.

Chapter Thirty-One

The face matched the photos. This, Kay realized, was the real Eugene Fanning. Strangely, in some ways, he reminded her of Seifer. They were about the same age and had a similar build. She guessed that Fanning didn't allow the typical sedentary work of an attorney prevent him from regular exercise. His gray-flecked hair was similar to that of the man called Gentleman Jimmy, although the latter, no doubt, had colored his to match Fanning's. His cheeks were ruddy as if he had just returned from a walk in a blustery wind. But, she suspected, given the Irish or Scottish-sounding name, it was probably his Celtic heritage that accounted for the coloring. His eyes were blue, like Seifer's, and, again like Seifer, he hardly moved while she spoke. Kay recognized that familiar attribute of an experienced attorney: the ability to listen and to absorb before asking a question, much less come to any conclusion.

She looked across the polished oak desk at Fanning. "I suppose you want proof?"

Fanning, as he had done since she had sat in his office and began her story, remained silent. An hour previously, she had been escorted in by a puzzled secretary who had said, "Mr. Fanning, your nine o'clock appointment. Eh, Mike Bishop."

The attorney had displayed obvious surprise when Kay walked in. She quickly explained the subterfuge: she had had her deputy call and make the appointment. She worried that her phone was being monitored and decided against calling to make the appointment. Concerned also that Fanning's office suite was being watched, she had reserved a room in the Lenox Hotel, within walking distance of Fanning's building, in addition to the room in the hotel where Seifer had directed her. At eight A.M., she was already in the building, confident that even if Seifer and company were watching, they would not expect her to show up so early.

It had taken an hour to detail the entire story from the moment Seifer had entered her life. She brought events up to the present, to Janet's murder. But it was all hearsay. This was an attorney who had just been told he was in danger of being killed. Of course, he would want proof.

He reached for the phone and hit a button.

"Beth. Cancel the rest of the morning's appointments."

Surprised, Kay asked when he placed the receiver in its cradle, "You believe me?"

"Mrs. Daniels, I can't imagine what scheme you might be trying to perpetrate. Therefore, I have to take into consideration the possibility that you may well be telling the truth—however bizarre that truth may be. So yes, I would now like to see some proof."

She reached into a tote bag and withdrew the dossier.

"Here's what he gave me," she said, handing it to Fanning. "As preparation."

Fanning looked through it, maddeningly slowly. Kay took the opportunity to look around the office. It was at least twice the size of her own and decidedly more old-world: dark wood paneling, leather chairs for both attorney and client, a burgundy leather couch at one wall, soft lighting from expensive-looking lamps. The ambiance, though, she felt, suited a man a decade or two older than the one sitting across from her. The one anomalous touch was a fancy aquarium against a rear wall; tiny, multicolored fish darted amid the foliage and rocks of their own underwater world.

Finally, he finished and said, "Well, it's comprehensive enough. But in and of itself, it's merely a recap of my bio. It doesn't really corroborate what you have been telling me."

She knew his dossier wasn't going to be sufficient, so she reached into her bag a second time and withdrew a file folder.

"Seifer's greatest hits," she explained, passing it over.

Again he took his time, going through the printouts from Nexis that she had assembled. When he finished, he seemed a little less calm, a little less assured than he had been. An hour ago, she understood, he was the one in control. The archetypal expert to whom a member of the laity had come for advice and to bow before his greater knowledge. Now that equanimity had been disturbed, if only fractionally.

"Mrs. Daniels, I know you don't want to hear this, but the police have to be notified."

She shook her head. "No. Do that, and Kelley will die."

He was about to argue, but she cut him off. "Don't waste your time. I've just told you in detail what this man is capable of. The evidence is in front of you. He won't hesitate a second to do it."

He nodded. "Apparently. But what else do you expect me to do?"

"I expect you to fake your own death."

"What?"

"I have a plan. It's the only way this guy can be brought to justice. And first, he has to be convinced that I've done what he wanted me to do."

"Mrs. Daniels. I don't think I need to go to that extreme. I could just go into protective seclusion."

"Yes, if yours was the only life at stake. But do that, and Seifer will know I've warned you. Then, Kelley will die. And, as you surely understand by now, he'll just keep on with his system.

More people will be killed. Maybe not in a week or a month. But eventually, innocent people will continue to die."

Fanning was silent, his eyes, no longer at peace, moving from her to the folder and back again.

She pushed her advantage. "You realize I've saved your life?"

He stared at her. It was obvious that had not occurred to him.

She went on, "You realize if Seifer had assigned another beneficiary to you, *that* person would not be sitting here giving you a warning. He—or she—would walk up to you, on the street, in a store, in a restaurant, and use *this.*"

She took the bottle of sodium cyanide from the tote bag and held it up in front of him. Pointing at the aquarium, she asked, "How fond of those fish are you?"

"They're from New Guinea," he said. "Rainbowfish. Quite expensive."

She stood and walked over to the aquarium.

"So's your life." She held the bottle over the water. "May I?"

He hesitated only a moment, then nodded. She poured some of the liquid into the aquarium. In less than a minute, the half-dozen fish, inert motes of color, lay floating atop the water's surface.

Kay returned to her chair. "You realize what I'm saying? You owe me. Now all I'm asking you in return is to be inconvenienced for a few weeks. A month at the most."

"And what are you going to do?"

"I'm going to get my daughter back."

Chapter Thirty-Two

"This is *preposterous!*"

Kay disliked Amy Fanning even before she'd opened her mouth. It was the excessive jewelry worn in the daytime, the bulbous lips that had to be the result of frequent botox injections, the limp handshake when Eugene Fanning introduced his wife to Kay. And now that she did finally speak, it was, Kay thought, inevitably a whine of intolerance.

"This is some sort of scam," she went on, speaking to her husband and ignoring Kay, who sat on the couch next to her. "It has to be."

"Amy," said Fanning. "I've already decided."

Kay understood the surprise that appeared on the other woman's face. She, too, had been surprised by Fanning's relative lack of hesitation in agreeing to her proposal. Instead of giving her the bum's rush out of his office that morning, he had instead spent the afternoon debating the pros and cons of her plan. That he believed her was obvious. That he would agree to such a potentially embarrassing enterprise after a few hours of discussion was not. Perhaps he was confident that the labs at Harvard Medical School, where he used his connections to have the poison tested, would soon verify her claims.

"But think about the children. They'll be traumatized."

"I've already told you: we treat it as a charade. They'll stay at my mother's house in Miami until this is over. They'll know damn well that I'm safe. They'll miss a few weeks of school, but it can't be helped."

"I still don't understand why you can't go to the police."

Fanning glanced at Kay before replying: "Then this woman's daughter will die. And Seifer will remain free to continue as he has been doing: killing innocent people. We have a chance, a real chance, to bring this man to justice."

"That's not your responsibility! You're a lawyer in private practice. You're not in the District Attorney's office anymore. And you haven't been a police officer for twenty years. What's the matter with you—trying to recapture your past?"

Kay noticed the sharp intake of breath from Fanning. She couldn't possibly know, but she suspected his wife's last remark was a familiar rebuke.

Fanning said, "I need your cooperation—*obviously.* Otherwise we can't pull this off. So, are you willing to cooperate?"

The woman stood. "If it will speed up the divorce when this . . . *charade* is over, then yes."

Some residue of her breeding made her turn to Kay.

"Mrs. Daniels. Good day."

She left, not bothering to close the door behind her. Another familiar rebuke, Kay guessed.

Fanning closed the door, then went to an antique-looking drinks cabinet.

"Let me refill your glass," he said.

Kay smiled what she hoped would be seen as a gesture of support. "I think you're the one who needs a refill."

His own smile was rueful. "I never thought I'd admit this, but for once she's right. We really should get the police involved. No, don't say it. You're correct, of course. It would be disastrous for Kelley. But I'm not altogether sure our plan will work."

He brought the bottle of Glenlivet over to her and poured a large measure into her glass.

"Actually, I think it's *my* plan," she said. "You shouldn't have to take responsibility if it goes wrong."

He smiled again. With his wife out of the room, Kay saw, he had noticeably relaxed. What was the reason for the tension between them, she wondered? Who was really at fault in this troubled marriage? The news articles in the dossier had offered only speculation. The marriage had the privacy of the privileged and, in truth, she realized, only this man and his wife had the answers to the source of the conflict between them.

"Well," he said, "it's the only plan we've got. And it's worth the attempt. Frankly, I doubt the police could prove much anyway without the cooperation of the other beneficiaries. And the police are unlikely to sanction what we're about to try."

He shook his head. "I've got to hand it to this guy. It's an ingenious system. His hands are always clean. Someone else is always doing the dirty work."

Kay nodded. "I've been thinking about it a lot, as you can imagine. It's the *incentive* that makes it work. My situation is an anomaly. Merely threatening or blackmailing people might suffice most of the time, but it just takes one individual to balk and possibly expose him. But with this system of his, there's no need of the stick because the carrot is so substantial."

Fanning drained his glass and placed it on the coffee table.

"We have two full days until Wednesday," he said. "We need to go over it again. And again and again and again. Timing—in this situation—is not only everything. It's the only thing."

Chapter Thirty-Three

"You've come a long way," Johanna said.

"A journey I wouldn't want to repeat," replied Kay.

They were in the apartment on Cumberland Avenue. She had, as instructed, waited in the room at the Eliot Hotel for the phone call. Apparently satisfied at the news reports of Fanning's death, the call came at eight P.M. on Wednesday night. She had watched the local Six O'clock News herself. The death of the "prominent attorney" from cardiac arrhythmia that afternoon was the fourth story. The newscaster, a perky bottle-blonde, disposed of it in a couple of sentences and then turned to her colleague at the weather map for an update on the possible storm approaching from Canada. Johanna told Kay to come immediately to the apartment.

Kay was surprised that Seifer wasn't present, but Johanna had explained before she could ask the question. He had gone to fetch Kelley and would be back shortly. Johanna was visibly relaxed, Kay thought. And why not—she and her partner believed they had just guaranteed themselves another lucrative payday. Kay had done some research of her own and estimated that Fanning's net worth had to be around $10 million. Johanna had clearly been drinking and offered Kay a shot. Kay, wary of doing anything that could be construed as obstructionist, accepted.

"You should just have gone ahead and done it in the first place, Kay. It wasn't so difficult in the end, was it? Just a swipe of your finger on somebody's skin. Be grateful you didn't have to drive a car and knock someone down—like the earlier ones. Christ, I was always amazed that we never ran into problems."

Kay was startled at her tone of confidentiality, of . . . *collegiality,* even. It was as if they were now partners and, therefore, Johanna could let her guard down.

"What sort of problems?" Kay asked.

Johanna made a vague gesture with her glass, spilling some of the whiskey onto the carpet. "You know—what if the target was only seriously injured? I told MacBride it wasn't going to work every time. That we needed to come up with a better method."

MacBride? Kay felt a sudden surge of excitement and hoped it wasn't visible on her face. Seifer's real name was MacBride? This was a breakthrough, she thought.

Johanna pointed to her chest. "*I* was the one who came up with the idea of the poison. I did all the research. And I found some beauts: thallium, which paralyzes the face and makes you unable to talk before the heart and kidneys begin to degenerate. And barium, which causes heart failure within ten minutes. But I quickly realized there were two big obstacles."

Kay knew she should be listening carefully, but she had to fight hard not be distracted by the thought that a man who changes his name does so because he had done something under his original name. And if that *something* was egregious enough, there might be a police file somewhere that recorded it.

Johanna sloshed the bottle of whiskey into her glass, spilling some onto the coffee table.

"First," she explained, "there had to be some sort of social interaction between the target and the poisoner. And since it was part of the system that there could be no interaction, how could the poisoner give the poison? Second, it had to leave no residue to indicate that it *was* poison. That, too, was part of the system. The target had to die, but it couldn't be obvious that the cause was murder. So I had real problems to solve. But solve them, I did. Yes, I did."

She put down her glass and stared at Kay. It took Kay a few moments to realize Johanna was waiting for her to ask "How?" and she did so.

"Glad you asked. It seemed like what I needed to know was not in any book or on the Internet. Then I had a brainwave. I contacted some of our old friends in the Family. They mentioned a doctor who wasn't a doctor any longer, if you know what I mean. Seems he liked his little patients a bit too much, if you know what I mean. Anyway, he was disbarred or defrocked, or whatever it is they do with doctors. So we went to see him in Jersey City, and he was the one who pointed us in the right direction. From there, it was a simple matter to find a chemist who for the right amount of cash mixed up the ingredients and—there you have it. Foolproof. So don't you be worrying about Eugene Fanning, Kay. They'll never realize what happened, and you'll be off scot-free."

Kay heard the door being unlocked and quickly filed away in her mind: *the Family.* She stood, facing the door which opened to reveal Kelley and, immediately behind her, Seifer. Kay felt tears in her eyes, and she went to Kelley, who ran into her arms.

While they hugged and kissed, Kay was aware of Seifer closing the door. She stood and wiped tears from Kelley's cheeks. Kelley seemed none the worse for wear, but she felt her daughter squeezing her hand.

Seifer walked over to Johanna who had already poured him a glass of whiskey. After taking a quick sip, he said:

"As I told you before, Kay, several times—I always do what I promise. Things can be so simple if people would only do what I tell them to do. Here's your daughter. Now the two of you can get back to your little suburb in Connecticut."

Kay had expected another obstacle, some further obligation. "That's it?"

Seifer glanced at Johanna, then laughed.

"What? You want a cut of the money?"

"No, of course not. I mean: Are we done? Should I expect to hear from you again?"

Seifer seemed puzzled. Then Kay understood. He didn't like a mess and retaining a hostage to keep her further in line would be extremely messy. As would disposing of them both. Two bodies, the wife and stepdaughter of a man who had been killed in a freak accident two years previously, would be very messy indeed. As before, they were all linked and the chain could be unraveled very quickly, exposing him. Besides—in his eyes—she was now as trapped as Marilyn Jarvis in Nebraska, as Jeff Reynolds in San Francisco, as all the other beneficiaries. Implicate Seifer, and she implicated herself. It was the system at its most ingenious.

"Whatever for?" Seifer replied. "No, we're done. You did a good job. I didn't have any doubts about you this time—for obvious reasons. Although I did visit the hospital this afternoon and made some discreet inquiries. Eugene Fanning was admitted just before one o'clock. He was dead fifteen minutes later."

Kay hoped she seemed distraught enough to convince them she was the culprit.

"As you said: it didn't take much. I bumped into him as he left his building for lunch."

"Ah. That reminds me. I'll take the bottle. I'm sure I'll be needing it more than you."

She removed it from her purse and handed it to him. As she turned toward the door, he spoke again.

"Kay, there is one final thing."

"Yes?"

"You will explain things to Kelley, won't you? How she needs to forget everything she has seen, and everyone she has met this past week."

"I'll take care of it."

"You do that. Because we don't want a mess. And you know how I feel about a mess."

Chapter Thirty-Four

They took a limousine to Logan Airport. Kay felt it would give her both the time and the privacy to prepare Kelley for what lay ahead. They couldn't discuss it in a taxi or while on the plane. So she made the most of the forty-five-minute journey.

"And he didn't hurt you?"

Kelley shook her head. "Nope. Didn't touch me at all. I got the impression he wanted me out of his life as quickly as possible. That I was just a nuisance."

"Thank God. Where were they holding you?"

"In a house. Somewhere in the suburbs."

Kay smiled. "How did you know that? I thought you said earlier they blindfolded you."

"Process of elimination, Mom. There was very little traffic noise. And no sounds of animals or stuff like that. So if it wasn't the city or the country, that left only one other possible place."

"What a smart daughter I have! I guess I've been sending you to the right schools, after all."

Kelley smiled. "Are you doing okay?"

"Yes, I'm fine. But it's you I'm more interested in. How did they get you to Boston?"

"When I came into the house, I felt some cloth or something put over my mouth. The next thing I knew, I woke up in the back of a van. My feet and hands were tied. And I figured we were on the highway because of the speed the van was going. When it finally stopped, it was dark and the woman opened the back door. She said she was going to put a blindfold on me. It looked like we were in a garage, but that's all I saw of the house."

"They kept the blindfold on all the time you were there?"

"No. I was in a bedroom, but there were big heavy drapes covering the windows, so I couldn't see out. Plus, they had me tied, so I couldn't get up to look."

"You poor darling. I'm so sorry you've had to go through all this."

"You know what the worst part of it all was?"

"What?"

"Having to watch game shows all day. I guess they couldn't afford cable."

Kay laughed and put her arm around Kelley. "Silly goose."

Kelley hugged her, then said, "So what happens now, Mom?"

This was the moment Kay had been dreading. She suspected that Kelley was unaware of Janet's death. Kelley certainly would have mentioned it if she had noticed her aunt's body when she'd entered the house. But apparently she had been drugged almost immediately. So, Kay felt, it was too soon after the trauma of the last several days to tell her what had happened to Janet. As it was, the dislocation of the next month was going to be disorienting enough for the teenager. So she focused on that and would deal with Janet's death at the appropriate time.

"You're going to make Carol and all your other friends jealous."

"Huh? How come?"

"For the next few weeks, I expect you to work very hard on your suntan."

Miami was brighter than Kay expected and cooler than she hoped. But, as Fanning explained when he picked them up at Dade Airport, it was late autumn.

"The best time for a visit," he said.

Kelley, Kay was delighted to see, seemed energized and expectant. After being reassured about missing school, she embraced the notion of spending some time in Florida. She asked little about Fanning, although Kay suspected she would have plenty of questions after he left them to themselves.

Kay was impressed by the Mediterranean-style house. More compound than house though, she thought, when Fanning pulled into the central bay of a three-car garage. Fanning explained it was his mother's home but Kay wondered if he was the actual owner. It hardly seemed the typical retirement home of the typical senior citizen. The swimming pool was Olympic-size while the tennis court could probably handle two games simultaneously. There had to be at least five bedrooms, Kay thought, as Fanning showed them to their rooms. Kay figured this would be where Fanning would move when it came time for him to retire.

Mrs. Fanning was white-haired, ruddy-faced like her son and, at seventy-two, didn't wear glasses. Kay said to her, "I can only pray I look half as good as you when I'm retired."

The older woman laughed, displaying perfectly straight, white teeth.

"I looked like this when I was forty, Kay. So what I've gained at the back end, I lost at the front."

Kay laughed easily, as if they were friends. For the first time in weeks, perhaps months, she felt something like her own self. Only a few hours here, and this was how she felt, she marveled.

"You're terribly kind to allow us to stay."

"Not at all. Gene has told me all about it. I was kind of shocked initially, as you can imagine, but I agree with him it's the best thing to do."

"We'll try to keep out of your way."

"Nonsense. I love company, the younger the better. Kelley and I will have a ball."

She turned to the teenager. "You like to swim, sweetheart?"

"I love to."

Fanning said, "Kelley, would you believe Mom was a champion at synchronized swimming?"

Kelley seemed genuinely impressed. "Wow! I'd love to be able to do that."

Mrs. Fanning winked. "Let's go find you a costume, sweetie. Your first lesson starts now."

After they'd left, Kay said to Fanning, "Something tells me your mom has already bought a costume that fits a fifteen-year-old girl."

He smiled. "Yep."

"She seems one hell of a lady."

"Always prepared. That's Roslyn Fanning for you."

"You told her everything?"

He nodded. "I had to. Besides, she's not just a former swimming champion. She was also a pretty mean cop in her time."

"Oh. Both your parents were in the police? I hadn't realized."

"Seifer omitted that in his dossier."

Now that the real reason they were there had arisen, Kay felt her gay spirits sag. She sighed.

"I can't believe we pulled it off. I was waiting for him to say he knew you were faking it."

"In my experience, the best lies are the ones that come closest to the truth. We thought it through and figured out the exact steps that would happen in such an occurrence. We merely were role-players in a game. Our own game."

"Yes. But it was the other players I was concerned about. How on earth did you manage to persuade the hospital to cooperate?"

Fanning made the universal sign for "money talks" by rubbing a thumb across two fingers.

"I'm on the advisory board of directors. When it comes to

fund-raising, let's say I'm as good a champion as Mom ever was in the water."

"They didn't pry into your motives for such a bizarre request?"

"They know me. They know I wouldn't do anything, however bizarre, without some good reason. And that I would never do anything to embarrass the hospital. I told them it was important. And that was sufficient. I also assured them that everything would be revealed next month."

She smiled. "Mr. Big Shot, eh?"

He smiled back. "Kay, I'm one of the biggest shots in Beantown."

After lunch, while Mrs. Fanning took a nap, they sat under an umbrella on the deck and watched Fanning's two boys, supervised by Kelley, play in the pool.

"So now we wait," said Kay.

"You're confident he'll contact Amy in a month?"

She shrugged. "He showed up at my office about four weeks after the funeral. I've always thought that was the minimum he'd give himself. I imagine that even people who were at odds with their spouses would need a few weeks to get over even some fragment of grief."

He chuckled. "Sometimes I think Amy would get over it after five minutes."

"Then why do you stay together?"

He gestured toward the pool. "The usual reason. I've always believed that kids need a mother and a father. Especially at *their* age. Besides, it's a small sacrifice. I can tolerate a little nagging if it means they're happy."

Kay suspected he tolerated a great deal more from living with Amy Fanning, but, surprised at his candor, declined to question him further. She changed the subject back to Seifer.

"Do you think his confession will be enough for the police to arrest him?"

"Well, it won't actually be a confession. Assuming this man does show up and confront Amy."

Kay was startled. Surely Fanning still didn't have doubts about Seifer? Why, otherwise, would he have agreed to her plan?

She said, "Oh, I think he will definitely show up."

"Okay, so he shows up. And reveals himself. Reveals that he was responsible for the death of Eugene Fanning. And we get it all on tape, as we've planned. That's not a confession. It's an unsubstantiated assertion. However, with your testimony, that you're the . . . *instrument* of his conspiracy, we should be at least able to get him for attempted murder. To say nothing of attempted blackmail. That will put him away for several years."

"It might also encourage some of the other beneficiaries to come forward."

"I would hope so. But I really doubt it. Murder is murder. Despite the extenuating circumstances, each of these people entered into their bargain willingly. The district attorneys in each city would probably be willing to cut some sort of deal, especially if it nails Seifer even further, but all those beneficiaries can expect jail time."

"Even if they don't come forward, you're going to disclose everything, aren't you? I mean, in the folder I gave you."

"I'm an officer of the court, Kay. I'm obliged to. You shouldn't feel any sympathy for them." He looked at her with what she felt was some tenderness. "None of them had the fortitude you did. None of them had the conscience. Or the courage."

"I know. But . . ." Why was it so difficult to explain? "It's just that I know what it's like. I know what they went through. You're bereft and simultaneously, you're free of a great weight. It's a dizzying time. And then, in waltzes Nikolas Seifer. You give him the money partly to make him go away and partly because you feel guilty that it's yours in the first place."

"But then he comes back for his pound of flesh. At that point, even if they had yielded and given him the money, they still had the opportunity to defy him."

"At a cost."

Fanning nodded. "Ah, yes. The right thing to do always comes with some cost."

He turned away, a look of sadness on his face, and although she couldn't be sure, Kay suspected that whatever he was now staring at was not directly in front of him.

That night, Kay started what became a nightly ritual. After the others had retired for the evening, she went down to the pool area. Initially, her thought had been merely to sit and wait for her body to become tired. Her sleeping patterns for the previous weeks had been disjointed, and it was well past midnight before she felt herself dozing off. She had tried watching the inanities of late-night TV, but sleep had apparently fled in terror and made it even more difficult to relax. She had enjoyed the afternoon by the pool, chatting with Gene about their lives, about college and careers, movies and theater, books and travel. Just like regular people, she thought, with regular concerns. With the children's screams and laughter, the sun beating down and the warmth of the moist air, the afternoon had sped pleasantly by.

Now, perhaps to recapture that, she sat on the deck in the glow of the moonlit night. But almost immediately she felt the urge to swim. She went to her room, put on a one-piece swimming costume, and returned to the pool. Slipping into the warm water, her mood changed yet again and she instantly knew why. She was, she thought, cleansing herself of Seifer, of Johanna, of the filth and corruption they represented. In a matter of weeks, they would be placed where they belonged, behind bars. No longer would they be free to coerce and kill. She was confident her plan would work. If Gene Fanning, with more than twenty years of experience in the law, believed in it sufficiently to take the enormous steps he had just taken, there could, she felt, be only one satisfactory outcome.

After several laps in the water, she allowed herself to float and then, feeling a languorous sense of fatigue, swam to the edge of the pool and knew she would have the first decent night's sleep in recent memory.

They scoured through the Web sites of all the newspapers in the greater Boston area. To Kay's surprise, Mrs. Fanning seemed to enjoy reading the stories about the private wake, funeral, and cremation of her only son. Her explanation was jovially simple.

"Cheer up, Kay. We know it's all bogus."

Fanning himself seemed disappointed at the paucity of articles. He made a face.

"I guess I didn't have as much an impact as I thought."

Kay laughed. "Don't worry. Your real obit will eventually tell how you were responsible for getting Nikolas Seifer off the streets."

"I suppose we should be grateful. If interest diminishes in the death of Gene Fanning, it will lull Seifer and he'll make his move."

"Let's hope so."

Amy Fanning checked in every day to speak to the children. She kept her husband abreast of other family matters, but of Nikolas Seifer there was no contact. Three weeks passed. The two families vacationed as one, a succession of long relaxing days of sun, sand, and water, visits to the Everglades, deep water fishing, and snorkeling in the turquoise ocean. In the relaxed environment, with the stresses of the previous two years now seemingly distant, Kay felt herself becoming attracted to

Fanning and looked forward to the time they were alone and could spend a little time together. It had been years, she realized, since she had been interested in a man. However, while always attentive and companionable, Fanning never gave any indication of anything more than friendship. Perhaps, Kay thought, as she completed her third lap of the pool one night, he doesn't want to jeopardize the equanimity of his children. He had mentioned the importance of their happiness to him, and to them, they still had a mother and a father.

"Any room in there for one more body?"

She looked up to see Fanning in swimming trunks at the pool's edge. Lost in her thoughts, she had not heard him approach and wondered how long he had been standing there.

She smiled. "Enough room for the entire U.S. Olympic team. Come on in."

She had assumed he would swim over to her but instead he moved, with swift, sure strokes from end to end, as if in some private competition. She floated and waited for some decision to be made, either by him or herself.

Finally, after a half-dozen rapid laps, he stopped and allowed himself to drift toward her.

"I have a confession to make," he said.

"You just peed in the pool?"

He laughed. "No!"

"See how my mind works? Three weeks with three children will do that. So, what do you have to confess?"

"I've been watching you. At nights. When you've been swimming."

"That's all? I was hoping for something juicier."

"How come you swim only at nights?"

"I didn't want you to see my fat ass."

His laughter was loud, surprisingly uninhibited. "Oh, stop. It's not fat."

"So you've been watching that, too?"

"No! I mean—I don't know what I mean. Anyway, that's my confession. I heard you leave your room the first night you arrived. And I looked out the window. That's all."

"So you look out your window every night now?"

"Yes. Looking out for you."

She smiled, wondering if he meant the alternative meaning to the phrase: looking *after* you.

In the silence, he said, "You've changed. Since you've been here."

"So have you."

He seemed startled. "In what way?"

"No more worry-wart face."

His smile was almost a shy one. "Was it that bad?"

" 'fraid so."

"Three weeks without Amy will do that to a man."

She said, "And me? How have I changed?"

"The same. There was a . . . tenseness about you. I saw it when you first came into my office. That's why I suspected you weren't trying to pull some scam. It was more than just nervousness. Almost an . . . apprehension. Anyway, that disappeared after you'd been here a while."

"Three weeks with Gene Fanning will do that to a woman."

He stared into her eyes. "Kay, I've never been unfaithful to her."

"I'm not asking you to be."

"I know. But I think *I* am."

They didn't kiss initially. They clasped and held onto each other, as if that was enough. As if each had found what they long ago had ceased looking for.

She lay sideways on the bed, her head propped against her left hand, and walked two fingers of her right hand in a circular motion around Fanning's belly button.

"What's this activity called?" she asked.

He smiled and shook his head. "Dunno."

"Navel Patrol."

He laughed.

"Kelley," she explained. "Age five-and-a-half."

"Oh God. I've got to get you away from the children for a few hours."

"*This* is all that would make me happy. Spending a few hours with you."

"We'll be spending more than a few hours together, I hope."

"I hope so, too."

She reached down and kissed his navel, then rested her head on his outstretched arm. He brushed her forehead with his lips.

"Something I've wanted to ask you for a while," he said after they'd been quiet for a few minutes.

"Ask away."

"Why do you retain your married name? Daniels?"

"No mystery. It's the name on the articles of incorporation of New Croydon Telecomm."

He didn't reply. Even though he wasn't a corporate attorney, she realized, he would be well aware that a simple filing would accommodate that problem. But he didn't pursue the matter further and that made her feel happy. He was giving her time to eventually answer that she didn't want her name to revert to that of her father. And if he was giving her time, it meant he expected they would have plenty of time.

"Hey," she said.

"What?"

"I've just received orders from HQ. A new mission."

"What's that?"

She ran her fingers along the inside of his thigh.

"Penis Patrol."

The next morning Kay came downstairs to find Mrs. Fanning herding the children into a station wagon.

Kelley waved and yelled, "See you later, Mom!"

"Where are they going?" she asked Fanning as the vehicle pulled out of the driveway.

"Disney World."

"Without us?"

"Yes. My plan. Now, change into some jeans and meet me in front of the garage."

"Why?"

"I told you we need to get you away from the kids for a little while. Today, it's adults only."

Ten minutes later, he appeared outside, dressed in jeans, a blue denim shirt with the sleeves rolled up, and, rather incongruously for such a patrician figure, brown leather cowboy boots.

Kay smiled and, unable to resist, said, "I get it: You're not a lawyer; you're a lawman."

He laughed. "Just be thankful my ten-gallon hat is at the cleaners."

She laughed, she felt, like a silly schoolgirl. But she didn't care. She couldn't remember when she last felt so relaxed, so uncaring.

They took a black Jeep Wrangler onto Route 27 and after half an hour reached a rural area outside a place called Miami Lakes. Ten minutes down a dirt road and they pulled into a property with a sign on the gate that read Fanning Horse Farm.

"Afternoon, Mr. Fanning!" It was a young man, calling from the doorway of what Kay guessed had to be stables. Fanning introduced Kay. The man's name was Johnny and with his young wife, Laura, who was nowhere to be seen. He ran the farm for the Fanning family.

"I saddled up Barney for the lady as you told me, Mr. Fanning," he said.

Kay turned to Fanning, actually startled. "Oh no! I don't know how to ride a horse."

"You know how to ride a bicycle, don't you?"

"Bicycles don't bite."

"Barney doesn't bite. More likely to lick you to death, he's so friendly. Come on. There's nothing to it."

Kay was terrified, but Fanning told her the most important thing was not to feel nervousness or the horse would sense it. The nearest Kay had ever been to a horse before was driving past a cop who rode one in the city streets. And even then she had been intimidated by its strange, living bulk. Now here was one up close, and it indeed seemed enormous, its hooves especially and, of course, the huge head. Not feel nervous, she thought? He had to be kidding.

Apparently, Fanning sensed it, too, for he said, "Here. Touch his nose."

"What!" Now she knew he was kidding. She felt if she put her hand anywhere near that mouth, she would soon be several fingers short of a fist. "No way."

"Come on. Trust me." He took her hand.

Perhaps Barney had been through this routine before, for he suddenly bowed his head and sniffed Kay's outstretched hand.

"Now, go on. Touch his nose."

She did, gingerly, and was surprised by its softness.

"It's like . . . velvet!"

"Yep. Not so bad, was it?"

She shook her head, feeling rather juvenile at her antics.

"All right. Now up you get on the saddle."

There was, she thought, no end to her Garden of Gethsemane

but, tired of displaying reluctance, allowed herself to be directed to what he called a mounting block. Strangely, from countless Westerns, she knew exactly what to do now: mount from the horse's left, hold onto the saddle with the left hand, left foot in the stirrup and swing the right leg up and over. It was definitely easier said than done, but with Fanning's support she actually managed it in one swoop.

Naturally she now felt like an idiot, clueless as to what to do next. She waited patiently while Fanning moved with practiced ease onto his own horse.

"Okay," he said. "Now, you're going to cluck and squeeze his sides."

She was about to commence clucking and squeezing, but he quickly said, "Wait! Not yet. We haven't covered steering and stopping."

He explained the childlike instructions for turning left or right and stopping. Unbelievably, she was actually to say "whoa" while pulling back the reins to stop. Well, she thought, this can't be that difficult. And it wasn't. A few sample baby steps and she began to feel some confidence. After fifteen minutes of advancing and stopping, turning left and right, Fanning said, "Okay, now let's go for a ride around that field."

Not a problem, she thought.

"And watch out for the alfalfa," he said.

"Huh?"

He was moving away and turned around in the saddle.

"Horses have a tendency to forget the rider when they see alfalfa."

She wouldn't know what alfalfa was if it bit her on the leg, so she clucked with alacrity and followed Fanning.

Within the hour she had convinced myself she could actually ride—Barney wasn't tempted too much by the alfalfa, thankfully. They didn't get out of sight of the house that afternoon but did manage to do a few circuits in the surrounding fields. The experience was new and left her eager for more.

After the horses were unsaddled and brought back to the stables, Johnny's wife appeared with tall glasses of cold lemonade. They sat on the porch, drank the tart drink, and watched the afternoon fade. The only noises were country noises; no speeding cars or honking horns, no klaxon sound from emergency vehicles, no boom-boxes or the harsh voices of strangers. It was that sort of moment when nothing needed to be said, a moment that only friends share.

They rode again the next two days. Mrs. Fanning appeared to be as accomplished a rider as much as a swimmer and supervised the children on their little ponies.

Kay sat on the porch and said suddenly, "I like being here."

"Yes. I love the farm."

"No, I meant Florida. I like being here. And . . . and I like being here with you."

He hesitated only a moment. "It goes without saying I like being here with you too."

He laughed at himself, shaking his head. "That phrase. *It goes without saying.* And then—"

"And then we always say it anyway!"

They both laughed.

"Do you think you'll ever move here?" Kay asked.

"I've thought about it. A lot." He turned and watched the children approach the stables. They waved and he waved back.

Still watching them, he said: "What about you? Do you think this could be home for you?"

Sometimes, Kay thought, even with people you know and are comfortable with, it's unclear what is being said. Was this a proposal and if it was, how should she reply? And if it wasn't, would she seem like a fool for thinking it so and be diminished in his eyes?

In the end, she thought the safest response was: "I think it could be. But only after things are taken care of."

He nodded. "Seifer."

Chapter Thirty-Five

The call came a few minutes before four o'clock on the twenty-seventh day following the funeral.

"It's me," Amy Fanning said. "He was here. He just left."

Her husband looked at Kay, who was sitting on the couch, and held up his right thumb.

"Did you have the tape running?" he asked.

"Yes. As soon as Maria told me who was at the door, I went into the library and started it. Then I waited for him there."

"Have you played it back? Did it work okay?"

"No. I called you right away."

"Put the phone down and play it now."

"All right, hold on."

She returned a few minutes later and said, "Yes, it worked."

Fanning let out a breath. "Great. All right. We'll leave right away. I'll call you from Logan when we arrive. Did he say when he wanted to meet with you again?"

"No."

Fanning glanced at Kay, puzzled. "Oh? How are you supposed to contact him?"

"He didn't say exactly. He just gave me a business card."

"Well, what *did* he say?"

"First, he introduced himself—"

"As Nikolas Seifer?"

"Yes. He said he knew you slightly, had done some business together. And wished to express his condolences. Then he left."

"That's all!"

"What should I do?"

"I—I don't know. Just stay there. I'll leave this evening if I can get a flight."

"What about the children?"

"They'll stay with Mom for the time being. This will all be over now very soon."

He hung up and turned to Kay. "All least, it would be over very soon if he had done what we had anticipated."

"Why? What's happened?"

He repeated what Amy had told him. Kay was equally confused.

"I don't get it. Why show up at the house of the widow for just a few moments and then leave? It doesn't sound like his usual procedure."

Fanning shrugged. "Maybe he was checking the lay of the land."

But Kay saw Fanning was disturbed. Could it be he still didn't fully believe her and, even now, held the tiniest morsel of doubt about her?

"He couldn't have noticed the microphone, could he?"

Fanning shook his head. "It was well hidden. I hired an expert to install it. No one would have spotted it."

"Well," said Kay, striving to find some optimism, "at least he's shown his hand. Given the money involved, I can't see him walking away from this opportunity."

Fanning still looked concerned. After a moment's thought, he said, "You better start packing. I'll call the airline."

They arrived at Logan Airport at eleven P.M. While Fanning called home, Kay phoned Kelley. She had told her daughter to go to bed at the normal time but Kelley insisted that she call when she landed in Boston.

"When is this going to be all over, Mom?"

"Soon, honey. Just be patient a little more. Okay?"

"Okay. Call me tomorrow."

"I will."

After she hung up, she turned to Fanning who clearly looked concerned.

"No answer," he said.

"Maybe she's asleep."

He made a face. "Amy is a night owl. It's not even close to her bedtime. Come on. Let's get the car."

They went to the long-term parking garage and retrieved his Lincoln Continental.

"Good thing it has tinted windows," Kay said as they headed for Fanning's Federal-style home in Beacon Hill. "If Seifer is watching the house, he won't know who's driving in at this time of night."

"Hopefully, even Mr. Seifer needs some beauty sleep."

Less than half an hour later, they pulled into the driveway of the house. Fanning touched a button on the dashboard and the garage door opened. The house, Kay noticed, was in darkness. The only light was a fluorescent bulb in the roof of the garage that had automatically triggered when the door opened.

"Hold on a moment," Fanning said, when they entered the house through a side door in the garage. "The drapes are still open."

Trying to avoid been seen through the living room windows, although Kay had noticed no activity on the street outside, he reached for the pull cord and closed the drapes. He then turned on the light and called out, "Amy!"

There was no response.

"Hold on," he said. "I'll check the bedroom."

Kay could hear him opening and closing doors on the second floor, his footsteps moving quickly, almost anxiously, she thought. Then he was treading back down the stairs.

He shook his head. "Nothing. The bed is still made."

"Anything been disturbed?"

"No, doesn't look like it."

"How about the maid? Maria."

A brief smile appeared on his lips. "Good thinking. Let me call her."

But Kay could see by his reaction that Maria was not going to provide any helpful information about her employer's location.

"All right, Maria. Thanks. Sorry for disturbing you so late. Why don't you take tomorrow off? . . . Yes, I insist."

"You look like you could do with a drink," Kay said when he hung up.

"Sounds good. Will you do the honors while I get the suitcases."

She went into the library where she had first been introduced to Amy Fanning. The room was at the rear of the house, facing another large home, but, following his lead, she pulled the drapes before turning on the light. After pouring the drinks, she looked around, trying to spot the microphone but even knowing it was there—somewhere—she found it impossible to locate.

Fanning came in and smiled when he saw her inspect the inlaid bookshelves.

"Not even warm," he said.

"Okay, I give up. Where is it?"

He picked up the glass of whiskey, took a sip, and pointed to a vase of artificial roses atop the center of the coffee table.

She sat down on the couch, then picked up the vase.

"No wires?"

He sat on one of the two burgundy armchairs that flanked the coffee table.

"The miracle of modern technology." He gestured toward a

desk in the corner of the room. "The recorder is in the center drawer. Don't ask me how it works. I experimented with it, and all I know is that it does."

He stood, then went to the desk. Kay asked, "What did Maria say?"

"She left at the usual time. Six-thirty. After she'd prepared dinner. We usually take care of the dishes ourselves, so she seldom hangs around once dinner is ready."

"Did she mention Seifer?"

"Described him to a T. Arrived before four o'clock and left just a few minutes later."

"Ah," Kay said. "There it is."

She'd removed the flowers and saw the silver device at the bottom of the vase. It was no bigger than her thumbnail.

"Unbelievable," she said. "And pretty clever putting it on the coffee table."

He nodded. "The installer's idea. It's the natural area where people would sit and talk. Now, let's see what Mr. Seifer has to say for himself."

The recorder was a small black oblong and, Kay thought, vaguely industrial looking. She had never seen the like in stores or catalogues. It had a rugged, rubbery exterior. She suspected it could be dropped on the ground and still function perfectly.

Fanning hit the larger of three buttons, then adjusted a knob that she guessed was the volume control. Initially, all Kay could hear was some voices in the background and was disappointed at the quality. They seemed remote, as if in a different room, but then she realized that was exactly correct. It was Maria and Seifer, out in the hall. Good Lord, she thought, this microphone could pick up sounds from that distance?

Then a clear, distinct voice. "Mr. Seifer, Ma'am."

"Thank you, Maria." Amy's voice, so clear she could almost be present now. "That will be all."

Kay heard the door close.

"Mrs. Fanning. How do you do? My name is Nikolas Seifer."

Kay looked up at Fanning, stared into his eyes, then nodded.

"How do you do?" Amy replied.

"Thank you for seeing me on such short notice."

"Quite all right. You said to the maid that you knew my husband?"

Kay waited for Seifer's response but it didn't come immediately. She glanced at Fanning who seemed equally puzzled.

"A . . . a little. We had some business once. I just wanted to express my condolences. I was unable to attend the funeral."

"No. It was a private affair. His mother preferred it that way."

"I see. Well, Mrs. Fanning. I was just passing through the city and thought I would drop by. Thank you for seeing me."

There were noises of people standing.

"Thank you for coming, Mr. Seifer."

"If I may, let me give you my business card."

"Certainly. Thank you."

Kay heard the door open, and the voices moved into the hallway. A few moments later, she heard footsteps and the door to the library close. Then, Amy's voice, clearly making a phone call.

"It's me. He was here. He just left."

Fanning reached down and hit the *Stop* button.

"Let's play it again," he said.

They listened to the tape, even to the end of Amy's phone conversation with her husband. But they were as puzzled as before.

"Where does that leave us?" Kay asked.

"I don't know, until we speak to Amy."

Kay looked at her watch. "It's almost midnight. She doesn't usually stay out this late, does she?"

He turned away. "Amy has . . . friends. Sometimes she

doesn't come home until after the kids have left for school."

Kay was startled by his response. He had never mentioned his marriage had deteriorated to this point. But she had already sensed while they were in Miami there were many things about his life he had not shared.

"How about her cell phone?" she asked.

"Right. I'll try it."

But it was evident that Amy was not answering. Fanning left a message, telling her he was at home.

He blew out a breath and said to Kay, "It's been a long day. You should get some sleep."

"What about you?"

"I'll wait up for a while. In case Amy calls. And I want to listen to that tape again."

Chapter Thirty-Six

Kay was awakened by the shrill ringing of her cell phone.

"Hi, it's Mike."

"Mike?" She looked at the clock on the bedside table. Eight A.M.

"Mike Bishop, your deputy."

"Oh. Hi, Mike. What's up?" He usually got in at eight sharp. So clearly it must be important for him to call right away.

"It's the regulatory commission in California."

"What about it?"

"They're balking at renewing the license."

"Oh dammit. Did they say why?"

"Paul Keating has all the details. You need to speak to him ASAP. He said he would be in his office early, waiting for you to call."

"Okay, I will." She closed the connection. Vacation's over, she thought. She called Paul's direct number.

"Kay, we need to get together right away. To plot a strategy. My contacts tell me that Alliance have a friend on the commission."

"Oh crap." She didn't need an attorney to tell her the advantage her competitor would have with a "friend" on the commission. More worrying was that any such friend would almost certainly be New Croydon Telecomm's enemy.

"Can you come in this morning?"

"This morning!" She almost laughed. "Paul, I'm in Boston."

"Oh goodness. Well, if you want to continue operating in the biggest market in the country, I suggest you start making your way back to Connecticut as soon as humanly possible."

She sighed. "Let me think. Give me an hour, Paul, to get washed and dressed, and I'll call you back."

She heard him emit his own sigh. "Very well, Kay. I'll be waiting."

She got up, put on a robe and went out into the hallway. She had intended to go to Fanning's room but she noticed the lights were on downstairs, in the living room. As she made her way down the stairs, voices began to speak and then almost immediately stopped. Then they started again. She realized it was the tape, being played and then replayed.

When she walked into the living room, she was startled to see Fanning's appearance. It was obvious that he hadn't gone to bed. He was wearing the same clothes he had on the previous evening, and his face seemed lined with fatigue.

"Gene? What's going on?"

He turned and stared at her. She waited for him to respond, but he said nothing, merely gestured to the couch where she had sat listening to the tape last night.

She went and sat down. He played a short section of the tape, rewound it, and then played it again.

Thank you for seeing me on such short notice.

Quite all right. You said to the maid that you knew my husband?

A . . . a little. We had some business. I just wanted to express my condolences. I was unable to attend the funeral.

Fanning looked at her, and she stared back, then shrugged.

"What?"

He rewound it and played it again, stopping it at the same point.

She strained to hear whatever he was trying to convey, but she couldn't get it. He reached down to the volume control and turned it to the maximum.

He said, "Listen after the words *my husband.*"

She lowered her head toward the coffee table and closed her eyes, in the hope this would help focus on what it was he could hear and what she could not.

. . . *knew my husband.*

She waited for the pause that she had noticed the first time she had heard the recording. Then, expecting a short silence, instead she heard something. The volume was now so high that she could plainly hear a noise that she had missed before.

"Play it again," she said. "Just before and after the pause."

He did so, then pushed the *Stop* button.

She said, "I heard it. It sounds like . . . like . . ."

He reached into his shirt pocket and removed a small piece of paper. He then unfolded it and re-folded it before placing it back in his pocket.

"Paper?" she said, then nodded. "Yes. Paper. But what sort of—Oh God."

"I've been listening to it all night. It took me a couple of hours but there's no mistake."

Kay stood up, alarmed. "She gave him a note."

Fanning looked away.

"Gene, she gave him a note! A message. She was warning him. That they were being taped. Jesus, why would she do that?"

"Because she wants Nikolas Seifer to kill me."

Chapter Thirty-Seven

"No!" But Kay already knew it was the truth.

"It's the only logical explanation," Fanning replied. "That's why he doesn't elaborate on why he showed up and leaves right away. And why he gave her the business card. So she could contact him. You've told me he's no fool. He must have instantly realized what her intentions were. Otherwise, why warn him?"

"Oh God. Now he knows you're alive. And that I told you."

She felt the return of the dread that, until Florida, had seemed to be a constant companion. She was such a fool, she thought. She had assumed it was almost over, that this man would soon be put away, and she and Kelley could get on with their lives. Now Seifer knew what she had done and was as free as ever. She went to the windows and moved the drapes a fraction.

"He's probably waiting outside now," she said.

"No, that's not his style. He doesn't get his fingers dirty."

"Not usually. But this is a different situation."

"How?"

"He's directly threatened. Before, he was always behind the scenes pulling the strings. Now, that won't work. He will have to get involved himself. As he did with Thomas Scanlon."

There was little activity outside. A few cars moved quickly past the house. No vehicles were parked on the exclusive street. She closed the drapes and went back to the couch.

"God, think of it," she said, suddenly angry. "He was within a minute of committing himself. And only because of Amy—"

She stopped and looked at Fanning. "Why? Why would Amy take the risk? Does she hate you that much?"

"You already know the answer. You've told me yourself. Why did all the other beneficiaries do it? Greed."

Kay shook her head, puzzled. "Wouldn't she have been well taken care of with the divorce?"

"Not well enough, apparently. But this way, instead of getting ten percent of my worth, she would get one hundred percent of my estate."

"Fifty percent. After Seifer got his share."

He nodded. "Right."

Something occurred to Kay. "But why did she bother turning on the tape recorder in the first place? If she didn't intend to stick with the plan, that wasn't necessary."

"To get me back here. Remember, we were going to remain in Florida until Seifer showed his face. The recording, even an abbreviated one, was the only thing that would get us to return."

The phone rang, and he jumped up to get it. But Kay soon realized it wasn't Amy. It was Fanning's mother. After reassuring her that everything was "fine" and then talking briefly with each of the boys, he hung up.

"No sense in alarming her," he explained to Kay.

"That reminds me. I got a phone call myself this morning."

She explained her discussion with her lawyer.

"What are you going to do?" he asked.

She shook her head, genuinely undecided. The future of her company may well lie in the balance, she realized. It wasn't just a matter of losing the California market, big as that was. It was the reputation that New Croydon Telecomm would acquire if it became known their application to continue offering service was denied. Other states might well look askance at the company and wonder, "Why?"

But could she really take off for New Croydon? Although, in truth, what could she contribute here now? Boston was Gene's home turf. He had money, influence, contacts. The sole rationale for her presence was to give testimony to the police following their disclosure of the tape. But now they had no evidence of Seifer's intentions, not even the "unsubstantiated assertion," as Fanning described it. They were back at the beginning, with only wild allegations and no concrete evidence.

"I think I'm going to have to get back, to deal with this. Hopefully, it won't take more than a day. Then I can return. If you want me."

He smiled. "Of course I want you."

He took her in his arms and kissed her.

"Anyway," he said. "I don't see how Seifer can pull off anything now. This *is* different. You were right. But it's different in our favor."

"How?"

"Think about it for a minute. How can he kill me now? Amy's plan might have worked—if we hadn't figured out that she must have given him a note of some kind. So all I have to do is confront her and tell her I know."

"Yes," said Kay, feeling more optimistic. "Besides, I was the designated beneficiary assigned to do the killing. Who else does he have?"

"All right. That's settled."

"But there's something else. The children. Amy will almost certainly tell him where you've been. We need to make sure that Seifer doesn't go after them."

"I'll call Mom and tell her to move to the farm for a few days. Johnny and his people will be on hand to protect them. I'll make the calls now. And you better get dressed—you can't go to Connecticut looking like that."

Chapter Thirty-Eight

It took three hours to make the trip from Boston, but Kay was hardly aware of time passing. When she pulled into the parking lot of Paul Keating's law offices, she called Gene from her cell phone. He had still heard nothing from Amy. His mother had already arrived at the farm, and the children were too excited to be staying there to be otherwise concerned. He told Kay he was considering calling a press conference to explain his motives for his disappearance.

"We have to get the spotlight on Seifer," he explained. "Even if we can't prove anything."

She agreed instantly. "Yes. I've been thinking about it on the drive here. He has no hold on me now. I burnt the phone bill and the hotel receipt. And Kelley is safe. Amy is unlikely to have told him about the farm, in any case."

"We may not be able to put him away. But by doing this, at least we can put him out of business. Hopefully it will make the national news. He won't dare show up at some person's door in the future having arranged the murder of that person's spouse."

"Given your prominence and the fact that you've done what you have, the police may well dig deep and investigate the other beneficiaries. The pressure may force one of them to talk."

"That would be crucial. It would only take one to confess. Just one. That, plus your testimony, should be sufficient to get Seifer to trial."

After they closed the connection, she went in to see Keating.

As it was lunchtime, he insisted on taking her out to his favorite seafood restaurant.

"So, should I close up shop or what?" she asked him when the waiter brought their shrimp cocktails.

Keating smiled. "Why so gloomy? I thought you were a glass-half-full person."

From the time she had initially hired him, Paul Keating had seemed like the kindly uncle she never had. He was tanned—permanently, it seemed—white-haired, although he was still a few years from fifty, and heavyset from the fine wine and food that was his only avocation. When he wasn't dining, it was rumored, he was working.

She replied, "Usually, I am. But these are not usual times."

Keating was, understandably, unaware to what she alluded.

He said, "As for me, I'm the type of person who asks: Was the glass full in the first place and can you prove it?"

She laughed. "So what's your advice, Paul? What can we do?"

He pointed at her untouched shrimp. "Eat! Eat! I've been on the phone all morning. You would be amazed how many of my Columbia classmates ended up in California."

It felt good discussing the business, Kay thought, as Paul shared his ideas. *This* was how she wanted to spend her time—building up her company, securing a future for herself and Kelley, and, who knows, preparing for a life with a man she could genuinely love instead of one who could be a surrogate father. She didn't want to spend another minute thinking about Seifer and his activities. She hoped that Gene's press conference would, once and for all, rid her of Nikolas Seifer.

After lunch, she headed to the office in a buoyant mood. Paul had reassured her that even in the worst possible scenario—denial of renewal—they could file an appeal that would put the spotlight on Alliance. She had smiled at Paul's use of the phrase—the exact one that Gene had used.

"People, especially unsavory types, hate the spotlight shone on their affairs, Kay. I think we'll be all right. New Croydon Telecomm's reputation speaks for itself. It might be a slog fighting, it but it will be worth it. And I suspect when it's obvious that we're not going to accept a fait accompli, Alliance might lose their stomach for the fight."

Everything at the company seemed perfectly routine. Given her long absence, she decided to call a staff meeting to catch up and to apprise all the executives of the problems that lay ahead. It was almost four o'clock before she made it to her own desk and confronted the mess of paperwork that had accumulated over the previous month. At six o'clock she called Kelley on her cell phone and was glad to hear that everyone had a fun day. She decided to wait until she arrived home and had some dinner before calling Gene. She wondered would he want her there to give moral support when he called the press conference, and decided almost certainly he would. Besides, she thought, as she pulled into her driveway, the press, and even the police, would probably want to interview her, a task that she would look forward to.

Oh damn, she thought, as she entered the house. She should have stopped at the store to pick up something up for dinner. She recalled she had discarded everything perishable in the fridge weeks before. Oh well, she thought, looks like the pizza guy is going to have to make a trip. She was too tired to turn around and go out again.

She opened the side door from the garage and went into the kitchen. Then she headed toward the hallway closet to hang up her coat. She realized a light was on in the living room. Oh crap, she thought. Had she left it on all this time, since she had headed for Boston to first encounter Gene all those weeks ago?

She walked into the living room and saw Amy Fanning sitting

upright on the couch, a carving knife buried to the hilt in her chest.

Chapter Thirty-Nine

"Mrs. Daniels, why did you call Eugene Fanning before you notified the police?"

Detective Frank Sinclair's manner and his questions were as unfriendly as before.

"I—I don't know. It was his wife. I guess I felt he needed to know right away."

"You've just spent a month with Mr. Fanning in Florida, is that correct?"

"Yes. And with his mother and two children. And my daughter."

"And you spent Monday night in his home, in Boston?"

"Yes. But we didn't—"

"Didn't what?"

"Nothing."

"You were having an affair with Mr. Fanning?"

"No. I mean—" An affair. Was it really an *affair,* she wondered? That word always implied something transitory. What she and Gene had was surely more, promised to be more. More than an affair.

"Either you were or you weren't. Now, were you having an affair with Eugene Fanning?"

"We had established a . . . a relationship."

"An intimate relationship?"

"I . . ." Why was she finding it so difficult to answer? Was she that unsure of him, of *them?*

"Mrs. Daniels. You agreed to cooperate with our investigation. To be interviewed. So we need you to cooperate. Now, were you having intercourse with Eugene Fanning?"

Intercourse. God, that sounded so soulless, so clinical. But what would it sound like to this man if she said she and Gene had made love, beautiful love like she had not experienced with any of the other men in her life?

Finally she nodded and said, "Yes."

"Was Mrs. Fanning aware of your relationship with her husband?"

"No." How could Amy be aware of it? She and Gene had only just met when she first encountered Amy.

"Then why did she drive all the way from Boston to confront you?"

"Confront me? She didn't confront me. I've told you already. I came home and found her."

"Well, why would she come all this way to see you?"

"She didn't come here voluntarily. I've already told you what I think happened."

"Ah. This Mr. . . . Seifer. He drove her here, all the way from Boston?"

"He probably coerced her." She remembered how they had transported Kelley such a long way. "Or drugged her."

Sinclair looked at the other woman present. Although her hair was now down to her shoulders and she wore makeup, it was, Kay felt certain, the detective who interviewed her about Mister Scanlon. But she was from Brooklyn, Kay recalled. What was she doing here in New Croydon?

Sinclair turned back to Kay. "So you're saying this man brought Mrs. Fanning here, to your home, and killed her? Drugged her. And brought her all the way from Boston. Is that what you're saying?"

"It's not what I'm *saying.* It's what happened. It's the only possible explanation."

"Mrs. Fanning's car is parked on the street outside your house. She could hardly drive while she was drugged."

"They drove it."

"And then they just left it? And walked away from the scene of the crime?"

"No. I don't know. *She* probably drove it. Johanna. And Seifer drove another vehicle, probably a van with Amy in the back. I don't know."

"What about your knife?"

"My knife?"

"The knife used to kill Mrs. Fanning. It matched the set of knives in your kitchen."

"I—I don't know. I didn't touch it."

"Did you wipe the handle of that knife? To remove the fingerprints?"

"I told you. I didn't touch it. I was too frightened. I called Gene. And he—he told me to call the police. And I did."

"Why would this man, this . . . Seifer bring Mrs. Fanning to your home and kill her?"

That was the one question for which she had no answer. To all the other questions, she could offer reasonable responses. She could guess how Amy had been brought here, how they had driven more than one vehicle, how they had cleaned the knife handle to remove fingerprints. Even if she didn't actually *know,* she could infer. But why Seifer had perpetrated this . . . mess, she couldn't fathom.

"To implicate me, I assume."

"Implicate you in what?"

Was that the correct word? Hardly. It would imply that something demonstrable was evident. But the genius of his system was that nothing untoward was ever evident. So, then, why did he kill Amy Fanning?

"In his schemes. His blackmailing. And his murders."

"But if that were the case, he would be implicating himself, wouldn't he?"

"I don't know. I don't know why he did it. It doesn't make sense. I don't know." God, she was so tired. She hadn't slept. She had reached Paul Keating after calling the police and stayed at his house for the night, but she hadn't been able to sleep. The sight of Amy Fanning's dead eyes staring at nothing wouldn't leave her. The uniformed police officers had interviewed her first and then Paul had shown up as he'd promised when she'd called. He convinced them that she would report first thing in the morning to the police department to cooperate with their investigation, and they had let her go under his recognizance.

"Where can we find this Mr. Seifer?"

She shook her head. "I don't know. I don't know anything about him, where he's from, where he lives."

Detective Sinclair sat back, then abruptly stood. He left the room, followed by the female detective. A few minutes later, they returned.

"Mrs. Daniels," he said. "I'm giving you a chance to help yourself. I'm going to forget everything we've already discussed this morning. And we're going to start again. Right now. But from this point on, you need to be honest with me and tell me the truth."

"But I—"

"The truth! Now, why did you kill Amy Fanning?"

Chapter Forty

My husband is not dead. This conversation is being taped by a hidden microphone.

Life was funny sometimes, Seifer thought. It was funny to look back and see the things that proved to be turning points. A dog chasing a rodent into the woods. A story about an automobile accident in a foreign newspaper. A disgraced pediatrician desperate for money. And now, the wife of a rich man who got too greedy. That, though, was the final turning point.

"All good things come to an end," Johanna had said when he showed her Amy Fanning's note. And she was right. She knew immediately, as did he when he left the Fanning home on Beacon Hill.

He had scanned the surrounding houses and vehicles but could detect nothing out of the ordinary. But Eugene Fanning was presumably somewhere in the vicinity, Seifer assumed. And, undoubtedly, so were the police. As he always did throughout his career, even as far back as when on an assignment in Northern Ireland, he went through the escape routes already mapped before entering the city. The simplest would be to abandon their car in the apartment complex's parking garage and get a taxi to the airport, or even better, Back Bay train station. He doubted the police knew where they were staying, but if they were following him now, he would lead them to Johanna. His debate with himself whether he should head directly to the train station and abandon her or call her now to warn her was interrupted by the buzz of his cell phone.

"Yes?"

"It's . . . Amy Fanning."

"Where are you calling from?" he asked, concerned that her conversation was being taped by the hidden microphone.

"My bedroom. On a cell phone. The tape recorder is in the library, downstairs."

"Your husband, he's not there?"

"No. He's in Florida but he'll be returning tonight. Now that—now that you've shown up."

Florida. Why so far, Seifer wondered?

"And the police?"

"They don't know about any of this."

Relief surged through him. It was understandable though, he realized. The police wouldn't allow themselves to be party to such an extravagant pretense.

"But your husband intended to go to them with the tape?"

"Yes."

"You knew all about me? From Kay Daniels?"

Of course it was Kay who had somehow persuaded Fanning and his wife to concoct this farce. But Fanning's wife, clearly, didn't want to be part of it. She had warned Seifer. The thought made him smile. His research was always thorough, his analysis always correct. He knew enough about the Fannings' marriage to know that she would be amenable to him when he came calling. But Kay Daniels had stuck her nose in and upset the plan. Depriving Amy of all those millions. Or perhaps not. She had decided to warn Seifer because she wanted Seifer free. Free to conclude his business with her husband.

"Yes. She explained everything. How you work. What you do."

"And you're comfortable with that, I assume."

"I am. So I suggest we discuss this matter further as soon as possible."

He thought it through, then said, "Yes. Do you have a pen? I'll give you an address where we can meet."

He gave her directions to the house in Brookline where they had kept the Daniels girl. They agreed on a time, six o'clock, and before closing the connection, he asked, "Kay Daniels. Where is she?"

"She's in Florida, too. With my husband."

"Will she be returning tonight as well?"

"I expect so. The plan was for her to provide testimony to the police when they were given the tape."

A thought that had bothered him for several weeks prompted a final question.

"Your children? They're in Florida, too?"

"Yes."

Of course. A passing mention in a newspaper report had indicated the two boys would be staying with their grandmother after the funeral. Seifer had wondered about it briefly but had then dismissed it. It was, in hindsight, a red flag that he and Johanna should have focused upon. There was little plausible reason why the children should stay away from their widowed mother for so lengthy a period. But now it made sense. If the intention was to soothe the children's confusion about their father being "dead" by having them stay with him, it was a mistake. Fanning and Kay had made a mistake, just as they had made a mistake on underestimating Amy Fanning.

"All right," he said. "We'll talk further at six."

He drove to the Cumberland Avenue apartment and showed Johanna the note from Amy Fanning.

"Yes indeed," he said, in response to her reaction. "It was too much to expect it to last."

"She's crazy if she thinks we're going to kill her husband now."

He nodded. "Too many strands are unraveling. Kay's sister. Now, Fanning."

"He's got nothing. The tape is worthless. That leaves only Kay and her allegations."

"Yet he believed her. He's got enough clout in this city to stir things up. Even if nothing can be proved. Pity. He was worth so much."

"If it wasn't for that bitch, Kay. Jesus, I'd like to strangle her."

He didn't respond, merely sat staring into space.

She continued, "We'd better pack. Get out of here right away. Before Fanning arrives from Florida."

"Yes," said Seifer, coming to a decision. "But first, let's leave Kay Daniels a farewell present."

Chapter Forty-One

"Vengeance."

Kay looked at Gene Fanning and didn't respond.

"Or vindictiveness," he continued. "What else could it be?"

Paul Keating said, "Well, there certainly seems no monetary motive for his actions."

They sat in the conference room at Keating's law firm. Earlier in the day, he had secured a one-million-dollar bond that allowed Kay her freedom until the trial. At the district attorney's insistence, however, her passport had been retained by the court.

Fanning nodded. "He hadn't implicated himself on the tape. He wasn't in any immediate danger of arrest. So why else would he bring Amy all the way to Kay's house and kill her?"

The two attorneys seemed to have forgotten Kay was present. But, perhaps, she understood. She was no longer an equal. She was now a client, a defendant, a less-than-free person. Someone not like them.

"God, the nihilism of the man," said Keating. "To murder a woman out of . . . spite."

Kay suddenly realized that neither Gene nor Paul had ever met Seifer. What they knew of him was her telling. Her depiction. They seemed flummoxed by his behavior, but she had had so many encounters with him, she was the only one present who fully understood.

"He was sending a message," she said.

They looked at her as if they had forgotten her presence.

"What message?"

Yes, of course, she realized, now convinced of it. "That he was . . . retired."

"Retired?"

"Yes. No poison this time. No attempt to disguise the cause of death. Instead, a great deal of trouble to bring his victim across the state line. Then to stage the murder in my home. All to entrap me."

"But—why retire?" asked Keating.

"Why not? Consider what he's accumulated over the past decade. I alone gave him two million."

"Kay's correct," said Fanning. "Besides, it was inevitable that someone would start making connections. It was almost inevitable, too, that someone, sometime, would balk and fight back." He looked at her. "Someone like you."

Kay said, "There's too much attention now. He had to have known that a prominent attorney like Gene wouldn't do what he had done and then let matters rest. Even if was only publicity, it meant Seifer's entire system was exposed. So he's decided to stop."

Keating said, "Well, let's focus on the immediate problem. Kay, you know I'm not a trial lawyer. Gene is going to defend you."

"No."

"Kay, Gene's a former prosecutor. He's ideal for the task."

"Yes, Kay," said Fanning. "I insist."

"No. There are plenty of good trial lawyers we can hire. If Gene is defending me in court, he's not going to have the time to find Seifer."

"Find Seifer? What are you talking about?"

"We have to find him," she said with conviction. No longer was she alone. No longer did Seifer have the whip hand. Things were different now. Oh yes, she may well be headed for trial.

But now the spotlight was on him, and it was just a matter of finding Seifer and keeping him in that light. "For me. And Amy. And all the others."

But especially, she thought, for Janet.

Chapter Forty-Two

"What do you think?" Mo asked.

"I think it's highly unlikely," Sinclair replied.

"Maybe there's some truth to what she's saying."

"Mo, you've been suspicious of this woman from the get-go. Ever since Thomas Scanlon disappeared. After *she* hired him. Now you think she's as pure as the driven snow?"

"I'm not saying that. I'm only saying that this guy, this Seifer character—"

"If he exists."

She nodded. "If he exists. This Seifer guy would explain everything."

"If he exists."

"But why make it up? Why not come up with some more plausible explanation? It's too . . . detailed, too elaborate."

"She's got a good imagination. What can I tell you?"

"We have time, you know."

"What do you mean, we have time?"

"Henderson. He's got his case ready, neat and tidy. He'd to go to trial tomorrow if he could."

Sinclair shrugged. Roger Henderson was a refugee from the corporate world. He held an MBA before he went back to school to get his law degree. So he liked *efficiency,* he had said at the meeting earlier in the day. He liked a *packaged* case.

"And this, my friends," he'd said to the two detectives earlier that morning, "is a very nice package. Second-degree murder.

No, I don't think the Daniels woman planned it. But when Amy Fanning showed up, it's obvious what happened: words turned to recriminations, then escalation, rage, a typical domestic dispute. The culprit picks up the nearest weapon at hand. And there you have it."

Sinclair didn't feel he was the one who should point out that a carving knife was hardly "at hand" in the living room of Kay Daniels's house. Or that Amy Fanning was in a sitting position on the couch when the knife was thrust between her third and fourth rib, the closest route to the heart.

Mo went on, "So, Henderson feels he's already got enough to get a conviction. We have time to do some more exploring."

"Exploring?"

"What else would you call it?"

"Fishing?"

"Well, let's do some fishing."

Sinclair sighed, knew she was right. "All right. Where do you want to start?"

Chapter Forty-Three

Matthew Staunton was not what Kay anticipated. When Fanning told her Staunton was one of "Boston's best," she'd expected to meet a gray-haired patrician of the old school, accustomed to doing battle in a courtroom—equipped with the guile of a fox and the tenacity of a bulldog. Instead, she met with a man who seemed a decade younger than Gene, whose hair—blow-dried with blonde highlights—and cream-colored suit hardly seemed the outfit of a distinguished trial attorney. Kay thought he could be a young executive at an advertising agency.

"I'm listening," he said when she had paused a moment to allow his note-taking to catch up to her recitation. "I'm listening. Don't wait for me, Mrs. Daniels. Keep going; keep going."

He tapped the fingers of his left hand onto the desk like some deranged, one-armed piano player. Kay could hardly keep her eyes away from the motion.

"Uhmmm . . . so then I called Gene. He told me to call the police. And I did."

"Okay, okay. Did you touch the body?"

"No."

"Did you touch the knife?"

"No. I went to the front door and opened it. Waiting for the police."

"You didn't look throughout the house?"

She shook her head, puzzled by the question. "Why?"

"The killer could have still have been there."

"Oh. I didn't think of that."

"Well, the prosecutor will think of it. And, more importantly, he'll be asking it."

"Well, it's the truth."

"Mrs. Daniels, murder trials are not about the truth. They're about what the jury believes actually happened. And we have to explain to them why they should believe that a woman who finds a murder victim in her living room wouldn't check the rest of her house—if *she* didn't commit the murder."

Kay shrugged. "Well, what can I say? That's what happened."

"All right, all right. Let's move on. The police arrived. What happened then?"

Kay went through the events of the evening and following morning. Staunton made an anguished face when she acknowledged talking to Sinclair and Lipinski without her attorney present.

"Why did you do that?"

"I had nothing to hide. I wanted them to know what happened and about Seifer. Since he was almost certainly responsible."

Staunton bobbled his head. "Ah yes, the mysterious Mr. Seifer. But, of course, they didn't believe he exists."

"How do you know that?"

"Because they arrested you."

She lowered her head, discouraged, and feeling stupid. Of course if they had believed her story about Seifer, they wouldn't have arrested her. They would have begun an immediate manhunt for a pathological killer.

She sighed. "So, what do you think?"

He glanced at his watch, then, evidently satisfied he had the time, said, "First of all, there's Mrs. Fanning's Lexus. Found outside your house. If someone brought her there, as you claim, then how did they get away? Second, there's the knife. You acknowledge it's from a set in your kitchen. Third, there's your affair with the dead woman's husband. Certainly, no one actually *saw* you stab Amy Fanning. But the circumstantial evidence is damaging. And your only real explanation for all of this is that some mystery man is behind it."

He looked at her for more than a moment. "That's a tough sell for any defense attorney, even the best."

Kay didn't need Matthew Staunton—or Gene Fanning—to tell her that Staunton considered himself the best. But beyond the posing and the affectation, there was a clear indication that Staunton was concerned. Whether the concern was for her being found guilty or for *him* finally losing a case—Gene had said he had a one-hundred-percent success record—was immaterial. The simple issue remained: he *was* worried.

"What will our defense be, then?" she asked.

"We have none—if we don't find Seifer. Oh, certainly, I can put some niggling doubts in the mind of the jury. Such as the fact that Mrs. Fanning *forced* the confrontation by driving all the way from Boston. That you and she had met only once and had no prior adversarial relationship. That you had no real motive—she was going to divorce her husband in a matter of months anyway. But all this still doesn't negate what will be the prosecutor's argument: a dispute occurred between a man's wife and his mistress, it escalated to violence, and you stabbed her."

"But a kitchen knife? In the living room? Gene said that domestic disputes resulting in injury are almost always spontaneous. The attacker picks up the nearest weapon to hand. I would have had to go into the kitchen, locate the knife, and return to the living room. He said any reasonable juror would accept that anger could dissipate in the time that would have passed. He also said the fact that she was in a sitting position when she was stabbed was a crucial issue."

Staunton nodded several times.

"Indeed. As I just said: niggling doubts. But not insurmountable for a clever prosecutor to overcome. And Roger Henderson is, by all accounts, a very clever fellow. However, we keep coming back to what is—on the surface—a straightforward scenario. Juries, Mrs. Daniels—"

"Please. Call me Kay. We're in this for the long haul, it seems, so we may as well be on first-name terms."

A polite smile appeared, then disappeared on Staunton's face. Time, evidently, was of the essence and didn't allow for even the smaller courtesies.

"Of course. And please call me Matthew. Well, as I was saying—Kay. Juries are not stupid. But they're also not terribly imaginative. They will find it difficult to imagine a man like Seifer. They will need to *see* Mr. Seifer. They will want to *hear* from him. Or failing that, they will want to hear him *referenced* by someone other than you or your defense attorney. They will want to hear from a police officer that Seifer exists. They will want to see a witness testify that Seifer not only exists, but that the witness himself has knowledge of the man and his schemes and his ruthlessness. If we don't have that, we have nothing. We have merely your claims. Even Gene Fanning never met Seifer. And his testimony, unfortunately, will be tainted. Or will be perceived as being tainted."

"We have the audiotape."

"Yes. But Seifer doesn't implicate himself. He gives nothing away."

"What about the realtor? She sold him the house on Primrose Lane. And Marge Haynes, who bought the house. She met Seifer and Johanna. Plus, we have the photos from the security cameras."

"Yes, but the prosecutor will point out it's not Seifer on trial.

Furthermore, it still *proves* nothing. Or, of more relevance, it *doesn't* prove he is the master criminal you claim him to be."

Staunton paused to gather his notes together by shaping them against the desktop.

"So, to summarize: Not only do we have to locate this man, but we then have to *prove* what he was up to. And that still doesn't change your situation: Amy Fanning was found in your house with one of your kitchen knives in her chest. There's no evidence that this man Seifer did it. And plenty of circumstantial evidence that *you* did. And last—and certainly not least—not helping us is the fact that juries are more inclined to convict in a second-degree murder trial because they don't have the burden of the death penalty to bear."

He saw the discouragement in her faraway look. But his job was not to give false hope.

"Let me be frank," he said. "In every case, I always ask the same question. Knowing what we know—now that we have the discovery materials—and barring any last minute surprises by the prosecutor, I usually ask the question of myself and of my staff."

"Yes?"

"If you were a juror, how would you vote?"

"And how *would* you vote?"

He didn't hesitate. "Guilty."

Chapter Forty-Four

"Well, it starts tomorrow," Kay said. "Staunton says it looks bleak."

Fanning nodded. He seemed saddened, too saddened even to respond. Despite three months of effort, including hiring a private investigation team comprised of former FBI agents, the search for Seifer had been fruitless. He had disappeared. Whether it was experience, natural cunning, or simply his accumulated wealth, the tools he possessed to conceal himself from prying eyes were all too successful.

Kay went on, "You were a former prosecutor, Gene. Do we have a chance?"

He didn't hesitate. "No. Given your background and lack of criminal history, the jury will accept that it wasn't premeditated. Even the DA acknowledges that. But the fact remains: there is a murder victim in your home and no other possible suspects. If they're like any jury I've ever encountered, they will have a hard time cutting you any slack at all."

Kay was struck by his focusing on the exact same point as Staunton. They thought alike, of course. It's how they were trained to think. And no doubt, in the same fraternity, so would Roger Henderson, the district attorney.

"That's what Staunton says. Gene, we only have one chance. We have to find Seifer."

"Yes. But we've already tried everything."

"We haven't tried Carlo Sentora."

The color left Fanning's face. "What are you talking about?"

"I had a long talk with your mom. At the farm. A couple of days before we came back to Boston. You were out riding with the kids that afternoon, remember? I stayed behind because I'd hurt my ankle the day before. Anyway, we were relaxing on the porch, just chit-chatting, lazing the afternoon away."

She recalled the warm afternoon, the languorous feeling she felt. She and Gene had made love that morning, and it seemed as natural as between husband and wife. He had said a curious thing moments after entering her. *It just . . . feels right.* Strangely, she knew what he meant—not a sensation of physicality, but the realization that he was for her, and she was for him. Of course, she understood at the time, how could they know that? Even if such a thing *was* possible, which for so long she had believed was the realm only of the movies and the romance novels. But they knew, she was convinced. They knew.

"I had been asking her about you. What you were like as a kid. That type of stuff. It was harmless. But . . ."

"Yes?"

"I think she realized you'd changed. She remarked on it. I think she saw the effect I was having on you. The effect we were having on each other. She said she hadn't seen you so happy in years. Then, she told me about Carlo Sentora."

"I suppose, in my defense, I could say I was young and stupid."

She didn't press him, allowed him to proceed at his own pace. Would he tell her? But why wouldn't he—if his own mother had revealed what had occurred?

He went on, "And I probably was. But that still doesn't make it right." He smiled, without any humor. "It's strange, but it didn't seem very complicated at the time. The simple issue was: my wife's father was looking at prison time. And all *I* had to do was—nothing. Just keep my lips sealed. Say nothing. Say nothing about how he was using his own law firm's connections to launder dirty money for one of Boston's worst mob bosses."

He paused, and Kay felt he wanted her to ask questions, to clarify, to make what was now complicated, as uncomplicated as it had appeared to be ten years previously.

"Connections?"

"With other firms. Sullivan, Myers & Connolly go back, far back. Established in the Thirties. They're not just prominent. They're international. Connections, relationships, with other firms in Canada, the Caribbean, London. How he got involved with Sentora in the first place, I never found out. I suspect it was when the firm defended Sentora's nephew for murder. Tommy Sullivan got him off. Tommy Sullivan got nearly everyone off. That was what he was renowned for. He was the best in the city, and he employed only the best. That's how I ended up working for him. He approached me. I was very content to make seventy thousand a year working for the government for the rest of my career. A poor Irish boy whose father and grandfather had been cops? That, to me, was paradise. But he said, 'Kid, you can make six times that in your first year alone working for me.'

"As I mentioned, I was young and stupid. I allowed myself to be persuaded. And it went well for a couple of years. I met Amy at one of his parties. She was different then. Oh sure, it was obvious she was spoiled and was accustomed to the best. But she was fun, lively. And not stupid. She had been to Harvard and could have been a success in any profession. But she gets restless easily, bored quickly. She left in her senior year, didn't bother to graduate. However, I liked her. She liked me. We ended up at the altar.

"I don't even think she ever knew about it. Her dad and Sentora, I mean. I certainly didn't tell her. That was the reason I stayed silent in the first place—for her. Not for him. He was a big boy. He could handle himself. I doubt he told her, either. How could he explain it, in any event? Why on earth get involved? But, I suspect it was the money. He was wealthy, of course. The Sentora money, though, was big, *big* money. Millions. Tens of millions. And for his involvement, he was no doubt getting a hefty cut.

"Tommy had a boat, you see. As you can imagine, it was not some little dinghy but an ocean-going, luxury yacht with the works. It was a great scam, I have to admit. You can't land in the Caymans in a commercial plane—or even a private plane—with a suitcase full of cash. The authorities are under enormous pressure from Washington to control the laundering of drug money. But on these small islands, the authorities can't monitor every beach, every cove, every inlet. It went on for a couple of years, Tommy taking a 'vacation' on his yacht to the Caribbean. Just him and a few fishing buddies. Once they were on the island, he would then simply visit the law firm and with their connections, the money was transferred from their accounts into other accounts until finally ending up in Sentora's accounts. It worked perfectly. Year in, year out. Until—"

"Until you found out about it."

Fanning nodded. "Tommy made a mistake. He took me along. For pleasure. He loved to fish. He had become so cocky that the trips were now only partly for the money laundering. Once it had been the sole rationale for the trips. But now, it had become merely a chore on the way to more enjoyable activities.

"Anyway, I saw him. Saw him with the money. As I said, I was a poor Irish kid from Dorchester. I was never on a yacht before. I couldn't find my sea-legs and felt miserable that night. It was well past midnight, but I couldn't even sleep. So I went up on deck to get some fresh air. I saw him through a porthole. With the money, the suitcase open on his bunk. It was beyond belief the number of bank notes. They were pouring out of the suitcase onto the bed and onto the floor. I think he might have been drinking—Tommy always liked his Jameson's. That was probably why he was so careless. And it was late. Probably he assumed everyone on board was asleep. Anyway, he felt comfortable enough to have the suitcase open. Maybe he was counting it. Maybe he was skimming from it. But it was damn obvious that something illegal was going on. There was no legitimate reason why he would be handling such large amounts of cash on a pleasure cruise."

"Did you confront him?"

"No. I followed him. My seasickness was a perfect cover. He assumed I was still in my cabin recovering. So the next morning I followed him into George Town. Watched him head into the law firm. Then I watched how he left the building, empty-handed. He went to a bar, so I headed back quickly to the boat, searched his cabin but the money was gone. I said nothing. He said nothing. We spent a few days doing touristy stuff. Then we went fishing, visited some of the other islands. Went gambling at the casinos. Tommy was a born gambler, naturally. Played blackjack with thousand-dollar chips. Then we came back home. And—"

"Yes?"

"I hired a private investigator."

"What?"

He shook his head, grim-faced. "To follow my own father-in-law. Shameful. The guy was a good investigator, a former cop I knew from the Force. But he didn't need to be. God, Tommy had become so careless. He went straight to Sentora's house in the North End on a Sunday morning after Mass. It was then obvious what was going on. But I couldn't prove it of course. I couldn't sleep, couldn't eat. Finally, I even went to my mom and asked for advice."

"She told you to go to the police?"

He smiled. "You're two of a kind. No wonder she's confiding in you. Yes, she told me that I should go to the police. But I couldn't. I just couldn't. So I went to Sentora."

"Good Lord."

"I told him that I knew everything. He seemed unsure what I was doing there. He had to know I was no longer in the District Attorney's office. Before I could continue with my offer, he said, *Bring me down, counselor, and you bring down your wife's old man.* He knew that Tommy would almost certainly plea-bargain and admit what he had done—given my testimony. And if Tommy confessed, Sentora was looking at jail time, too. Tommy deserved it, of course. There was no justification for his behavior. He had plenty of money. It was wrong. It was illegal. And it was greedy. He deserved to go to jail. And yet—I loved Amy. She had just become pregnant with the twins. I knew this would devastate her. Not just her father going to jail. The shame of it for the family. Her mother left alone. I was also worried about what the stresses of a trial would do to her physically. In the end, it was for her and not Tommy that I came up with a solution."

"What was that?"

"I told Sentora I was going to remain silent. On one condition. That it was over. He was never to deal with Tommy ever again. And Tommy was not to know why. Sentora seemed pleased, even relieved. He offered me a glass of wine to seal the deal. I refused and then left."

"It was soon after that you left the firm and went out on your own?"

"Yes. And that was when the problems began with Amy. She couldn't understand why I was leaving the most prestigious firm in Boston, where I was certainly destined to become partner. She questioned me, hounded me actually. But I never told her. And Tommy didn't enlighten her because he didn't know why he was no longer being used by Sentora. Three years later, the issue became moot."

"Why?"

"Tommy died. Too much booze, too much high-living. Amy was devastated, not least because he left her virtually nothing. Because he *had* virtually nothing by that stage. He was a gambler, as I said."

Kay placed a hand on Fanning's arm. "Gene, I think you did the right thing."

"I certainly hope so. But, in any event, what relevance does any of that have with Seifer and your trial?"

"Remember I told you what Johanna let slip in the apartment? While we were waiting for Seifer to bring Kelley? She referred to him as 'MacBride.' Clearly that is his real name."

Fanning nodded. "I'd always thought 'Seifer' was an alias. But still, knowing his real name—even if *is* his real name—is not a whole lot to go on."

"I know. But she also said, 'We contacted some friends in the Family.' No. 'Some *old friends* in the Family.' That can only mean the Mafia."

Fanning was clearly dubious. "Mmm. Seifer's game hardly seems typical of the Mafia. They don't have the patience for something like that."

"Perhaps not. But clearly there is some connection. Or was. After all, how many ordinary people have *old* friends in the Mob?"

"Even so. Carlo Sentora is based in Boston. He wouldn't necessarily know Seifer—or MacBride—if he was indeed involved somehow with the New York mob."

"That's right. It's a desperate measure. But, Gene, I'm pretty desperate right now."

Chapter Forty-Five

Henderson's first witness was his first surprise. When the clerk swore in Philip Maguire, Kay noticed the looks exchanged by Staunton and Paul Keating, who was sitting at the defense table to give her moral support.

Keating, in a lowered voice, explained: "Prosecutors don't usually begin their case with a forensics expert. Such testimony is used to *support* a case, not to initiate it."

In a brisk series of introductory questions, Maguire's credentials as a forensics examiner were established. He had the academic qualifications—two degrees—and practical experience—a dozen years in the Connecticut State Police—that would impress any jury. Another series of questions, equally brisk, established the context in which Maguire examined the scene of Amy Fanning's murder.

"Now, Mr. Maguire," said Henderson. "You examined the Lexus that was parked outside 14 Ridgewood Court in New Croydon on January 27. Is that correct?"

Maguire, a middle-aged man whose tidy beard and large eyeglasses gave him a professorial look, replied, "Yes, I was called in by the New Croydon police as they did not have an experienced forensics examiner in the department."

"Did the police inspect the car in any way prior to your arrival?"

"The office in charge on the scene assured me that no one had inspected the car."

"Very good. Now, in collecting trace evidence inside the car, did you find any hairs in the driver's seat?"

"Yes, I did."

"Were you able to determine if they were human hairs?"

"Yes. That is straightforward to determine. Animal hair is characterized by unique patterns of the medulla, the central core of hair. Human hair has no medulla, or it is fragmented. Animals typically have a continuous medulla. The samples taken from the driver's seat had no medulla."

"All right, good. Was there evidence of more than one type of hair?"

"No. The hair was unique, consistent with that from a single individual."

"Were you able to match this hair with any other?"

"Yes. It matched the hair from Amy Fanning."

"You took hair samples from Amy Fanning and matched them to the hair in the driver's seat, is that correct?"

"Yes."

"Did you find any hairs in the back seat of the car?"

"Yes. I was able to find hair from two distinct individuals."

"Could either of these individuals be adults?"

"No. The hair was consistent with that of a child."

Paul Keating leaned toward Kay. "The clever bastard."

"What?" she asked.

"Now it makes sense. He's preempting our defense even before we offer it. Mitigating the damage. He knows damn well it's the only defense we've got."

"How?"

"By establishing that Amy drove the car. If she drove the car herself, then Seifer couldn't have brought her."

Henderson continued the questioning. "Mr. Maguire, how can you be so sure that the hairs found in the back seat belonged to children?"

"A child's hair is always finer than that of an adult's. But in this case, there is an even easier reason to be sure."

"Please share with the court what that reason is."

"DNA. Roots of hair specimens contain follicular tissue which is used for DNA testing. The DNA of the hair from the back seat matched the DNA of Mrs. Fanning's two children."

"You had DNA from the two children with which to compare?"

"Yes. Their father, Eugene Fanning, acceded to our request for samples."

"Apart from the hair specimens from these three individuals—Amy Fanning and her two children—did you find any other human hair in the car?"

"No."

"In your experience, have criminals—aware of the dangers of leaving such trace evidence—tried to dispose of such evidence at a crime scene?"

"I'm aware of a number of instances where clever criminals have tried to do that."

"Is it possible that hair samples from another individual were removed from the driver's seat of the car?

"Apart from the amount of time it would take, I should say it would be impossible to be that exact—to remove all samples of specific hair specimens."

"Did you find any other trace evidence in the driver's seat?"

"I found fibers from clothing material."

"Were you able you match the fibers?"

"Yes. The fibers matched the beige pants worn by Amy Fanning at the time of her death."

"So, to summarize: you found hair from three individuals in the car and none from another individual. You found fibers of clothing in the driver's seat that matched the clothing worn by Amy Fanning. Correct?"

"Yes, correct."

"Do you have an opinion as to who drove the Lexus to New Croydon on January 27?"

"Yes."

"What is that opinion?"

"Amy Fanning drove the car."

Chapter Forty-Six

Carlo Sentora, apart from a little gray at the sides of his hair, didn't seem to have aged in the ten years since Fanning had last seen him. But, Fanning thought, why should he? Sentora lived a life of ease. Head of a Family of one hundred mobsters, he had under-bosses, counselors, and lawyers to handle the dirty day-to-day affairs of his business. Like any other CEO, he reaped the rewards of the sweat and toil of others under his dominion.

Nor was Fanning surprised that Sentora agreed to see him as soon as he had phoned Sentora's attorney. Apart from a trivial incident as a teenager, he had never been touched by the law. He was insulated, cosseted, protected. Untouchable. Except the one time he had allowed himself to be exposed by using the willing services of a civilian. Tommy Sullivan. And it was Gene Fanning he could thank for bailing him out.

"Nice to see you again, counselor," Sentora said.

The mob boss had little education, Fanning thought, but he certainly did have taste. Everything in Sentora's library appeared authentic: the figurines were antique, the lamps with their twin-shades of emerald and ruby-stained glass were surely Tiffany, the small watercolors on the elegantly patterned walls were originals, the furniture had the hand-tooled look of European craftsmen.

Fanning nodded. "Ten years."

"Yep. Ten years it is. Sorry to hear about your wife."

Sentora appeared sincere, but Fanning couldn't bring himself to say "Thanks." Instead he nodded again and replied, "That's what I've come to see you about."

Sentora held up both hands. "Hey, we had nothing to do with it. You gotta be kiddin' me if you think we did."

"No. I realize that. But you might be able to help me find the man who did."

"I thought the cops already had someone? Her trial started yesterday, didn't it? I saw it on the news last night."

"She didn't do it."

"That's what they all say."

"This time it's the truth. I know. I also know who did it. I just have to find him."

"And that's where I come in?"

"Yes."

"Well, sure, counselor. I can lend a hand—if I'm able. But it's hardly down our alley, know what I'm saying?"

"The man I'm looking for. His name—at least one of them—is MacBride. And I believe he was involved at some point with one of the Families in New York or New Jersey."

"Whoa. Whoa. Wait a minute. I said I'd lend a hand—for your wife. For Tommy Sullivan's girl. For old times' sake. But Family business is somethin' else. If it was some black boy who went after some white meat, we could help track him down. Or some asswipe burglar working above his station who knifed the lady of the house—okay, we'd help find him. But there's no way I can finger somebody in another Family. What's the matter with you? You were a prosecutor. You know how the world works."

"I think he was only in the life. He wasn't actually part of any Family."

"But you just said—"

"With a name like *MacBride?*"

Fanning knew after the Donnie Brasco disaster in the Eighties that full membership to the Mob was now limited to those of Italian or Sicilian descent.

He went on, "He wasn't a made man. Couldn't have been. He was a connected guy—at best."

Sentora was silent for more than a few moments. "Okay. But still. Even a connected guy."

"I think—almost certainly—he's no longer doing work for any Family. He's now a private operator. And has been for some time—several years. I should imagine he's owed nothing."

"Still, it's a hell of a favor to ask someone like me."

"I did you a hell of a favor ten years ago."

"Seems to me, counselor, you were helping Tommy Boy a lot more than me."

"Seems to me, you both benefited by my silence."

Sentora bobbled his head from side to side, as if in sync to a tune only he could hear. "Maybe. Maybe."

"If it makes it any easier, you wouldn't have to indicate who is asking for the information."

Sentora laughed. "I'd imagine they'd add two and two together when you put a bullet in this guy's head once you find him."

Fanning was surprised. He hadn't conceived of that. He realized now it wasn't vengeance he sought by finding MacBride. It was to protect Kay Daniels.

"That's not going to happen," he said.

"And if I still say 'No'? What will you do, counselor? Nothing stupid, I hope."

Tommy Sullivan was dead. So was his daughter. There was no reason to remain silent now. No one to protect. Fanning's testimony would hardly convict Sentora a decade after the events. Yes, he had the file prepared by the private investigator. And yes, the P.I. was still alive; he had used him on a number of other, non-criminal investigations. But there was no physical proof, no money, no suitcases full of dirty bank notes. Fanning had no leverage at all.

He shrugged. "A man in grief sometimes does stupid things."

Chapter Forty-Seven

"Detective Sinclair, you interviewed Kay Daniels the morning after the body of Amy Fanning was discovered. Is that correct?"

Roger Henderson, Kay thought, had the persona of a super-salesman—it was more than confidence in his product, more than self-assurance in his ability. It was the *certainty* that oozed out of him. He was certain the accused sitting across from him was guilty of murder. Now all he had to do was sell his certainty to the jury. She liked his unctuousness even less the first time she had encountered him. To save time and the city the expense of a trial, he had offered Staunton a plea bargain. Kay would plead guilty, and Henderson would recommend leniency, a possible sentence of ten years, maximum. Staunton was in favor. Kay refused.

Sinclair answered, "Yes."

"What was Mrs. Daniels's explanation for what had transpired in her home?"

Sinclair, as he had presumably been directed, addressed the jury more than the prosecutor. He told them about her denials, her story about Seifer, about her husband's accident, how Seifer's *system* worked. Already Kay could see the disbelief in their faces. The foreperson—a primly dressed woman whose wedding finger held no band—gave her a derisive glance when Sinclair testified about Kay's admission of intercourse with the dead woman's husband while his children were in the same house.

"Mrs. Daniels made available to you photographs of this man

taken by security cameras at her place of business, is that not true?"

"Yes."

"You showed these photographs to Dorothy Kramer, the realtor who sold the house on 38 Primrose Lane and to Margaret Haynes, the woman who bought the house?"

"Yes."

"Did Linda Kramer identify the man in the photos as the individual who purchased the property?"

"Yes."

"Did Margaret Haynes identify the man in the photos as the individual who purchased the property?"

"Yes."

"Did either of these two women identify the man as Nikolas Seifer?"

"No."

"In fact, the photographs merely confirm that William Johnson visited New Croydon Telecomm at some unknown time?"

"That's correct."

"Did Mrs. Daniels tell you about this man, this Nikolas Seifer, when her husband was killed in an automobile accident?

"No. She never mentioned him."

"How many times did you interview Mrs. Daniels after her husband died?"

"At least six times."

"And she never once mentioned Nikolas Seifer?"

"No."

After evidently ridiculing the existence of Seifer, Henderson now proceeded to eliminate him from the proceedings altogether.

"How many years have you been a police officer, Detective?"

"Sixteen."

"And for how many of those years have you been a detective?"

"Twelve."

"Now, despite the lack of evidence indicating the existence of this man Nikolas Seifer, your sixteen years experience as a police officer nevertheless made you investigate this possible suspect. Correct?"

"Yes, that's correct."

"Please tell the Court what steps you took to locate this . . . mystery man."

Sinclair testified for another hour. Kay was startled by the intensity of the hunt that Sinclair had conducted, and she began to look at the man in a new light. From the beginning, he had clearly suspected her of wrongdoing in Bernard's death. He had always been cold, and, when interrogating her about Amy, his manner was hostile enough to frighten her. And yet, she marveled, here he was describing his exhaustive search for Seifer. She was especially dazed when he recounted contacting Interpol in connection with the death of that man in the swimming pool in San Francisco. Had Sinclair actually believed her at some point? But, no, apparently not, she realized; otherwise, he would hardly be sitting there recounting his failure to locate Seifer.

Henderson asked, "And after all that, you were never able to locate this Nikolas Seifer?"

"No."

"And you were never able to connect any of these deaths throughout the country to Nikolas Seifer?"

"No."

"And, as far as you could determine, there was no evidence that foul play was involved in any of these deaths?"

"Not as far as I could determine."

"Very well, Detective. A final question. With sixteen years of experience in law enforcement under your belt, do you now believe in the existence of this man, Nikolas Seifer?"

"No."

"Detective Sinclair," Staunton said, "when you interviewed Kay Daniels the morning after Mrs. Fanning's body was discovered, did she have an attorney present?"

"No."

"You made her aware of her rights, I assume? That she was not obligated to speak in the absence of her attorney?"

"Of course I did. She said she didn't need an attorney."

"The District Attorney has pointed out numerous times that you have been a police officer for sixteen years. In your sixteen years of experience in law enforcement, do murderers offer to speak to the police without an attorney present?"

"Only the stupid ones."

Staunton didn't seem perturbed by the laughter in the court, even by the smiles from several jury members.

"You interviewed Mrs. Daniels several times. Did she ever strike you as being stupid?"

"No."

"All right. Now, you stated this morning you were unable to locate Nikolas Seifer."

"Yes."

"Were you able to locate William Johnson?"

"No."

"Were you able to establish his place of employment while he was living in Primrose Lane for six months?"

"No."

"Margaret Haynes told you that Johnson said he worked in insurance."

"Yes."

"Did you contact any insurance companies in the state?"

"There are hundreds. We contacted the major companies."

"Did they employ William Johnson?"

"No."

"So you were never able to locate this man at all? His place of business? Where he'd come from? Where he went?"

"That's correct."

"As District Attorney Henderson might say: William Johnson—like Nikolas Seifer—seems to be a bit of a mystery man."

"Your words, not mine."

"Now, Detective Sinclair. You've already testified that Mrs. Daniels gave you a list of alleged victims of Mr. Seifer."

"Yes."

"You contacted the police departments in the jurisdictions where these individuals died?"

"Yes. I already testified to that this morning."

"Indeed. You also testified that you requested copies of the investigation files conducted into the deaths of these individuals?"

"Yes."

"And in the majority of the cases, the cause of death was deemed to be cardiac arrhythmia. Isn't that so?"

"Yes.

"Didn't that strike you as strange?"

"Not necessarily strange."

"Well, let's say 'unusual'?"

"Possibly."

"Come, come, Detective. Mrs. Daniels had no connection with any of these individuals, had never visited most of the states where they'd lived. And yet every single one of the people she claims was actually poisoned, died of cardiac arrhythmia?"

"What's your question?"

"Mrs. Daniels told you that most of these individuals were poisoned, did she not?"

"Yes."

"Poisoned with sodium cyanide?"

"Yes. But Amy Fanning wasn't killed by cyanide poisoning."

Chapter Forty-Eight

The sign on the door of the pawnshop indicated it was closed. But the man on the phone had told Fanning to ring the bell anyway. Feeling self-conscious and foolish, Fanning did so. A light in a back room came on, and in a few moments a small man with a cigarette in the corner of his mouth opened the door.

Fanning gave his name. "I believe you're expecting me."

The man gestured toward the inside of the shop with a nod of his head. Fanning crossed the portal and, because the shop was in darkness, even though it was only mid-morning, assumed he should head to the lighted back room. The proprietor, who seemed to have a problem with his foot or leg, shuffled behind him, then closed the door of what presumably was his office.

The man sat and looked at Fanning. After several moments of this silence, Fanning guessed the proprietor was not going to commit himself with even a simple introduction.

He said, "What can you tell me about a man named MacBride?"

"Whadya want to know?"

Fanning was surprised by the response. He had anticipated little cooperation, if not outright stonewalling. But perhaps Carlo Sentora's long arm reached even into the New York areas of mob activity.

"Everything you have."

"You a cop?"

The question was puzzling. Sentora would never vouch for a police officer.

"No. A lawyer. I believe this man killed my wife."

"Oh. I can see why you'd be interested then."

The pawnbroker took a Marlboro from a pack on the table and lit it with the stub of the cigarette he'd been smoking.

"Well," he said, "knowing MacBride, he didn't do it for laughs."

"What do you mean by that?"

"I mean, he never killed no one for nothin'. If there was money in it for him, then he's your man. He was a mercenary. The Real McCoy."

"I—I don't quite understand. You mean a . . . a soldier?"

"Yeah. Well, nah, not exactly. IRA. Came over here after they got their shit together in the old country."

"IRA? Why on earth would Angelo Delacroce have an IRA man on the payroll?"

Fanning knew there were more than enough hardened killers available to any Mob family. The rules of initiation, even, called for a made man to perform two hits. Not the least of the reasons was to avoid a repeat of the Brasco affair—the Mob knew that the FBI would not condone one of their agents committing murder in order to infiltrate the Mafia.

"Why? Because MacBride was efficient, that's why. Those other shooters were brutes, idiots. *No subtlety,* Mr. Delacroce used to say. MacBride was different. He was used for specific jobs. Any idiot could entice some bozo into a cellar and put two slugs into his head. But MacBride was never used for anything like that. Just the real important stuff. He could use a sniper rifle, could rig explosives. And he was good with a knife."

"How about poison?"

"Poison? Nah, I never heard him get involved with poison. Why? He poison your wife?"

"No. Stabbed her."

"Yep. That sounds like our boy, all right."

"So what happened to him?"

"Ankle Express."

"What?"

"Took a walk one day and never came back. Left his apartment and all his stuff behind. I went over there when we didn't hear from him in a couple of weeks. Clothes, furniture, bathroom stuff, everything. We figured he'd been hit. But after Mr. Delacroce put the word out on the street, it was clear nobody did nothin' to MacBride. He'd just disappeared. And the broad, too."

"Johanna?"

"Yeah, right. Johanna. Smart-alec little trollop. But a good thief, I have to say."

"Did you try to locate him?"

"Not really. Mr. Delacroce was pissed. He liked the guy, but he wasn't going to spend much time or money finding a guy who didn't want to be found."

"What about you?" Fanning sensed there was some connection between the two men, that it was not all business, all the time. Besides, it was to the pawnshop owner he'd been directed to get answers to his questions. "Did you try to locate him?"

The man shrugged. "I made a few phone calls. Checked out his old haunts. But turned up nothin'."

"His old haunts? What sort of haunts? What did he like to do?"

A smile of genuine warmth appeared on the man's face. "He loved AC."

"AC? What's that?"

The man rolled his eyes. "Atlantic City."

Fanning felt a surge of excitement. He remembered how Seifer had contacted Kay the second time. In Las Vegas.

"MacBride liked casinos? Liked to gamble?"

"*Loved* to gamble. He used to say they didn't have casinos in the old country. First time I took him, I could see it in his eyes. He liked the *unpredictability* of it, he used to say. The *treadmill to oblivion,* he called the roulette wheel. He could be a regular fuckin' poet sometimes."

The revelation puzzled Fanning. Gambling on the roll of a dice or the spin of a wheel hardly seemed compatible with the man described by Kay. His continual talk of *systems* and abhorrence of a *mess* conflicted with the image of a devoted gambler. But perhaps it was the ostensible excitement that casinos offered. After all, he reasoned, MacBride's profession was killing. It was not something he did on a daily basis. He would need some sort of other adrenaline rush in its stead, and gambling—however tame by comparison—might well provide it. Something Kay said about Seifer came to Fanning. *He's sending a message . . . He's retired.* Could it be possible? Could MacBride have *retired* to Vegas? Well, why not, Fanning reasoned? It would be unlikely he'd move to Atlantic City—so close to New York—where he might be spotted by former cronies. Thirty million people visited Las Vegas every year. What better place to disappear than among those throngs?

The phone rang, and the man stood without excusing himself. Fanning took the time to think it through. That Seifer was dangerous, Kay had made obvious a long time ago. But this added dimension was especially disturbing. A man who received his apprenticeship in killing in a terrorist organization and then moved into the world of organized crime as a specialist in assassination was far worse than Fanning had anticipated. Even if Kay was to be found not guilty, such a man, now exposed by her testimony, was out there and, if he desired, would be well capable of disposing of her without conscience or remorse. Fanning's grim mood, if it was possible, he thought, became grimmer.

The pawnbroker hung up the phone. "Got any more questions?"

Fanning shook his head, then stood. If this man didn't know where Seifer was, no one would. "Thanks for your help."

"No problem." He gestured toward the phone. "That was Mr. Delacroce. He wanted to know have you eaten yet?"

"Eaten? No."

"Well then, he'd like you to join him for lunch."

Chapter Forty-Nine

"Detective Sinclair, I'd like to ask you about your testimony yesterday concerning the knife that killed Amy Fanning."

"All right."

Staunton had spent the afternoon of the first day cross-examining Detective Sinclair. But he had told the judge that he had further questions for the detective. On the drive to the courthouse, Paul Keating explained the rationale to Kay.

"There's no ambiguity about the cause of death. Amy Fanning died from a stab wound. There are no forensics to dispute. No experts to quiz. No psychologists to explicate behavior. Sinclair is vital. He's the lead investigator. The jury sees him as the representative of the police, and by extension, representative of the law. If cracks can be made to appear in his testimony, cracks will appear in the entire case. So he needs to be squeezed for all he's got because we have so little otherwise."

Staunton asked the detective, "You stated that the handle of the knife had no fingerprints?"

"Yes."

"Obviously the killer wiped the handle clean?"

"Obviously."

"Do you believe Kay Daniels wiped the handle of the knife?"

"I do."

"Do you have proof that Mrs. Daniels cleaned the knife?"

"No"

"No, you don't. But in your testimony yesterday you stated

that Mrs. Daniels cleaned the knife."

"I was making a logical assumption."

"No, you were manufacturing a fact."

"What?"

"You took two facts and manufactured a third. It was Mrs. Daniels's knife. It was Mrs. Daniels's house. You then made a leap and came up with a third fact that is not a fact—isn't that true?"

"I think it is a reasonable assumption in the context of the events."

Staunton made almost an unconscious nod to himself. Most observers probably didn't notice it, but Kay, alerted by Keating as to where Staunton was driving, recognized it.

"Is it a reasonable assumption—as you testified yesterday—that an argument took place and that in an agitated state Mrs. Daniels stabbed Amy Fanning?"

"Yes, it is."

"But you've just testified that it is also a reasonable assumption that Mrs. Daniels cleaned the knife."

"So?"

"So Mrs. Daniels would have had to be agitated enough to stab the victim but then be calm enough to wipe the handle."

"Well, I—"

"And remain calm to then call the police and agree to be questioned without her lawyer present?"

"But—"

"Please share with the jury your *assumption* about when exactly the agitation ceased and the calm commenced."

Chapter Fifty

Henry Pierce tried to focus on the article in the Sunday edition of the *Chicago Tribune* but the pain in the front of his temple was so severe it caused his eyes to tear, making it difficult to read the tiny print.

Sunday morning had always been his favorite time of the week. Even when he was a reluctant employee of Barlow & Co., his late wife's company, facing the imminence of another dreaded Monday, he loved to sit in his leather club chair with the large cup of coffee and read the thick paper from front to back. Now he was a wealthy man of leisure, but he still loved the weekly ritual. The headaches, though, would not go away, and the pills that two doctors had prescribed did little to help.

Guilt, he supposed the culprit was. But he couldn't admit that to the doctors. They would ask the inevitable question: Why? They eliminated stress—he didn't work, had plenty of money now that Julia was gone, and had no external stressors. His genes were good: no evidence of high blood pressure or heart problems in his ancestors. So the doctors gave him the pills and told him to come back if the migraines continued.

Had they increased since the trial of Kay Daniels began, he wondered? No, they'd been pretty much continual for the previous few months. Funny, he thought. They hadn't begun after he had murdered poor Elizabeth Carlisle. He and a lady friend of some two scores years younger had taken a wonderfully relaxing trip to the Antilles. When they'd returned, he conducted some stock market business with his new broker and solicited estimates for remodeling his home. He'd bought a Mercedes convertible with every available option. Life was good. But then the migraines began.

He glanced at the antique clock on the mantle of the marble fireplace. He's taken the first of the day's pills at eight A.M. That was less than two hours ago, but to hell with it, he thought. He opened the pillbox and swallowed the little blue cylinder with a mouthful of coffee. Then he picked up the paper and forced himself to finish the article that summarized the week's events at Kay Daniels's trial in Connecticut.

Four days had passed. Brick by brick, Henry read, piece by piece, District Attorney Henderson made his case. The prosecutor called Fanning's mother to confirm that Kay had spent several weeks in the same house as the dead woman's husband. He called Maria Gonzalez, the Fannings' maid, who testified that Kay had met Amy Fanning and that she'd heard voices raised in the library during her visit. Staunton countered by having the maid admit she couldn't detect what the argument was about or, behind the closed door, whose female voice it was. But another piece of Henderson's mosaic had been laid.

He then called Kay's neighbors. The rich men's houses, however, with their huge lots, were deliberately set far apart, and the owners were not the typical middle class. They commuted to Manhattan early in the morning and seldom returned until early evening. Their children were driven to ballet classes and piano lessons and diverse other activities after school. No one saw Amy Fanning drive her Lexus down Ridgewood Court the day of her death, and no one, Henderson made certain to point out, had seen someone else drive it. Nor did anyone in the neighborhood see a drugged woman carried into Kay Daniels's home. As always, Henderson undermined Staunton's argument before Staunton could make the argument.

Photographs of the murder victim were introduced during the testimony of the medical examiner. Experts quoted in the article voiced their opinion that it was a tactic merely to shock the jury and diminish any residue of sympathy they might have for Kay Daniels. There was no issue of contention with the cause of death, no real reason for the photographs, enlarged and ghastly, to be displayed. But display them, Henderson did, and everyone saw the reaction of the jury.

But it was the testimony about the security system that the article's author—having discussed the matter with legal observers—noted was especially bad news for Kay Daniels. The disconnected alarm, it was always assumed, was the defense's ace-in-the-hole. A defeated alarm meant an illegal break-in, giving credence to Kay's claims of innocence. After all, a typical homeowner doesn't disconnect the electronic leads of her own alarm. But Henderson had prepared even for that.

Kay Daniels, he demonstrated, was not a typical homeowner. The typical homeowner doesn't *own* a telecommunications company. Kay Daniels had become an expert on the telecommunications industry, he was able to establish. Her company had expanded beyond landline phone service. New Croydon Telecomm had, in the previous twelve months, begun to offer cell phone service, Internet access and, most recently, security systems. It was a natural fit—New Croydon Telecomm already had a substantial call center manned by scores of employees. And what was an alarm company, other than a call center monitoring alarm consoles? If anybody knew how to defeat a household alarm system, he pointed out, it was the accused.

That was the final piece of Henderson's mosaic; the complete picture that showed Kay Daniels, and only Kay Daniels, as the murderer of Amy Fanning.

★ ★ ★ ★ ★

Henry Pierce finished the main article, then turned to the sidebar that listed capsule biographies of the main players in the courtroom drama: the widowed defendant trying to raise a child and run a business all by herself; opposing her, the prosecutor's main witness, the detective, himself a widower with a beloved wife lost to a brutal cancer, who didn't even believe the woman's story but had tried to locate the mystery man; the young but experienced attorney with the one-hundred-percent winning record; and finally, the ambitious DA who was surely destined for higher office.

"Who Will Prevail?" read the headline in the box. Who indeed? Henry Pierce wondered. It looked bad for the Daniels woman, he had to admit. But Matthew Staunton, apparently, had something up his sleeve. Henry went back to the main article and re-read the final sentence.

"Sources familiar with the defense team say that a 'desperate maneuver' to make a breakthrough will be attempted within twenty-four hours."

Chapter Fifty-One

"Jesus fucking Christ!" Seifer flung the newspaper across the living room.

"What's the matter?" Johanna asked, and went to fetch the paper. But even before she picked it up, she understood his anger: the *Las Vegas Sun* had landed with the full-page ad facing up.

$1 MILLION REWARD. HAVE YOU SEEN JOHN MacBRIDE?

Beneath this was his photograph. It was crude, in black-and-white, but it was clearly him.

WANTED FOR MURDER. BELIEVED TO CURRENTLY RESIDE IN LAS VEGAS. DO NOT ATTEMPT TO APPROACH THIS MAN. KNOWN TO BE ARMED AND DANGEROUS.

The name and a phone number of a Boston law firm were displayed at the bottom of the page.

"Oh my God," said Johanna. "Your picture! And they know your name! And that we're in Vegas! How do they know all that? How the hell do they know all that?"

"I don't know."

"Oh God. A million dollars reward. Oh Christ. This is a disaster."

He had made a mistake, he realized. A huge mistake. It was so uncharacteristic, he knew, even as he had brought Amy Fanning all the way from Boston to Kay Daniels's house. He'd even had second thoughts as they'd crossed the Massachusetts state line and considered just aborting the plan. But it had such elegance, was such a fitting culmination to the system that he decided it was worth the risk. Causing a mess for Kay Daniels was, he felt, fitting revenge for the mess she had caused him. He didn't want her dead—that would be easy enough to accomplish. But he didn't want her anguish to be temporary. He wanted it to be continuous. He wanted her to spend the bulk of the rest of her life in prison. He was aware that sentencing guidelines mandated a term of twenty-five years for second-degree murder. He wanted her to spend all of that time growing old in a foul jail cell, cut off from her daughter, knowing all the time, as the long years slowly passed, not only that she was innocent, but that he was the one who'd put her there. That was why it had to be perfect. That was why he spent so much effort getting it just right. The speculation in the papers that he had drugged Amy Fanning was wildly inaccurate. The fools. He didn't have to drug her. She had driven the Lexus herself, following him all the way from Boston. The stupid, greedy woman had bought his story about how he was going to take care of her husband. And allowed herself to be convinced that a trip to Kay Daniels's house was a crucial part of the scenario, to lure Gene Fanning.

And then once they'd got into the house, Johanna, as planned, kept her talking while he went to the kitchen. He had selected the best knife and, so that she would be unaware of what was to happen, to prevent her screaming and not to have any marks or scratches on her, he had simply returned to the living room with the knife concealed, walked behind her as she talked, then reached over her shoulder and thrust in the knife. A huge gasp was all she could manage, such was the surprise. He'd worn gloves, but he deliberately wiped the handle clean. MacBride had dealt with enough crooked cops in New York to know the importance of trace evidence and the power of scanning electron microscopes and infrared spectrophotometers. He and Johanna spent an hour eliminating all fiber, hair, and shoeprint evidence and then left, five minutes apart.

But now, he conceded, it was a mistake. The articles about the trial in the newspapers had mentioned him, naturally. But he never used the name Nikolas Seifer, much less John MacBride, in his legitimate business affairs. Their luxury condominium on the Strip was bought in the name he used for all his dealings with the conventional world. His credentials—driver's license, Social Security card, even a passport, all crafted by the best forgers in Los Angeles—carried the same alias. The business card with the Seifer name and a phone number were for cell phones bought at a department store with prepaid minutes, and discarded after each job. Without a name, a photograph, a location, the authorities had nothing, and he felt supremely safe. Until this morning, when he'd opened the *Sun* and seen the huge ad.

"Every lowlife from here to New York will come out of the woodwork for that type of money," he said.

"We can get disguises," Johanna said. "We know people we can trust. Wigs. Plastic surgery."

"I don't want to *disguise* myself. I don't want to live my life hiding behind a mask. Or cowering in some hole. Waiting for some nonentity to finger me so he can become rich. That was the entire rationale with the system: never expose yourself, allow the mark to do the deed, pull the strings behind the scenes. That was the *essence* of it all."

"Well, we'll have to go abroad, then. Mexico or South America."

"I'm not living in exile. And I'm too old to learn foreign languages. No, there's only one way to put an end to this."

"How?"

"End the trial right now. End the publicity. And the purpose for any more advertisements."

"How do you hope to do that?"

"Kill Kay Daniels. If there's no defendant, there's no reason to have a trial."

Chapter Fifty-Two

Staunton began by calling Kay to the stand.

"She's not our only witness," he had told Keating. "But she *is* our only defense."

As they had rehearsed, Staunton led Kay through the events of her life beginning far from the night of January 27. In a quiet but firm voice, she recounted her departure from her father's home, her struggle to better herself, her life as a single mother in Manhattan, the marriage to Bernard Daniels, and the creation of New Croydon Telecomm.

Staunton's intention was to continue to shine the light on Seifer but to do so from the point of view of Kay Daniels. No one else in the courtroom had encountered Seifer. No one present had been under the duress or felt the coercion that Kay had endured. Staunton knew this, in and of itself, was not a defense for a unpremeditated murder done in anger, but by helping the jury see the passage of events through Kay's eyes, he hoped they would conclude not that she was innocent as much as that Seifer was guilty.

Once again the jury heard the narrative of Nikolas Seifer, but now it was directly from her lips and not second-hand from a prosecution witness. As Sinclair had done, she addressed the jury when she spoke. After revealing the contents of the watch-box, even the forewoman, she saw, reacted with disgust. Staunton, intentionally, had positioned himself so he too could see the jury's reaction. This was the "pivot point," he believed, in

Kay's behavior. If the jurors could accept what had happened to Thomas Scanlon, they would understand what Kay had gone through and what Seifer was capable of.

"Why didn't you go to the police at that point?" Staunton asked.

"I was afraid. Afraid of him. What he was capable of doing to my daughter."

"You were not afraid for yourself?"

"No. I thought only of her."

Staunton then had her recount the events following her payoff to Seifer. She told them about tracking down William Johnson as the owner of 38 Primrose Lane. Her trip to Las Vegas and Seifer's reappearance. Her refusal to kill Gene Fanning and her plan to expose Seifer.

After six hours on the stand, she was exhausted, but she sensed that the jury had responded, that there was credence in the fact that what had occurred may not necessarily have been a domestic dispute ending in tragedy but a carefully calculated murder by a devious man.

Staunton, well aware of the time because he had planned it that way, allowing no opportunity for the prosecutor to pose even one question, asked Kay one final thing.

"Did you kill Amy Fanning?"

"No."

"Mrs. Daniels," said Roger Henderson. "You testified yesterday that the finger you allegedly saw in the watch box belonged to Thomas Scanlon."

Staunton glanced at Keating and smiled. Henderson, too, was aware of the pivot point.

"Yes," Kay replied.

"How do you know it belonged to Thomas Scanlon?"

"I saw the ring. The big World Series ring he had worn in my office."

"How do you know it was the same ring?"

"I—It looked the same."

"Had you personally handled Mr. Scanlon's ring in your office?"

"Handled it? No."

"Did Mr. Scanlon take the ring off and give it to you for inspection?"

"No. I never said that."

"But you do say that a ring you saw for a matter of moments in your office was exactly the same ring as the one in the watch box?"

"Yes. I'm sure of it."

"Do you have the ring now?"

"No. I gave it to Seifer when I handed over the money."

Henderson smiled without mirth. "Naturally."

He walked back to his desk to retrieve something, but Kay, briefed by Staunton, knew it was a standard tactic to allow the jury time to absorb the point he had just made.

Henderson then announced the object in his hand as one of the exhibits.

"Mrs. Daniels, please take a look at Exhibit 42 and describe it for the jury."

Kay took the object and immediately felt the encroachment of tears. She pressed her lips together and said to herself, *Hang on. Hang on. Hang on.*

"Mrs. Daniels? Are you having a problem describing the exhibit?"

"No."

"Well, then, please tell the court what you are holding in your hand."

"It's a . . . a ring."

"What sort of ring?"

"A . . . World Series ring."

"What year is inscribed on the ring?"

"1999."

"Is this the ring you saw on either Thomas Scanlon in your office or on the finger in the watch box?"

"I . . . don't know. It looks the same. It could be."

"Mrs. Daniels, are you aware that replicas of World Series rings may be bought in sports specialty stores or on the Internet?"

"No. I didn't know that."

Henderson introduced another exhibit and said, "Please take a look at Exhibit 43 and tell us what it is."

She read the document and sighed. "It's a receipt for a replica of a World Series ring made out to you."

"Mrs. Daniels. You don't know if the ring in the box belonged to Thomas Scanlon, do you?"

"No."

"You don't even know if the finger—assuming there *was* a finger—was Thomas Scanlon's, do you?"

"No."

"In fact, you don't know what happened to Thomas Scanlon at all, do you?"

"I can assume what happened to him."

"But you don't *actually* know. Is that not true?"

She hesitated, then nodded her head.

The court reporter typed: "Witness indicated assent."

Chapter Fifty-Three

"You'll have to do it," MacBride had told Johanna. "I doubt they'd expect *me* to waltz into the courthouse. But the focus up to now has been on me. It's a miracle they've hardly mentioned you. Besides, my picture is now in every major newspaper."

That certainly was true. The size of the reward and the context of the offer even made the national news broadcasts on television. MacBride's photograph—crude and grainy as it was—had been seen by millions.

He was correct, Johanna acknowledged. He was always correct. She had to be the one to kill Kay Daniels. But it was unnerving to go up the wide steps of the Bridgeport courthouse and into the building. This was the third time she had been inside any courthouse—the first two were her appearances for breaking-and-entering in Nassau. The trial wouldn't resume until ten A.M., for some technical reason. But that was perfect. It gave her the time and opportunity to study the layout of the place.

Kay's trial was occurring in courtroom number eight, on the third floor. Johanna passed the armed guard and went through the metal detector in the lobby. She had no obvious weapons—the poison was in a perfume bottle in her pocketbook—and the device sounded no alarm. She wore nondescript clothes—an old black sweater and equally old blue jeans under a khaki jacket. Her hair was dyed black and tied in a severe bun. She wore no makeup. The eyeglasses with clear lenses contributed to the overall effect she was trying to establish. "You don't want any man glancing at your legs, your breasts, or your face," MacBride explained. "The outfit is not just a *disguise* to protect your identity if they look at you. It's to make you look unattractive enough and uninteresting enough so they will look *away* from you."

She took the elevator to the third floor and asked another guard for directions to the ladies' room. He was uniformed but unarmed and, to her irritation, her appearance didn't seem to diminish some interest from him. He was young and reed-thin, with a wisp of a moustache no doubt grown to make him appear older than he was. He smiled more than was necessary while giving her directions. She walked quickly away, certain his eyes followed her down the hallway.

The third floor was surprisingly busy with well-dressed men and women moving with purpose, and whether these people were employees or visitors involved with other cases, none of them paid her any attention. And that was all her appearance deserved anyway, she thought.

She went to the ladies' room and was relieved there was no one present. It was going to have to be here, they had decided. It would be unlikely that Kay would expect MacBride or Johanna to show up at the court, but at the very least she would have people around as they made their way to and from the courtroom. It wouldn't be impossible to get to her but it would be difficult, and success couldn't be guaranteed. But the most important reason for not attacking Kay in a corridor or while exiting the building was the difficulty of escape. Kay could easily recognize Johanna, and if she realized what had been done to her, a call of alarm would almost certainly cause her associates or the guards to make a grab for Johanna.

The problem, of course, then became whether Kay Daniels would feel the urge to visit the rest room at some point. But the trial thus far had lasted all day of each of the five days. It was not an unlikely gamble that Kay at some point would head to the ladies' room. And when she did, Johanna intended to be laying in wait in one of the stalls. But first, she had to acquire a seat in the rear of the courtroom and wait for her target to get up from her place.

There were a half-dozen spectators already in the courtroom but as avid trial aficionados, they had come early to secure the best seats at the front of the room. Johanna sat next to the aisle in the last row of the ancient wooden benches. Over the next forty-five minutes the courtroom gradually filled until all available spaces were occupied. The prosecution team entered just minutes before Kay and her companions showed up. Johanna rested her chin in the cup of her right hand, obscuring the bottom half of her face. Even if Kay was not preoccupied enough to glance her way as she moved up the aisle toward the front of the courtroom, Johanna doubted she would be recognizable. Nevertheless, she was thankful that the group merely continued to their places and sat down.

The judge entered from his chambers at exactly ten o'clock, and, almost immediately, the defense attorney called Eugene Fanning. His testimony was an exercise in futility, Johanna thought with amusement. By the end of the day, Kay Daniels would probably be dead and anything he had to contribute to her defense would die with her. Although Johanna continued to listen to the question-and-answer session as it tiresomely unfolded, her gaze was directed solely toward Kay. At the first sign of movement, she intended to get up and head to the ladies' room. But to her irritation, there was no such movement. At noon, the judge announced a two-hour lunch break, and Johanna was the first out of the room. But after waiting twenty minutes in the rest room, none of the women that entered was Kay. Realizing the defense team had probably left the building for lunch, Johanna made her way down to the food stalls set up by enterprising vendors on the streets outside the court building. She grabbed a soda and a hot dog, consumed them as she took a walk around the building, then went back to the third floor.

Oh no, she thought, as she got off the elevator. The young guard who had given her directions earlier was walking toward her. What to do, she wondered? A brief smile to be polite and keep moving? Or ignore him completely, even if he spoke to her? The brush-off might hurt his feelings and cause some form of lingering resentment that would exacerbate his focus upon her. But smiling would only encourage him, probably with the same result. Before she had come to a decision, he was upon her and stopped with a wide smile.

"Afternoon, Miss!"

He couldn't have been more than twenty, she guessed. The moustache's scrawniness was explained by his receding hair. The green nametag on his shirt pocket read "Welch."

"Good afternoon," she said without emphasis and looked over his shoulder as if she was searching for someone.

"I see you found a seat easily enough. I knew you would."

Oh Christ, she thought. He had noticed where she headed after leaving the ladies' room this morning.

"Yes, thanks." She looked at her watch. "It will be starting soon. Better get going if I want to keep my seat."

"Not to worry. If you'll be coming every day, I'll be sure to save you a seat. Just let me know. My name's Billy."

"Great, thanks." She nodded and walked around him. She headed quickly to the courtroom and took her seat with relief. She consoled herself that he was interested in her for one reason only. She had shown him some interest that morning, however fleeting, and like many lonely men, he took it for more than it actually was. He was a lowly guard, not even given the responsibility of a firearm, surrounded on a daily basis by high-powered lawyers and judges. He was insignificant, and her inquiry this morning had given him some significance. He would remember her, though, she sensed. But at least her appearance was sufficiently different from her normal look that she decided not to dwell further on the guy. She had a job to do, and she needed to focus.

The afternoon session began promptly at two o'clock. She let out a silent sigh. Now she had to listen to the prosecutor cross-examine Fanning.

"Mr. Fanning. You testified this morning that you fabricated your own death in order to help Mrs. Daniels lure this Nikolas Seifer into the open. Is that correct?"

"Yes, it is."

"You went to a great deal of trouble and risked considerable personal embarrassment with this . . . stratagem."

"I felt it was worth it."

"No doubt you should be commended for your behavior. But is it not true that you undertook all this merely on Mrs. Daniels's say-so?"

"Yes."

"The fact that you went to the extraordinary measure of fabricating your own death doesn't mean that Mrs. Daniels was telling the truth, does it?"

"No, I suppose not."

"The fact that you acceded to her request merely meant that you believed her?"

"Yes, I did believe her."

"But if Mrs. Daniels was telling a lie and believed in that lie herself, it would mean you did what you did for a lie. Isn't that correct?"

"I suppose so. *If* it was a lie."

On and on they droned, the hours passing as attorneys from

both sides split hairs on interpretation and inflection, on motivation and speculation. Thank God she wasn't a juror, Johanna thought. How were they going to come to a decision based on this sort of testimony? Either the defendant did it or she didn't. As the minute hand on her watch slowly made its way toward the four o'clock mark, Johanna sensed it was not going to happen this afternoon. She understood that proceedings usually finished around five P.M.

Then she realized something unusual was happening at the defense table where her attention, as before, was focused on Kay. While the attorney, Staunton, stood in the front of the witness box asking more questions on re-direct, the white-haired man sitting next to Kay suddenly reached into his pocket and pulled out something. He stared at it with great interest and then—it was as if he had been struck—reacted with a gasp. He touched Kay on the arm and, when she turned, he showed her the object. Johanna could now see that it was a cell phone. Someone had evidently sent a text message. The man had to be Paul Keating, Johanna realized, remembering the newspaper articles she had read. He and Kay exchanged some words and then he stood up and walked down the aisle toward the door. Johanna saw a smile on the man's face.

The questioning of the witness continued despite this brief interruption. Johanna hardly paid any attention. She decided she would wait until four-forty-five and then leave. It would have to be done all over again tomorrow. Or perhaps MacBride might come up with an alternative method to get to Kay Daniels. It was always going to be difficult, and she had little confidence in the plan. There was too much risk of exposure, too little of the protection they were accustomed to. She suppressed a sigh and continued to wait.

The next time she looked at her watch it was four-forty-three. Two more minutes and then she could get out of here. In the front row, someone else apparently had decided they'd had enough. A young woman stood and excused herself to the other spectators, then made her way down the aisle. As she reached the last row of benches, she stopped. Johanna, staring at Kay, was peripherally aware of the girl halting and, disinterested, glanced at her. The girl yelled.

"Hey!"

Oh fuck! Johanna thought. It was Kay's daughter. She had recognized her. The girl ran back up the aisle, yelling.

"It's her! It's her! She's here!"

The judge called for order. The bailiff stood, then ran toward Kelley. Kay was on her feet, her head moving rapidly from Kelley to where her daughter was pointing. Johanna looked directly into Kay's eyes. She saw the moment of recognition but then couldn't wait. She had to leave—now.

The majority of the spectators had also stood but as she was in the last row, there was no one blocking the door. She pushed through the doors and ran down the corridor away from the elevators. Before she entered the courtroom that morning, she had determined where the stairs were located. MacBride had trained her well, she now realized. Always be aware of the bolt holes.

She was fit—the daily calisthenics that MacBride insisted on for them both saw to that—and she carried little extra weight. Within seconds she had reached the door to the stairs, but as her hand touched the handle, she was jerked back, almost falling.

"What's going on here?"

It was that fool guard, Welch. He had pulled her by the jacket collar. There was still hope, she saw by the look on his face. Suspicion fought with sympathy. She only had a moment before the people in the court—the bailiff, Kay, who knows who else?—would be upon them. She had to do it. There was no option, she would tell MacBride. She had to do it.

"Them!" She pointed behind him. Naive, inexperienced, he did the natural thing. He turned his head a fraction, but it was enough. She struck the left side of his face with the heel of her taut palm—a blow learned from MacBride—driving Welch's cheekbone into his eye. He collapsed without a sound.

She went through the door and took the concrete stairs two at a time. It was only three floors. She strained to control her breathing, knowing she had to slow down when she reached the lobby door. She couldn't burst through gasping for breath. One more floor. Would someone in Courtroom Eight be smart enough to phone downstairs to alert them? Was there some kind of panic button on the bench the judge would push? She didn't know. She didn't have time to guess, to worry. The door stenciled "Lobby" was already approaching. One further deep inhalation, and she opened it.

There was no alarm, no yelling, no unusual movement. Everything seemed as normal as she had observed earlier in the day. The armed guard, in fact, was looking toward the front door, his back to the lobby. She exhaled, took another deep breath, and forced herself to walk toward the door.

At this late hour, the majority of people in the lobby seemed as if they were leaving the building. Of course, she realized. It was approaching closing time for the courts and the support staff. They would all be heading home. But apparently someone still had business in the building. As she went through one of the front doors, she noticed two men reach the top of the steps headed for the lobby. She gasped, recognizing them both. One was the white-haired man from the defense table, Paul Keating. The other was a ruddy-faced man, looking nervously around him. Gentleman Jimmy Doyle.

Chapter Fifty-Four

"Will they let you go now, Mom?"

Kay smiled. "Not exactly. But things look a whole lot better than they have been."

They were eating dinner in their hotel room. Armed bodyguards hired by Staunton stood outside.

"But she killed that security man. They have to believe you, now."

"Well, that doesn't prove she killed Amy Fanning."

Kay was not surprised she was now able to distinguish the nuances of how an attorney thought. Surrounded by lawyers for the past few months and immersed in the hair-splitting that passed for the adversarial process of the trial, she knew that Johanna killing the security guard was helpful to her case but it wasn't enough to set her free.

Of far greater value was the impending testimony of Jimmy Doyle. "A million dollars puts people's loyalty to the test," Gene had said. And Gentleman Jimmy had failed that test. He had called the 800-number and agreed to testify against Seifer.

"Why did they cancel the trial for tomorrow? Didn't Mr. Staunton introduce him as a witness?" Kelley asked.

"Not technically. He merely told the judge that he had a new witness that would verify the existence of Seifer. He had to question Jimmy Doyle at length to prepare him for his testimony. He needed time, and given the importance of the witness, the judge agreed."

"Did you see the look on Mr. Henderson's face? I thought he was going to faint!"

Kay smiled again. "Yes. He realized Doyle will verify the existence of Seifer and what he does for a living. With that testimony and the murder of the security guard right outside the courtroom, I should imagine even the most hostile of jurors would have a hard time voting guilty."

At least that's what Staunton had told her after the judge closed that day's session. He also insisted that she and Kelley stay in a hotel room in the city rather than return home.

"God, I hope so. I wish—" Kelley looked down at her plate, moving the food around with her fork.

"What, sweetie? What do you wish?"

"I wish we could go back to Florida and get away from it all."

"Soon. Mr. Staunton said it will be over very soon."

"And then we can go back to Florida for good?"

"It depends."

"On what?"

It depended on her selling the business, but also it depended on Gene. What were his intentions? Would he feel as she now did—that it was time for a change? Too much had happened to return to her old life. Or would he want to return to his firm and continue as before?

She pointed at Kelley's plate. "On you finishing your vegetables. Now, eat those carrots."

Chapter Fifty-Five

Old habits really do die hard, Seifer thought when Gentleman Jimmy Doyle walked into the bar. A million dollars was waiting for him in a matter of days, but he still couldn't control his urges. Thank Christ for that.

The music in the bar was not just ear splitting. It was almost physical in its assault. How the hell were you supposed to pick up someone in a place like this, Seifer wondered? And yet it didn't seem to inhibit the majority of the people here. The place was mobbed with men, young and old, fat and thin, some dancing in intimate proximity, the majority talking, persuading, seducing strangers to leave together for the night.

When Johanna told him about Doyle and they had watched reports on the Six O'clock News about Staunton's "surprise witness," he had immediately tried to identify the gay pick-up places in central Bridgeport. He knew Jimmy, who lived in Manhattan, didn't own a car, so it would have to be somewhere central within walking distance or perhaps a cab-ride away. But Jimmy was always discreet and wouldn't have wanted a stranger knowing where he had been taken. So it had to be within walking distance of one of the few hotels in the small city.

It was Johanna who had extracted the information from the desk clerk at the motel where they were staying. A smile, a swish of her hips, and the clerk was more than happy to disclose the gay and lesbian places in the area. It was the O-zone on Whitney Street that Seifer felt was the safest bet. Johanna waited in a car outside the other possibility, four blocks away.

He got there early but even in midweek, it was busy. Requiring a table in a corner, he was relieved that one of them was occupied solely by a heavyset man in his fifties, balding, and dressed in a well-tailored blue suit. Perfect, thought Seifer, and walked over to the table.

"Mind if I join you?" he asked the man.

A smile of relief appeared on the man's face. "Not at all. I really am coming apart."

Seifer stared at him, not understanding. The man smiled again and explained: *"Join me. I'm coming apart."* He shrugged, now embarrassed. "Sorry. I make jokes when I'm nervous."

Seifer forced himself to smile. "No need to be nervous. I don't bite."

"Damn. I was hoping you like to bite. Oh hell, there I go again."

Seifer felt he needed to control this man right away. He sensed a physical response would facilitate that. He touched the man on his right arm, a reassuring pat.

"No need to be nervous at all. You're probably more experienced than I am, anyway."

The man looked at him as if he were a piece of meat. "I don't know about that."

Seifer wore a pressed pair of blue jeans and a black leather jacket and boots. He had no idea what a typical gay man found attractive but decided he couldn't go too far wrong in that outfit. He suspected his muscular physique would more than compensate for any slip-up in attire.

"Well," he said, "let's have a drink and compare histories, shall we?"

The man nodded his head several times, his eagerness all too obvious. He gestured toward a waiter and ordered two bottles of Stella Artois.

An hour passed. Seifer let the man, whose name was Donald, do the majority of the talking. A salesman, he was married and "exploring his real side," he confided to Seifer. He was based in Minneapolis, peddling software on the east coast for a company that Seifer had never heard of. As he babbled on, Seifer, who had positioned himself against the wall and directly behind Donald and the front door, was aware of everyone who entered. Each table had little red candles in ornate bronze bowls that illuminated the faces of those at the tables. Almost immediately, he had extinguished the candle. Donald had given him a puzzled look, but it was momentary.

At a few minutes past ten, Gentleman Jimmy Doyle entered the bar. Seifer, on a visit to the rest room at the opposite side of the bar, had already established that a newcomer would be hard-pressed to distinguish anyone at Donald's table. The combination of the pulsing, colored lights and the crush of dancers in the middle of the floor made it difficult to make out anybody in the corners. That the candle on the table had been extinguished also helped. But to further conceal himself, Seifer leaned in close to Donald so that the other man's bulk also afforded him some protective cover.

Jimmy, dapper as ever in a blue blazer with bright shiny buttons, pressed charcoal slacks and a crimson cravat, did what Jimmy always did. He headed toward the roughest looking men in the place. One of them evidently had come directly from a construction site. Blonde, in his mid-twenties, with holes in his jeans, he was Jimmy's target. Within minutes, no doubt flashing promises along with his wallet, Jimmy was entangled around the man as they danced to a slow song by some unfamiliar girl group.

Seifer suppressed a smile. Jimmy had earned his nickname not just because of his manners or his always-spiffy outfits. He disliked men like himself, men who knew where the forks went on the dinner table, men who enjoyed museums and galleries, men who had education. He preferred what he called "rough trade."

Let's hope he's already found it, Seifer thought. Donald was getting equally amorous and suggesting Seifer accompany him back to his hotel. But Seifer continued to stall, waiting to see where Jimmy went because he intended to follow.

Perhaps Jimmy was pressed for time because he had to get up early to testify at the trial tomorrow, but it seemed mere minutes passed before he and his new friend made their way to the door. As the door closed behind them, Seifer stood.

"I've got to go," he said to Donald. "I'll be back in a few minutes."

Donald was clearly disappointed but nodded, looking forlorn. Seifer struggled to push his way to the door through the throng of dancers. When he finally made it outside, he was startled by the sudden silence. His head ached from the music and the lights, and the cool night air was refreshing. He looked around but saw no one on the sidewalk in either direction. Realizing the construction worker probably arrived in a vehicle, he jogged around to the parking lot at the rear of the building. There they were, headed toward a filthy pick-up trick.

He looked around. The lighting from a single lamppost was meager. But he had no alternative. He had to risk the possibility of someone in neighboring buildings observing what was about to happen. He consoled himself that this was a business district and the buildings were unlikely to house anybody at this hour.

The two men had almost reached the truck. He would have to take care of the younger man first. The guy appeared strong, no doubt conditioned from the daily physical labor, and even if uncouth and unprofessional, could be muscular enough to cause a problem. Yes, Seifer decided, him first because he had the advantage of surprise. He reached down to his right leg, pulled up the jeans and removed a hunter's knife from its sheath.

The two men had eyes only for each other and were unaware of Seifer as he jogged up to them.

"Hey," he said, tapping the young man on the left shoulder.

Seifer knew the vast majority of men were right-handed and were at a disadvantage if they turned around to their left. The man indeed reflexively turned, allowing Seifer a clear view of his neck. Seifer brought the scalpel-sharp knife in a short arc across the man's windpipe, stepping back immediately to avoid the spurt of blood.

The man tried to say something and simultaneously reach a hand to his neck. Seifer ignored him and moved toward Jimmy who had remained motionless, staring not at Seifer but at his companion who had now dropped to his knees, both hands pressed against his neck.

Seifer never wasted words during an attack. It was pointless to ask Jimmy "Why?" or to condemn him with a curse. A waste of words, and a waste of time. He buried the knife into Jimmy's chest. Jimmy said a long "Nooooo" but ignoring him, Seifer removed the knife and plunged it twice more into Jimmy's belly. Then he pushed him to the ground.

The younger man had now fallen onto his side in a vaguely fetal position. He was still alive but was dying with the rapid loss of blood and probably was aware he was dying. Seifer looked back at Jimmy. The Gentleman was already dead.

"What's going on here? What's happening?"

Seifer turned. It was Donald. The fool! Why couldn't he stay inside? No doubt he suspected Seifer was not coming back and had pursued him. Too bad.

Donald said, "Oh my God! Those men. What's happened?"

He looked at the bodies on the ground and then gasped when he saw the knife in Seifer's hand.

"You've attacked them? Why?"

Seifer had to end this as quickly as possible. He didn't answer the question, and walked toward Donald.

"No!" said Donald. To Seifer's astonishment, Donald reached under his coat and removed a gun.

Jesus, thought Seifer, staring at the Thirty-Eight Special now pointed at him. It was ridiculous—to go out to a fat, bald idiot in a parking lot of a faggot bar. No, it was not going to happen. Donald, he realized immediately, hadn't flicked the safety. No doubt he carried the gun for protection on his travels and was not a professional.

Seifer flung the knife underhand at Donald, the substantial bulk of the man offering an easy target. Perhaps the layers of fat diminished the impact of the blow reaching his brain. Donald merely looked down in surprise at the knife sticking in his chest and then raised his head to look curiously at Seifer. But Seifer had already moved. Not seeing Seifer, the man looked down again at the knife, then moved his left hand toward it. Seifer was now behind him. He placed his right leg immediately in front of Donald's left, and pushed him hard. The large man went facedown, the weight of his body forcing the knife fully into his chest. Seifer rolled him over, then felt his neck pulse. There was no movement.

He removed the knife, wiped it clean on Donald's jacket and replaced it in the sheath. Then he walked the four blocks to where Johanna was waiting in the parked car.

Chapter Fifty-Six

"He exists," said Sinclair. "And he's in this city. There can't be any doubt about it now."

"That still doesn't help Kay Daniels," replied Mo. "Henderson wants his pound of flesh."

Jimmy Doyle was never a witness, had never given any testimony; therefore his claims were inadmissible. Staunton pleaded in the judge's chambers that the obvious murder of the key witness clearly substantiated Kay's claim. He saw sympathy in the judge's face but the judge was obligated to honor the letter of the law, as Henderson argued. The judge even reminded Staunton not to introduce Doyle's murder into the summary argument.

Staunton's final witnesses were disposed of in a single day. Kay's broker testified about the transfer of $2 million from her accounts. Henderson made short work of the witness. The money transfer meant nothing in the context of Amy Fanning's death. Business owners dealt with that type of money on a daily basis. The final witness, a doctor, tried to make much of the location of the stab wound—between the second and third rib, the closest route to the heart—and the depth of penetration, arguing about the strength required to inflict it. But again Henderson swatted the arguments away with little effort. Staunton closed his defense and Henderson began his summary argument.

Mo and Sinclair sat in the court and listened to the prosecutor. When Henderson finished, both knew the summation was devastating and, even to the most objective juror, certainly decisive. To his credit, the prosecutor focused on the facts, making it so evident that Kay Daniels had killed Amy Fanning there was no need to speculate on what occurred in Ridgewood Court on January 27. The jury could come to its own conclusion, and that conclusion was obvious to the two detectives.

It was late afternoon when Henderson returned to his seat. The judge decided to end the session for the day. Staunton would have his say in the morning.

"Let's go get a drink," said Sinclair, and they headed to the Gallery Bar down the street from the courthouse.

"I hope you feel as bad as I do," Mo said when they had been served their Rolling Rock.

"Of course I do."

Of course he felt horrible. He had never believed Kay Daniels, even about her husband's death. It was his testimony that had done plenty of damage. But it was clear that she had been telling the truth. What other explanation could there possibly be for the death of Jimmy Doyle and the other two men? It was beyond coincidence that the key witness had so conveniently been murdered. And in such a manner. Three men all killed by a knife. That one man could have done all that convinced Sinclair of the existence of Kay's mystery man. He'd even gone to Henderson and asked for time to investigate the murder of three men outside the bar. But the district attorney had pushed back.

"I'm not going to stop the trial. That's not going to happen, Detective. This Doyle getting himself killed still doesn't prove Kay Daniels is innocent."

Mo took a swallow of beer, then said, "We'll keep looking for him. It won't end even if she does go to prison."

"We've been looking for him for so long. And never been

able to find him."

"But now he's had to do his own killings. He's coming out of the shadows."

"That's what I find puzzling. Why he bothered to kill Doyle. Sure Doyle's testimony would have helped the defense, but so what? If Kay Daniels is found not guilty, it doesn't put Seifer in jeopardy."

"Not by her. But we'd have to investigate Doyle's claims. After all, it would be sworn testimony in a murder trial. And if we were able to arrest Seifer at some point, Doyle would then be a witness against him. Besides, clearly Seifer has it in for Kay Daniels. He wants her found guilty."

"Well, we'll work the bar angle. A few of the men there saw him. We now have a description. Time is on our side."

"It's not on Kay Daniels's side."

The following morning, the trial began at nine o'clock sharp. Staunton stood and immediately requested a conference in the judge's chambers. He and Henderson then disappeared with the judge and didn't return for fifteen minutes. Henderson was red-faced as he walked to his seat.

The judge said, "Mr. Staunton."

"Your honor. With your permission, I wish to re-open the defense case."

"Very well. Carry on."

"Your honor, I call Henry Pierce to the stand."

Chapter Fifty-Seven

"Mr. Pierce, do you know of a man who calls himself Nikolas Seifer?"

"I do."

"How do you know him?"

"He murdered my wife. And he persuaded me to murder a woman by the name of Elizabeth Carlisle."

The entire group of spectators seemed to gasp as one. Even the jury members, Kay noticed, reacted as if they had been struck. And why not? She, too, had been startled when Staunton rushed to her hotel room last night to tell her that Detective Frank Sinclair had called him. A man, identifying himself as a beneficiary, had contacted Sinclair and wished to testify at the trial. Kay was puzzled when Staunton related the man's name. "Henry Pierce" was unfamiliar to her. It was not among Seifer's newspaper clippings; of that she was fairly certain. But then she realized: Of course! Pierce must have been the next beneficiary after her!

"You're going to go free, Kay!" Staunton said, clearly excited. "This is dynamite testimony."

"You believe me now?" she asked. She had wondered from the first if the young lawyer ever really believed her story. Defense attorneys, she knew, didn't need to believe in their clients to put on a vigorous defense. But she had always sensed there was a doubt, however marginal, in Staunton's mind.

Staunton grinned, the first time she had seen him do so.

"I always believed you, Kay. My problem was knowing how difficult it would be to persuade the jury to believe you."

Henry Pierce, Kay thought, was a funny-looking man. Bald-headed, with enormous spectacles, he had an intelligent face but his eyes appeared to roam as he spoke. He was small in stature, seemingly undistinguished in appearance, but apparently he had a fine mind, and it was that which Julia Barlow had found attractive when they'd met at a meeting of the development committee at the University Art Gallery.

"I was the Curator of Babylonian art," he explained in response to Staunton's question. "I had acquired my PhD at the University and I began work at the gallery immediately after. I was also an adjunct professor teaching an undergraduate course. You could say I've spent most of my adult life at the University. I was very happy."

"How old were you when you met Ms. Barlow?"

"Thirty-five."

"Were you married?"

"Gracious, no. I never held much attraction for the fairer sex."

"But you established a relationship with Ms. Barlow?"

"Yes."

"How old was she?"

"When we met, she was forty-eight years old."

"Had she ever been married, to your knowledge?"

"She told me she had not."

"You were unaware of her wealth and the wealth of her family, is that not correct?"

"Yes." He seemed embarrassed. His eyes stopped roaming and remained fixed on a spot next to Staunton's feet. "I was fairly . . . unsophisticated about such matters. My interests were in art, my research, and my teaching."

"But Ms. Barlow approached you after that initial committee

meeting and suggested you have luncheon together?"

"Yes, that's correct. We had luncheon and then several dinner engagements. A few months passed and she . . . she proposed."

"Why did Ms. Barlow propose to you?"

Henry shrugged. "I never really knew. I suspected it was because I didn't pursue her. She found me . . . unthreatening, I imagine."

"Would you say Ms. Barlow was a physically attractive woman?"

"No. She herself said she was 'ugly as a stump.' "

"Did you love her?"

"I . . . I don't know what love is, really. I imagine so."

"How long were you married to Ms. Barlow?"

"Twenty years. Then Nikolas Seifer came into our lives."

"Please tell the court the circumstances."

Henry sighed. "Things were not going well with Julia and me. She had insisted I leave the University and work for her company. Her father had passed away, and she was suspicious of the man who was now running the business. It was absurd. I had no financial knowledge. I was an academic. But she insisted, and when Julia insisted, she tended to get her way."

"So you became managing director of a merchant bank?"

"Yes. As I said, it was absurd. Naturally, things went from bad to worse. The business started to decline. We had acrimonious fights. She was worried that the company her great-grandfather had founded was in danger. There was tension between us continually. I made a decision to bring in an experienced man from Wall Street. She fought it for reasons I never understood. I later suspected it was because he was . . . he was Jewish. In any event, she forced him to leave after a few months. The incident made the newspapers, I understand. He was a highly regarded professional in the financial world and had to be compensated substantially when his contract was terminated prematurely. Then there was gossip in the society pages when Julia and I had an argument at an opera premiere at the Court Theater. I can only assume these incidents brought us to the attention of Mr. Seifer."

"Please tell the court how Nikolas Seifer contacted you."

"It was about a month after I had buried Julia. She had died of cardiac arrhythmia. She had been shopping at Marshall Fields—shopping gave her great pleasure—and she collapsed in the store."

"Did your wife have a history of heart problems?"

"Some slight blood pressure issues, but she took medication to control it."

"Was an autopsy performed?"

"No."

"All right. So how did Seifer approach you?"

"He came to my office—at the bank. He said he had some important information to share about my wife. So I agreed to see him without an appointment. That's when he told me he had . . . he had killed her."

"Did he say how he had killed her?"

"Yes. He said an associate of his had poisoned her with a substance that mimicked the symptoms of cardiac arrhythmia."

"Did he explain why he murdered your wife?"

"Yes. He explained it all. He called it his *system.*"

Kay was mesmerized. It was almost like Seifer had a prepared speech, a rehearsed presentation even. The arguments, the examples, the rationales that Henry Pierce now recited were the same as those Seifer had used on her in Juno's.

When Henry paused, Staunton asked, "How did you react when this man demanded half of your assets?"

"I refused, of course. I felt he was a charlatan."

"But you changed your mind?"

"Yes. I . . . I felt I had no choice. He showed me the poison. I felt . . . coerced. I also felt—"

"Yes? What else, Mr. Pierce?"

"Well, I felt . . . free. Mr. Seifer kept repeating that point. That I was now free. That I was wealthy. And I had him to thank. I began to think about it and realized perhaps he had in fact helped me. I wasn't sure if Julia was contemplating divorce, but if she had done so, I had signed a prenuptial agreement. I would have been a fifty-five-year-old ex-academic without a pension and very few assets of my own."

"But despite the prenuptial agreement, your wife left you her fortune in her will?"

"Actually she had never made a will. Under Illinois law, when a person dies intestate, the surviving spouse gets everything."

"So you acquiesced to Mr. Seifer's demands?"

"Yes. Not initially. But after thinking about it, I decided it was the safest thing to do."

"All right. So how did things proceed from that point?"

"I liquidated all the assets. Sold the bank to a larger institution. I then gave Mr. Seifer half of the proceeds."

"Did he leave you alone at that point?"

"Yes. He left, and I didn't hear from him again until about two years later."

"What were the circumstances of that reappearance?"

"He came to my home. He gave me a folder with information about a woman in New York. Elizabeth Carlisle. He told me he expected me to kill her."

"How did you respond?"

"I refused, naturally. Told him he was being ridiculous, that I could never do such a thing. But I felt threatened. By him and by the police."

"The police threatened you?"

"No, not in that fashion. I meant, Mr. Seifer invoked the police. That he would furnish them with information proving I was responsible for my wife's death. He called it 'circumstantial evidence.' "

"Did he clarify what exactly this evidence was?"

"The bottle of poison. When he'd first shown up at my office, he had given me the bottle of poison to inspect. I had foolishly taken it from him. And so my fingerprints were on it. Then there was the matter of selling the company so rapidly after my wife's death. He was very persuasive. The accumulation of detail was overwhelming. That, plus the fact that I felt under duress from him physically, made up my mind. Besides, he explained how . . . how easy it would be."

Tears came to his eyes. "I'm terribly sorry. I'm so terribly ashamed."

Staunton requested a brief recess to allow the distraught man to recompose himself. The judge agreed.

"Now, Mr. Pierce," asked Staunton, fifteen minutes later. "Please tell the court how Elizabeth Carlisle died."

Henry detailed the events in St. Patrick's Cathedral from six months before. Kay noted even the judge seemed rapt at the little man in the witness box. She felt sorry for Henry Pierce, realized the pressures he had been under and how easy it was to succumb. She had almost given in herself, but after Janet was killed and Kelley was taken from her, she had found the resolve not to allow Seifer to continue. She had remained quiet with her own father's atrocities and had not confronted him or brought him to the attention of the authorities. Instead she had run from the problem. And she had run from Bernard instead of standing and confronting him. So she vowed, *never again.* Innocent people would no longer suffer because of her.

Staunton finished his questioning and turned to the prosecutor.

"Your witness."

★ ★ ★ ★ ★

"Mr. Pierce, is everything you've told the court today the truth?" asked Henderson.

"Yes. I took the oath to tell the truth."

"You're telling the court that you knew your wife was murdered and didn't inform the police?"

"Yes."

"You're telling the court that you then killed a complete stranger because this man Seifer requested you to do so?"

"Yes."

"Do you know the defendant, Kay Daniels?"

"No. We've never met."

"Have you ever been to Connecticut before?"

"No."

"But you've come here today for the million-dollar reward, haven't you?"

Henry seemed puzzled. "No. I'm worth several million dollars. I don't need a reward."

Henderson's face again went red. "Mr. Pierce, if you *are* telling the truth, you're aware that your testimony will almost certainly mean you'll be arrested for first-degree murder?"

"I'm aware of that."

For the first time since he had strode so confidently into the courtroom on the opening day, Henderson seemed at a loss for words.

"But—but why would you do that?"

Henry shrugged. "It's time."

Kay stared at him. *It's time.* What did that mean? Had Pierce argued with himself over what he had done? Had he discovered a conscience? Even pitied her in her predicament, knowing surely what she had gone through with Seifer?

The prosecutor seemed lost. He shook his head slightly. Then he tried a different tack.

"Mr. Pierce, did you kill Amy Fanning?"

"No."

"Did you witness Nikolas Seifer kill Amy Fanning?"

"No."

"Did Nikolas Seifer admit to you that he killed Amy Fanning?"

"No."

"So to your knowledge, the defendant Kay Daniels is not innocent of the charges against her?"

"I have no knowledge of Kay Daniels. I only have knowledge of Nikolas Seifer."

Chapter Fifty-Eight

". . . one week after being found not guilty, Kay Daniels is believed to be in Florida at the horse farm of Boston attorney Eugene Fanning. Sources tell *Action News Nine* that a July wedding is planned by the couple. Meanwhile, an FBI spokesman confirmed that a nationwide manhunt is now underway for the man known variously as Nikolas Seifer or John MacBride, believed responsible for multiple killings, and his accomplice, known as Mary Ellis or Johanna Ellis.

"In a related development, Henry Pierce of Chicago has waived his rights to rapid extradition to New York City. NYPD has confirmed that Mr. Pierce will be charged with first-degree murder in the death of socialite Elizabeth Carlisle last year. And now, back to the studio . . ."

As she had done for the previous five days, Kay clung to the haunches of the stallion as it thundered through the fields toward the Atlantic shore. She felt the now-familiar surge of power in the animal beneath her, felt the joy of her control of this half-ton meld of bone, muscle, and flesh, and—most intensely—felt an almost forgotten sense of freedom.

This is how it should be for everyone, she thought. Unencumbered by fear and anxiety, free to experience the sensation of being alive. How close it had come to all being taken away from her! Not just her freedom but Kelley and Gene. Thank God for Matthew Staunton. And thank God, especially, for Henry

Pierce. Why had he done it? Why had he come forward and traded his freedom for hers? He had smiled at her as he walked from the witness stand that afternoon. She didn't see him again. But she promised herself she would visit him in prison to try to arrive at some understanding.

The only other mystery remaining, she thought, was Mr. Scanlon. Neither his body nor his car had been located. She and Gene had discussed it during the celebratory dinner the night of the verdict. Their best guess was that Scanlon, in tracking Marilyn Jarvis, had visited her "college classmate" in Primrose Lane and Seifer—already aware he had been followed from Juno's—no doubt invited the investigator into the house. A touch of cyanide, a knife in the back, whatever means was at hand was surely enough to take care of the unsuspecting investigator.

So it was over. She and Gene and Kelley could get on with a new life. She sensed Barney was tiring at the extreme workout. Kay felt pleased with herself that she was now able to sense these things. How different she felt! A few short months ago, she'd been terrified of horses. Now she had embraced riding as a passionate avocation. But it was just one little thing of the many things she intended to change about her life.

She saw the pearly turquoise of the ocean's edge ahead and slowed the horse to a canter. She knew Barney was well aware of the hollow with the abundance of alfalfa that was approaching. It was his new treat for allowing her to work him out so vigorously. She brought the horse to a stop and with easy elegance, dismounted and walked him over to the thick undergrowth. She patted his shanks as he ate with gusto.

"Not too much, Barney," she said. "You don't want to get a fat ass like mine."

The noise Seifer made was slight, but she was expecting it, and turned to face him as he came from behind a screen of bushes and approached her.

"Strange," he said. "You don't seem your nervous self anymore."

Kay looked at Seifer, at the long, serrated knife he held in his right hand. "I don't need to be frightened anymore."

"Oh? Well you should be, Kay. You really should be. You've caused me so much trouble. Such a mess. Such a bloody fucking mess."

There was an instant when she had to swallow her terror, to trust her instincts, to simply *believe.* He walked toward her, then stopped a half-dozen paces from her. A look of puzzlement moved over his face.

"You're remarkably calm for someone confronting her own death."

"I'm not confronting my own death. I'm confronting yours."

She raised her arm and pointed toward a bluff atop the dunes about two hundred yards away.

"I'm told professional hunters call it a *hide.*"

Seifer looked uncertain and turned in the direction where her arm pointed.

"What are you talking about?"

"Angelo Delacroce says hello."

"What?"

"Unlike everyone else, Mr. Delacroce doesn't want you arrested. Apparently, you'd have too much to tell. Even a murderer like you might tempt the district attorney into a plea bargain given that you know where so many Mafia bodies are buried—so to say. Mr. Delacroce doesn't look forward to that. So he asked my friend Gene if I would do him a favor."

Seifer looked at her, at the shrubbery on the bluff, and then back at her. "What favor?"

"To be a sitting duck. To lure you." She smiled for the first time in all their encounters, a smile of genuine warmth. "I told him I'd be delighted. Apparently the Delacroce Family has found someone like you. To replace you. A former military man, funny enough. A professional."

The first shot, intended to prevent further motor activity, severed his spinal cord near the second cervical vertebra. He fell to his knees with a piercing scream.

Kay forced herself not to turn away. She looked down at him, no pity in her heart, at the face twisted in agony. "A professional sniper."

The second bullet shattered his cerebellum, flinging shards of bone, brains, and bloody tissue across the hollow.

She turned away from the dead man and walked toward her horse. Johanna, she'd been told, was waiting in a hotel twelve miles away in Miramar. If not already, she would be picked up and, with Seifer, would end up in the Atlantic Ocean. That was the deal. Kay had agreed to it, agreed to the daily pattern the Delacroce man had outlined. So every day since she had arrived, she left the farm and the bodyguards behind and, the only time of day or night she would be alone, took the horse out on the same route. If Seifer was watching—and they all expected he was—there was only one obvious place, the hollow with the alfalfa where she always stopped, where he could confront her.

She picked up the reins. "Come on, Barney. Let's go home."

The reaction didn't *really* set in until she was safely in Gene's arms, able to *allow* herself to react, to be normal . . . or at least as normal as she could be, given the circumstances.

Gene stayed silent, at first. Merely held her, comforted her, before eventually putting it all into words

"It had to be done," he said eventually. "And it was done, and you're safe—thank God—and if you ever, ever, put yourself at risk for *anything*, ever again, I will . . ." Whereupon he stopped. He knew her, now . . . knew her strengths, but also her vulnerabilities. He wasn't even going to *suggest* paddling her ass, which was what he'd been about to say.

And she knew it. They were that close, now; she was coming to know his speech patterns, his way of thinking.

"You weren't worried about me—you were just worried about covering your own butt," Kay said with a chuckle. "And I don't blame you. After all, a sworn officer of the court helping to organize an assassination . . ."

"I can live with it. Sometimes the law doesn't work . . . *can't* work the way it should." Gene sighed, pulled her even closer, were that possible. "God I was worried about you, Kay. Now that it's over I can't even imagine how I could have *let* you set yourself up as bait like that."

"It was safe enough," she replied, the words emerging in a mumble against his chest.

And, she insisted to herself, it had been. Delacroce's current hit man had assured her of that and she had believed him.

Gene's first reaction to Angelo Delacroce's plan was to refuse to put Kay in such obvious danger, but she convinced him—eventually—to see the sense of letting her be the bait.

"How can you be sure he won't just shoot you from cover?" An obvious question, but that one, at least, could be easily countered.

"Look at his record," she said. "He's a knife man. Always has been."

"And a knife can be *thrown,* in case you haven't thought of that." Gene shook his head as if the gesture could add emphasis to his words. "How can you be so goddamned certain he'll give Delacroce's guy time for a shot?"

"Trust me on that one." And, strangely enough, Kay trusted *herself* on that point. Totally. Enough to risk her life. She knew Seifer; he would have to brag, have to explain to her—probably in gloating, lurid detail—what gruesome plans he had for her. He would *have* to do that, wouldn't be able not to do it.

Easy enough to believe now that it was over.

Epilogue

"Where the fu—" Mo caught herself, aware of Frank's opinion of her language. "Where the hell are you taking me?" she asked, pointing to the highway sign. "Ossining? I thought we were going on a nice Sunday drive."

"You'll see," he replied, and eased the Chevy down Exit 47 off I-95.

"There's only one thing to see in Ossining, Frankie. A prison."

"Just wait, can't you?"

"Sing Sing? This is your notion of a date? I have to say, Frankie, I'm not very impressed."

"We'll have plenty of time for dates."

"Well, that's a relief."

After they reached the prison, she waited in the car while he dealt at some administrative office outside the largest building on the site. Apparently it was arranged, for just minutes later he returned and escorted her a few hundred yards to the rear of the factory-like structure.

"A cemetery?" Mo asked when she saw the sign and the area beyond the fence. "Boy, Frankie, I wonder how you show a girl a *bad* time?"

He tried to make his look harsh. "Sometimes you deserve a good spanking."

She batted her eyes. "I should be so lucky." And she added: "Tease."

Again, prior arrangements must have been made for he spoke

briefly to a custodian at the gate who gave him a map with a location highlighted in red ink. They walked through the surprisingly tidy landscape.

Finally, he stopped and pointed. The headstone was small, as was the plot, clearly recently dug. Not quite a pauper's grave, but almost. The inscription was just as curt:

HENRY PIERCE. 1952–2009.

Sinclair spoke. "He gave all his money to charity. He said this was as good a place to be buried as anywhere."

"One thing I've never understood," said Mo.

"The reason he came forward?"

"No, that's obvious now. Terminal cancer. But why did he come forward to *you?*"

It was the one element, Sinclair realized, that Seifer had never anticipated in the system. It was an almost perfect scam. Victims with cast-iron alibis, plenty of money in reward, no possible relationships with the perpetrator and the victim. Perfect.

Almost.

As long as the beneficiaries were able to enjoy the benefits, it was perfect. But what if they were diagnosed with terminal cancer? After all, if someone was facing his own imminent death, there was no reason *not* to come forward. The wrath of the Law—or Seifer—would hold no fear for such a person.

Sinclair answered, *"Glioblastoma multiforme."*

She turned and looked at him. "Your wife. Didn't she—"

He nodded. "Pierce read about it in the papers."

"But—but—what are the odds?"

"Don't sweat it," he said, smiling. "God is good."

ABOUT THE AUTHOR

John Moran has tended bar in London, harvested grapes in the south of France, and worked in journalism on the East Coast. He lives in Connecticut where he is currently writing his second novel.